Luck or Cunning?

by Samuel Butler

First paperback edition by Golden Eagle Publishing 2019

Book and covers design by Golden Eagle Publishing

www.goldeneaglepublishing.us

fb.me/GoldenEaglePublishing

Proudly Created in the United States of America

Luck or Cunning?, by Samuel Butler

1922 Jonathan Cape edition.

LUCK, OR CUNNING AS THE MAIN MEANS OF ORGANIC MODIFICATION

NOTE

This second edition of *Luck, or Cunning?* is a reprint of the first edition, dated 1887, but actually published in November, 1886. The only alterations of any consequence are in the Index, which has been enlarged by the incorporation of several entries made by the author in a copy of the book which came into my possession on the death of his literary executor, Mr. R. A. Streatfeild. I thank Mr. G. W. Webb, of the University Library, Cambridge, for the care and skill with which he has made the necessary alterations; it was a troublesome job because owing to the re-setting, the pagination was no longer the same.

Luck, or Cunning? is the fourth of Butler's evolution books; it was followed in 1890 by three articles in *The Universal Review* entitled "The Deadlock in Darwinism" (republished in *The Humour of Homer),*after which he published no more upon that subject.

In this book, as he says in his Introduction, he insists upon two main points: (1) the substantial identity between heredity and memory, and (2) the reintroduction of design into organic development; and these two points he treats as though they have something of that physical life with which they are so closely associated. He was aware that what he had to say was likely to prove more interesting to future generations than to his immediate public, "but any book that desires to see out a literary three-score years and ten must offer something to future generations as well as to its own." By next year one half of the three-score years and ten will have passed, and the new generation by their constant enquiries for the work have already begun to show their appreciation of Butler's method of treating the subject, and their readiness to listen to what was addressed to them as well as to their fathers.

HENRY FESTING JONES.
March, 1920.

AUTHOR'S PREFACE TO FIRST EDITION

This book, as I have said in my concluding chapter, has turned out very different from the one I had it in my mind to write when I began it. It arose out of a conversation with the late Mr. Alfred Tylor soon after his paper on the growth of trees and protoplasmic continuity was read before the Linnean Society - that is to say, in December, 1884 - and I proposed to make the theory concerning the subdivision of organic life into animal and vegetable, which I have broached in my concluding chapter, the main feature of the book. One afternoon, on leaving Mr. Tylor's bedside, much touched at the deep disappointment he evidently felt at being unable to complete the work he had begun so ably, it occurred to me that it might be some pleasure to him if I promised to dedicate my own book to him, and thus, however unworthy it might be, connect it with his name. It occurred to me, of course, also that the honour to my own book would be greater than any it could confer, but the time was not one for balancing considerations nicely, and when I made my suggestion to Mr. Tylor on the last occasion that I ever saw him, the manner in which he received it settled the question. If he had lived I should no doubt have kept more closely to my plan, and should probably have been furnished by him with much that would have enriched the book and made it more worthy of his acceptance; but this was not to be.

In the course of writing I became more and more convinced that no progress could be made towards a sounder view of the theory of descent until people came to understand what the late Mr. Charles Darwin's theory of natural selection amounted to, and how it was that it ever came to be propounded. Until the mindless theory of Charles Darwinian natural selection was finally discredited, and a mindful theory of evolution was substituted in its place neither Mr. Tylor's experiments nor my own theories could stand much chance of being attended to. I therefore devoted myself mainly, as I had done in "Evolution Old and New," and in "Unconscious Memory," to considering whether the view taken by the late Mr. Darwin, or the one put forward by his three most illustrious predecessors, should most command our assent.

The deflection from my original purpose was increased by the appearance, about a year ago, of Mr. Grant Allen's "Charles Darwin," which I imagine to have had a very large circulation. So important, indeed, did I think it not to leave Mr. Allen's statements unchallenged, that in November last I recast my book completely, cutting out much that I had written, and practically starting anew. How far Mr. Tylor would have liked it, or even sanctioned its being dedicated to him, if he were now living, I cannot, of course, say. I never heard him speak of the late Mr. Darwin in any but terms of warm respect, and am by no means sure that he would have been well pleased at an attempt to connect him with a book so polemical as the present. On the other hand, a promise made and received as mine was, cannot be set aside lightly. The understanding was that my next book was to be dedicated to Mr. Tylor; I have written the best I could, and indeed never took so much pains with any other; to Mr. Tylor's memory, therefore, I have most respectfully, and regretfully, inscribed it.

Desiring that the responsibility for what has been done should rest with me, I have avoided saying anything about the book while it was in progress to any of Mr Tylor's family or representatives. They know nothing, therefore, of its contents, and if they did, would probably feel with myself very uncertain how far it is right to use Mr. Tylor's name in connection with it. I can only trust that, on the whole, they may think I have done most rightly in adhering to the letter of my promise.

October 15, 1886.

CHAPTER I - INTRODUCTION

I shall perhaps best promote the acceptance of the two main points on which I have been insisting for some years past, I mean, the substantial identity between heredity and memory, and the reintroduction of design into organic development, by treating them as if they had something of that physical life with which they are so closely connected. Ideas are like plants and animals in this respect also, as in so many others, that they are more fully understood when their relations to other ideas of their time, and the history of their development are known and borne in mind. By development I do not merely mean their growth in the minds of those who first advanced them but that larger development which consists in their subsequent good or evil fortunes - in their reception, favourable or otherwise, by those to whom they were presented. This is to an idea what its surroundings are to an organism, and throws much the same light upon it that knowledge of the conditions under which an organism lives throws upon the organism itself. I shall, therefore, begin this new work with a few remarks about its predecessors.

I am aware that what I may say on this head is likely to prove more interesting to future students of the literature of descent than to my immediate public, but any book that desires to see out a literary three-score years and ten must offer something to future generations as well as to its own. It is a condition of its survival that it shall do this, and herein lies one of the author's chief difficulties. If books only lived as long as men and women, we should know better how to grow them; as matters stand, however, the author lives for one or two generations, whom he comes in the end to understand fairly well, while the book, if reasonable pains have been taken with it, should live more or less usefully for a dozen. About the greater number of these generations the author is in the dark; but come what may, some of them are sure to have arrived at conclusions diametrically opposed to our own upon every subject connected with art, science, philosophy, and religion; it is plain, therefore, that if posterity is to be pleased, it can only be at the cost of repelling some present readers. Unwilling as I am to do this, I still hold it the lesser of two evils; I will be as brief, however, as the interests of the opinions I am supporting will allow.

In "Life and Habit" I contended that heredity was a mode of memory. I endeavoured to show that all hereditary traits, whether of mind or body, are inherited in virtue of, and as a manifestation of, the same power whereby we are able to remember intelligently what we did half an hour, yesterday, or a twelvemonth since, and this in no figurative but in a perfectly real sense. If life be compared to an equation of a hundred unknown quantities, I followed Professor Hering of Prague in reducing it to one of ninety-nine only, by showing two of the supposed unknown quantities to be so closely allied that they should count as one. I maintained that instinct was inherited memory, and this without admitting more exceptions and qualifying clauses than arise, as it were, by way of harmonics from every proposition, and must be neglected if thought and language are to be possible.

I showed that if the view for which I was contending was taken, many facts which, though familiar, were still without explanation or connection with our other ideas, would remain no longer isolated, but be seen at once as joined with the mainland of our most assured convictions. Among the things thus brought more comfortably home to us was the principle underlying longevity. It became apparent why some living beings should live longer than others, and how any race must be treated whose longevity it is desired to increase. Hitherto we had known that an elephant was a long-lived animal and a fly short-lived, but we could give no reason why the one should live longer than the other; that is to say, it did not follow in immediate coherence with, or as intimately associated with, any familiar principle that an animal which is late in the full development of its reproductive system will tend to live longer than one which reproduces early. If the theory of "Life and Habit" be admitted, the fact of a slow-growing animal being in general longer lived than a quick developer is seen to be connected with, and to follow as a matter of course from the fact of our being able to remember anything at all, and all the well-known traits of memory, as observed where we can best take note of them, are perceived to be reproduced with singular fidelity in the development of an animal from its embryonic stages to maturity.

Take this view, and the very general sterility of hybrids from being a *crux* of the theory of descent becomes a stronghold of defence. It appears as part of the same story as the benefit derived from judicious, and the mischief from injudicious, crossing; and this, in its turn, is seen as part of the same story, as the good we get from change of air and scene when we are overworked. I will not amplify; but reversion to long-lost, or feral, characteristics, the phenomena of old age, the fact of the reproductive system being generally the last to arrive at maturity - few further developments occurring in any organism after this has been attained - the sterility of many animals in confinement the development in both males and females under certain circumstances of the characteristics of the opposite sex, the latency of memory, the unconsciousness with which we grow, and indeed perform all familiar actions, these points, though hitherto, most of them, so apparently inexplicable that no one even attempted to explain them, became at once intelligible, if the contentions of "Life and Habit" were admitted.

Before I had finished writing this book I fell in with Professor Mivart's "Genesis of Species," and for the first time understood the distinction between the Lamarckian and Charles-Darwinian systems of evolution. This had not, so far as I then knew, been as yet made clear to us by any of our more prominent writers upon the subject of descent with modification; the distinction was unknown to the general public, and indeed is only now beginning to be widely understood. While reading Mr. Mivart's book, however, I became aware that I was being faced by two facts, each incontrovertible, but each, if its leading exponents were to be trusted, incompatible with the other.

On the one hand there was descent; we could not read Mr. Darwin's books and doubt that all, both animals and plants, were descended from a common source. On the other, there was design; we could not read Paley and refuse to admit that design, intelligence, adaptation of means to ends, must have had a large share in the development of the life we saw around us; it seemed indisputable that the minds and bodies of all living beings must have come to be what they are through a wise ordering and administering of their estates. We could not, therefore, dispense either with descent or with design, and yet it seemed impossible to keep both, for those who offered us descent stuck to it that we could have no design, and those, again, who spoke so wisely and so well about design would not for a moment hear of descent with modification.

Each, moreover, had a strong case. Who could reflect upon rudimentary organs, and grant Paley the kind of design that alone would content him? And yet who could examine the foot or the eye, and grant Mr. Darwin his denial of forethought and plan?

For that Mr. Darwin did deny skill and contrivance in connection with the greatly preponderating part of organic developments cannot be and is not now disputed. In the first chapter of "Evolution Old and New" I brought forward passages to show how completely he and his followers deny design, but will here quote one of the latest of the many that have appeared to the same effect since "Evolution Old and New" was published; it is by Mr. Romanes, and runs as follows:-

"It is the *very essence* of the Darwinian hypothesis that it only seeks to explain the *apparently* purposive variations, or variations of an adaptive kind." {17a}

The words "apparently purposive" show that those organs in animals and plants which at first sight seem to have been designed with a view to the work they have to do - that is to say, with a view to future function - had not, according to Mr. Darwin, in reality any connection with, or inception in, effort; effort involves purpose and design; they had therefore no inception in design, however much they might present the appearance of being designed; the appearance was delusive; Mr. Romanes correctly declares it to be "the very essence" of Mr. Darwin's system to attempt an explanation of these seemingly purposive variations which shall be compatible with their having arisen without being in any way connected with intelligence or design.

As it is indisputable that Mr. Darwin denied design, so neither can it be doubted that Paley denied descent with modification. What, then, were the wrong entries in these two sets of accounts, on the detection and removal of which they would be found to balance as they ought?

Paley's weakest place, as already implied, is in the matter of rudimentary organs; the almost universal presence in the higher organisms of useless, and sometimes even troublesome, organs is fatal to the kind of design he is trying to uphold; granted that there is design, still it cannot be so final and far-foreseeing as he wishes to make it out. Mr. Darwin's weak place, on the other hand, lies, firstly, in the supposition that because rudimentary organs imply no purpose now, they could never in time past have done so - that because they had clearly not been designed with an eye to all circumstances and all time, they never, therefore, could have been designed with an eye to any time or any circumstances; and, secondly, in maintaining that "accidental," "fortuitous," "spontaneous" variations could be accumulated at all except under conditions that have never been fulfilled yet, and never will be; in other words, his weak place lay in the contention (for it comes to this) that there can be sustained accumulation of bodily wealth, more than of wealth of any other kind, unless sustained experience, watchfulness, and good sense preside over the accumulation. In "Life and Habit," following Mr. Mivart, and, as I now find, Mr. Herbert Spencer, I showed (pp. 279-281) how impossible it was for variations to accumulate unless they were for the most part underlain by a sustained general principle; but this subject will be touched upon more fully later on.

The accumulation of accidental variations which owed nothing to mind either in their inception, or their accumulation, the pitchforking, in fact, of mind out of the universe, or at any rate its exclusion from all share worth talking about in the process of organic development, this was the pill Mr. Darwin had given us to swallow; but so thickly had he gilded it with descent with modification, that we did as we were told, swallowed it without a murmur, were lavish in our expressions of gratitude, and, for some twenty years or so, through the mouths of our leading biologists, ordered design peremptorily out of court, if she so much as dared to show herself. Indeed, we have even given life pensions to some of the most notable of these biologists, I suppose in order to reward them for having hoodwinked us so much to our satisfaction.

Happily the old saying, *Naturam expellas furcâ, tamen usque recurret,* still holds true, and the reaction that has been gaining force for some time will doubtless ere long brush aside the cobwebs with which those who have a vested interest in Mr. Darwin's reputation as a philosopher still try to fog our outlook. Professor Mivart was, as I have said, among the first to awaken us to Mr. Darwin's denial of design, and to the absurdity involved therein. He well showed how incredible Mr Darwin's system was found to be, as soon as it was fully realised, but there he rather left us. He seemed to say that we must have our descent and our design too, but he did not show how we were to manage this with rudimentary organs still staring us in the face. His work rather led up to the clearer statement of the difficulty than either put it before us in so many words, or tried to remove it. Nevertheless there can be no doubt that the "Genesis of Species" gave Natural Selection what will prove sooner or later to be its death-blow, in spite of the persistence with which many still declare that it has received no hurt, and the sixth edition of the" Origin of Species," published in the following year, bore abundant traces of the fray. Moreover, though Mr. Mivart gave us no overt aid, he pointed to the source from which help might come, by expressly saying that his most important objection to Neo-Darwinism had no force against Lamarck.

To Lamarck, therefore, I naturally turned, and soon saw that the theory on which I had been insisting in" Life and Habit" was in reality an easy corollary on his system, though one which he does not appear to have caught sight of. I saw also that his denial of design was only, so to speak, skin deep, and that his system was in reality teleological, inasmuch as, to use Isidore Geoffroy's words, it makes the organism design itself. In making variations depend on changed actions, and these, again, on changed views of life, efforts, and designs, in consequence of changed conditions of life, he in effect makes effort, intention, will, all of which involve design (or at any rate which taken together involve it), underlie progress in organic development. True, he did not know he was a teleologist, but he was none the less a teleologist for this. He was an unconscious teleologist, and as such perhaps more absolutely an upholder of teleology than Paley himself; but this is neither here nor there; our concern is not with what people think about themselves, but with what their reasoning makes it evident that they really hold.

How strange the irony that hides us from ourselves! When Isidore Geoffroy said that according to Lamarck organisms designed themselves, {20a} and endorsed this, as to a great extent he did, he still does not appear to have seen that either he or Lamarck were in reality reintroducing design into organism; he does not appear to have seen this more than Lamarck himself had seen it, but, on the contrary, like Lamarck, remained under the impression that he was opposing teleology or purposiveness.

Of course in one sense he did oppose it; so do we all, if the word design be taken to intend a very far-foreseeing o minute details, a riding out to meet trouble long before it comes, a provision on academic principles for contingencies that are little likely to arise. We can see no evidence of any such design as this in nature, and much everywhere that makes against it. There is no such improvidence as over providence, and whatever theories we may form about the origin and development of the universe, we may be sure that it is not the work of one who is unabl to understand how anything can possibly go right unless he sees to it himself. Nature works departmentally and by way of leaving details to subordinates. But though those who see nature thus do indeed deny design of th prescient-from-all-eternity order, they in no way impugn a method which is far more in accord with all that we commonly think of as design. A design which is as incredible as that a ewe should give birth to a lion becomes of piece with all that we observe most frequently if it be regarded rather as an aggregation of many small steps than as single large one. This principle is very simple, but it seems rather difficult to understand. It has taken several generations before people would admit it as regards organism even after it was pointed out to them, and those who saw it as regards organism still failed to understand it as regards design; an inexorable "Thus far shalt thou go and no farther" barred them from fruition of the harvest they should have been the first to reap. The very men wh most insisted that specific difference was the accumulation of differences so minute as to be often hardly, if at all perceptible, could not see that the striking and baffling phenomena of design in connection with organism admitted of exactly the same solution as the riddle of organic development, and should be seen not as a result reached*per saltum,* but as an accumulation of small steps or leaps in a given direction. It was as though those who had insisted on the derivation of all forms of the steam-engine from the common kettle, and who saw that this stands in mucl the same relations to the engines, we will say, of the Great Eastern steamship as the amœba to man, were to declare that the Great Eastern engines were not designed at all, on the ground that no one in the early kettle days had foreseen so great a future development, and were unable to understand that a piecemeal *solvitur ambulando* design is more omnipresent, all-seeing, and all-searching, and hence more truly in the strictest sense design, than any speculative leap of fancy, however bold and even at times successful.

From Lamarck I went on to Buffon and Erasmus Darwin - better men both of them than Lamarck, and treated by him much as he has himself been treated by those who have come after him - and found that the system of thes three writers, if considered rightly, and if the corollary that heredity is only a mode of memory were added, woul get us out of our dilemma as regards descent and design, and enable us to keep both. We could do this by making the design manifested in organism more like the only design of which we know anything, and therefore the only design of which we ought to speak - I mean our own.

Our own design is tentative, and neither very far-foreseeing nor very retrospective; it is a little of both, but much o neither; it is like a comet with a little light in front of the nucleus and a good deal more behind it, which ere long however, fades away into the darkness; it is of a kind that, though a little wise before the event, is apt to be much wiser after it, and to profit even by mischance so long as the disaster is not an overwhelming one; nevertheless, though it is so interwoven with luck, there is no doubt about its being design; why, then, should the design which must have attended organic development be other than this? If the thing that has been is the thing that also shall be must not the thing which is be that which also has been? Was there anything in the phenomena of organic life to militate against such a view of design as this? Not only was there nothing, but this view made things plain, as the connecting of heredity and memory had already done, which till now had been without explanation. Rudimentary organs were no longer a hindrance to our acceptance of design, they became weighty arguments in its favour.

I therefore wrote "Evolution Old and New," with the object partly of backing up "Life and Habit," and showing the easy rider it admitted, partly to show how superior the old view of descent had been to Mr. Darwin's, and partly to reintroduce design into organism. I wrote "Life and Habit" to show that our mental and bodily acquisitions were mainly stores of memory: I wrote "Evolution Old and New" to add that the memory must be a mindful anc designing memory.

I followed up these two books with "Unconscious Memory," the main object of which was to show how Professor Hering of Prague had treated the connection between memory and heredity; to show, again, how substantial was the difference between Von Hartmann and myself in spite of some little superficial resemblance; to put forward a suggestion as regards the physics of memory, and to meet the most plausible objection which I have yet seen brought against "Life and Habit."

Since writing these three books I have published nothing on the connection between heredity and memory, except a few pages of remarks on Mr. Romanes' "Mental Evolution in Animals" in my book, {23a} from which I will draw whatever seems to be more properly placed here. I have collected many facts that make my case stronger, but am precluded from publishing them by the reflection that it is strong enough already. I have said enough in "Life and Habit" to satisfy any who wish to be satisfied, and those who wish to be dissatisfied would probably fail to see the force of what I said, no matter how long and seriously I held forth to them; I believe, therefore, that I shall do well to keep my facts for my own private reading and for that of my executors.

I once saw a copy of "Life and Habit" on Mr. Bogue's counter, and was told by the very obliging shopman that a customer had just written something in it which I might like to see. I said of course I should like to see, and immediately taking the book read the following - which it occurs to me that I am not justified in publishing. What was written ran thus:-

"As a reminder of our pleasant hours on the broad Atlantic, will Mr. -- please accept this book (which I think contains more truth, and less evidence of it, than any other I have met with) from his friend -- ?"

I presume the gentleman had met with the Bible - a work which lays itself open to a somewhat similar comment. I was gratified, however, at what I had read, and take this opportunity of thanking the writer, an American, for having liked my book. It was so plain he had been relieved at not finding the case smothered to death in the weight of its own evidences, that I resolved not to forget the lesson his words had taught me.

The only writer in connection with "Life and Habit" to whom I am anxious to reply is Mr. Herbert Spencer, but before doing this I will conclude the present chapter with a consideration of some general complaints that have been so often brought against me that it may be worth while to notice them.

These general criticisms have resolved themselves mainly into two.

Firstly, it is said that I ought not to write about biology on the ground of my past career, which my critics declare to have been purely literary. I wish I might indulge a reasonable hope of one day becoming a literary man; the expression is not a good one, but there is no other in such common use, and this must excuse it; if a man can be properly called literary, he must have acquired the habit of reading accurately, thinking attentively, and expressing himself clearly. He must have endeavoured in all sorts of ways to enlarge the range of his sympathies so as to be able to put himself easily *en rapport* with those whom he is studying, and those whom he is addressing. If he cannot speak with tongues himself, he is the interpreter of those who can - without whom they might as well be silent. I wish I could see more signs of literary culture among my scientific opponents; I should find their books much more easy and agreeable reading if I could; and then they tell me to satirise the follies and abuses of the age, just as if it was not this that I was doing in writing about themselves.

What, I wonder, would they say if I were to declare that they ought not to write books at all, on the ground that their past career has been too purely scientific to entitle them to a hearing? They would reply with justice that I should not bring vague general condemnations, but should quote examples of their bad writing. I imagine that I have done this more than once as regards a good many of them, and I dare say I may do it again in the course of this book; but though I must own to thinking that the greater number of our scientific men write abominably, I should not bring this against them if I believed them to be doing their best to help us; many such men we happily have, and doubtless always shall have, but they are not those who push to the fore, and it is these last who are most angry with me for writing on the subjects I have chosen. They constantly tell me that I am not a man of science; no one knows this better than I do, and I am quite used to being told it, but I am not used to being confronted with the mistakes that I have made in matters of fact, and trust that this experience is one which I may continue to spare no pains in trying to avoid.

Nevertheless I again freely grant that I am not a man of science. I have never said I was. I was educated for the Church. I was once inside the Linnean Society's rooms, but have no present wish to go there again; though not a man of science, however, I have never affected indifference to the facts and arguments which men of science have made it their business to lay before us; on the contrary, I have given the greater part of my time to their consideration for several years past. I should not, however, say this unless led to do so by regard to the interests of theories which I believe to be as nearly important as any theories can be which do not directly involve money or bodily convenience.

The second complaint against me is to the effect that I have made no original experiments, but have taken all my facts at second hand. This is true, but I do not see what it has to do with the question. If the facts are sound, how can it matter whether A or B collected them? If Professor Huxley, for example, has made a series of valuable original observations (not that I know of his having done so), why am I to make them over again? What are fact-collectors worth if the fact co-ordinators may not rely upon them? It seems to me that no one need do more than go to the best sources for his facts, and tell his readers where he got them. If I had had occasion for more facts I daresay I should have taken the necessary steps to get hold of them, but there was no difficulty on this score; every text-book supplied me with all, and more than all, I wanted; my complaint was that the facts which Mr. Darwin supplied would not bear the construction he tried to put upon them; I tried, therefore, to make them bear another which seemed at once more sound and more commodious; rightly or wrongly I set up as a builder, not as a burner of bricks, and the complaint so often brought against me of not having made experiments is about as reasonable as complaint against an architect on the score of his not having quarried with his own hands a single one of the stone which he has used in building. Let my opponents show that the facts which they and I use in common are unsound, or that I have misapplied them, and I will gladly learn my mistake, but this has hardly, to my knowledge, been attempted. To me it seems that the chief difference between myself and some of my opponents lies in this, that I take my facts from them with acknowledgment, and they take their theories from me - without.

One word more and I have done. I should like to say that I do not return to the connection between memory and heredity under the impression that I shall do myself much good by doing so. My own share in the matter was very small. The theory that heredity is only a mode of memory is not mine, but Professor Hering's. He wrote in 1870, and I not till 1877. I should be only too glad if he would take his theory and follow it up himself; assuredly he could do so much better than I can; but with the exception of his one not lengthy address published some fifteen or sixteen years ago he has said nothing upon the subject, so far at least as I have been able to ascertain; I tried hard to draw him in 1880, but could get nothing out of him. If, again, any of our more influential writers, not a few of whom evidently think on this matter much as I do, would eschew ambiguities and tell us what they mean in plain language, I would let the matter rest in their abler hands, but of this there does not seem much chance at present.

I wish there was, for in spite of the interest I have felt in working the theory out and the information I have been able to collect while doing so, I must confess that I have found it somewhat of a white elephant. It has got me into the hottest of hot water, made a literary Ishmael of me, lost me friends whom I have been sorry to lose, cost me good deal of money, done everything to me, in fact, which a good theory ought not to do. Still, as it seems to have taken up with me, and no one else is inclined to treat it fairly, I shall continue to report its developments from time to time as long as life and health are spared me. Moreover, Ishmaels are not without their uses, and they are not a drug in the market just now.

I may now go on to Mr. Spencer.

CHAPTER II - MR. HERBERT SPENCER

Mr. Herbert Spencer wrote to the *Athenæum* (April 5, 1884), and quoted certain passages from the 1855 edition of his "Principles of Psychology," "the meanings and implications" from which he contended were sufficiently clear. The passages he quoted were as follows:-

Though it is manifest that reflex and instinctive sequences are not determined by the experiences of the *individual* organism manifesting them, yet there still remains the hypothesis that they are determined by the experiences of the *race* of organisms forming its ancestry, which by infinite repetition in countless successive generations have established these sequences as organic relations (p. 526).

are also bequeathed (p. 526).

That is to say, the tendencies to certain combinations of psychical changes have become organic (p. 527).

The doctrine that the connections among our ideas are determined by experience must, in consistency, be extended not only to all the connections established by the accumulated experiences of every individual, but to all those established by the accumulated experiences of every race (p. 529).

Here, then, we have one of the simpler forms of instinct which, under the requisite conditions, must necessarily be established by accumulated experiences (p. 547).

And manifestly, if the organisation of inner relations, in correspondence with outer relations, results from a continual registration of experiences, &c. (p. 551).

On the one hand, Instinct may be regarded as a kind of organised memory; on the other hand, Memory may be regarded as a kind of incipient instinct (pp. 555-6).

Memory, then, pertains to all that class of psychical states which are in process of being organised. It continues so long as the organising of them continues; and disappears when the organisation of them is complete. In the advance of the correspondence, each more complex class of phenomena which the organism acquires the power of recognising is responded to at first irregularly and uncertainly; and there is then a weak remembrance of the relations. By multiplication of experiences this remembrance becomes stronger, and the response more certain. By further multiplication of experiences the internal relations are at last automatically organised in correspondence with the external ones; and so conscious memory passes into unconscious or organic memory. At the same time, a new and still more complex order of experiences is thus rendered appreciable; the relations they present occupy the memory in place of the simpler one; they become gradually organised; and, like the previous ones, are succeeded by others more complex still (p. 563).

Just as we saw that the establishment of those compound reflex actions which we call instincts is comprehensible on the principle that inner relations are, by perpetual repetition, organised into correspondence with outer relations; so the establishment of those consolidated, those indissoluble, those instinctive mental relations constituting our ideas of Space and Time, is comprehensible on the same principle (p. 579).

In a book published a few weeks before Mr. Spencer's letter appeared {29a} I had said that though Mr. Spencer at times closely approached Professor Hering and "Life and Habit," he had nevertheless nowhere shown that he considered memory and heredity to be parts of the same story and parcel of one another. In his letter to the *Athenæum,* indeed, he does not profess to have upheld this view, except "by implications;" nor yet, though in the course of the six or seven years that had elapsed since "Life and Habit" was published I had brought out more than one book to support my earlier one, had he said anything during those years to lead me to suppose that I was trespassing upon ground already taken by himself. Nor, again, had he said anything which enabled me to appeal to his authority - which I should have been only too glad to do; at last, however, he wrote, as I have said, to the *Athenæum* a letter which, indeed, made no express claim, and nowhere mentioned myself, but "the meanings and implications" from which were this time as clear as could be desired, and amount to an order to Professor Hering and myself to stand aside.

The question is, whether the passages quoted by Mr. Spencer, or any others that can be found in his works, show that he regarded heredity in all its manifestations as a mode of memory. I submit that this conception is not derivable from Mr. Spencer's writings, and that even the passages in which he approaches it most closely are unintelligible till read by the light of Professor Hering's address and of "Life and Habit."

True, Mr. Spencer made abundant use of such expressions as "the experience of the race," "accumulated experiences," and others like them, but he did not explain - and it was here the difficulty lay - how a race could have any experience at all. We know what we mean when we say that an individual has had experience; we mean that he is the same person now (in the common use of the words), on the occasion of some present action, as the one who performed a like action at some past time or times, and that he remembers how he acted before, so as to be able to turn his past action to account, gaining in proficiency through practice. Continued personality and memory are the elements that constitute experience; where these are present there may, and commonly will, be experience; where they are absent the word "experience" cannot properly be used.

Formerly we used to see an individual as one, and a race as many. We now see that though this is true as far as it goes, it is by no means the whole truth, and that in certain important respects it is the race that is one, and the individual many. We all admit and understand this readily enough now, but it was not understood when Mr.

Spencer wrote the passages he adduced in the letter to the *Athenæum* above referred to. In the then state of our ideas a race was only a succession of individuals, each one of them new persons, and as such incapable of profiting by the experience of its predecessors except in the very limited number of cases where oral teaching, or, as in recent times writing, was possible. The thread of life was, as I have elsewhere said, remorselessly shorn between each successive generation, and the importance of the physical and psychical connection between parents and offspring had been quite, or nearly quite, lost sight of. It seems strange how this could ever have been allowed to come about, but it should be remembered that the Church in the Middle Ages would strongly discourage attempts to emphasize a connection that would raise troublesome questions as to who in a future state was to be responsible for what; and, after all, for nine purposes of life out of ten the generally received opinion that each person is himself and nobody else is on many grounds the most convenient. Every now and then, however, there comes a tenth purpose, for which the continued personality side of the connection between successive generations is as convenient as the new personality side is for the remaining nine, and these tenth purposes - some of which are not unimportant - are obscured and fulfilled amiss owing to the completeness with which the more commonly needed conception has overgrown the other.

Neither view is more true than the other, but the one was wanted every hour and minute of the day, and was therefore kept, so to speak, in stock, and in one of the most accessible places of our mental storehouse, while the other was so seldom asked for that it became not worth while to keep it. By-and-by it was found so troublesome to send out for it, and so hard to come by even then, that people left off selling it at all, and if any one wanted it he must think it out at home as best he could; this was troublesome, so by common consent the world decided no longer to busy itself with the continued personality of successive generations - which was all very well until it also decided to busy itself with the theory of descent with modification. On the introduction of a foe so inimical to many of our pre-existing ideas the balance of power among them was upset, and a readjustment became necessary which is still far from having attained the next settlement that seems likely to be reasonably permanent.

To change the illustration, the ordinary view is true for seven places of decimals, and this commonly is enough; occasions, however, have now arisen when the error caused by neglect of the omitted places is appreciably disturbing, and we must have three or four more. Mr. Spencer showed no more signs of seeing that he must supply these, and make personal identity continue between successive generations before talking about inherited (as opposed to post-natal and educational) experience, than others had done before him; the race with him, as with every one else till recently, was not one long individual living indeed in pulsations, so to speak, but no more losing continued personality by living in successive generations, than an individual loses it by living in consecutive days; a race was simply a succession of individuals, each one of which was held to be an entirely new person, and was regarded exclusively, or very nearly so, from this point of view.

When I wrote "Life and Habit" I knew that the words "experience of the race" sounded familiar, and were going about in magazines and newspapers, but I did not know where they came from; if I had, I should have given their source. To me they conveyed no meaning, and vexed me as an attempt to make me take stones instead of bread, and to palm off an illustration upon me as though it were an explanation. When I had worked the matter out in my own way, I saw that the illustration, with certain additions, would become an explanation, but I saw also that neither he who had adduced it nor any one else could have seen how right he was, till much had been said which had not, so far as 1 knew, been said yet, and which undoubtedly would have been said if people had seen their way to saying it.

"What is this talk," I wrote, "which is made about the experience of the race, as though the experience of one man could profit another who knows nothing about him? If a man eats his dinner it nourishes him and not his neighbour; if he learns a difficult art it is he that can do it and not his neighbour" ("Life and Habit," p. 49).

When I wrote thus in 1877, it was not generally seen that though the father is not nourished by the dinners that the son eats, yet the son was fed when the father ate before he begot him.

"Is there any way," I continued, "of showing that this experience of the race about which so much is said without the least attempt to show in what way it may, or does, become the experience of the individual, is in sober seriousness the experience of one single being only, who repeats on a great many different occasions, and in slightly different ways, certain performances with which he has already become exceedingly familiar?"

I felt, as every one else must have felt who reflected upon the expression in question, that it was fallacious till this was done. When I first began to write "Life and Habit" I did not believe it could be done, but when I had gone right up to the end, as it were, of my *cu de sac,* I saw the path which led straight to the point I had despaired of reaching - I mean I saw that personality could not be broken as between generations, without also breaking it between the years, days, and moments of a man's life. What differentiates "Life and Habit" from the "Principles of Psychology" is the prominence given to continued personal identity, and hence to *bonâ fide* memory, as between successive generations; but surely this makes the two books differ widely.

Ideas can be changed to almost any extent in almost any direction, if the change is brought about gradually and in accordance with the rules of all development. As in music we may take almost any possible discord with pleasing effect if we have prepared and resolved it rightly, so our ideas will outlive and outgrow almost any modification which is approached and quitted in such a way as to fuse the old and new harmoniously. Words are to ideas what the fairy invisible cloak was to the prince who wore it - only that the prince was seen till he put on the cloak, whereas ideas are unseen until they don the robe of words which reveals them to us; the words, however, and the ideas, should be such as fit each other and stick to one another in our minds as soon as they are brought together, or the ideas will fly off, and leave the words void of that spirit by the aid of which alone they can become transmuted into physical action and shape material things with their own impress. Whether a discord is too violent or no, depends on what we have been accustomed to, and on how widely the new differs from the old, but in no case can we fuse and assimilate more than a very little new at a time without exhausting our tempering power - and hence presently our temper.

Mr. Spencer appears to have forgotten that though *de minimis non curat lex*, - though all the laws fail when applied to trifles, - yet too sudden a change in the manner in which our ideas are associated is as cataclysmic and subversive of healthy evolution as are material convulsions, or too violent revolutions in politics. This must always be the case, for change is essentially miraculous, and the only lawful home of the miracle is in the microscopically small. Here, indeed, miracles were in the beginning, are now, and ever shall be, but we are deadened if they are required of us on a scale which is visible to the naked eye. If we are told to work them our hands fall nerveless down; if, come what may, we must do or die, we are more likely to die than to succeed in doing. If we are required to believe them - which only means to fuse them with our other ideas - we either take the law into our own hands, and our minds being in the dark fuse something easier of assimilation, and say we have fused the miracle; or if we play more fairly and insist on our minds swallowing and assimilating it, we weaken our judgments, and *pro tanto* kill our souls. If we stick out beyond a certain point we go mad, as fanatics, or at the best make Coleridges of ourselves; and yet upon a small scale these same miracles are the breath and essence of life; to cease to work them is to die. And by miracle I do not merely mean something new, strange, and not very easy of comprehension - I mean something which violates every canon of thought which in the palpable world we are accustomed to respect; something as alien to, and inconceivable by, us as contradiction in terms, the destructibility of force or matter, or the creation of something out of nothing. This, which when writ large maddens and kills, writ small is our meat and drink; it attends each minutest and most impalpable detail of the ceaseless fusion and diffusion in which change appears to us as consisting, and which we recognise as growth and decay, or as life and death.

Claude Bernard says, *Rien ne nait, rien ne se crée, tout se continue. La nature ne nous offre le spectacle d'aucune création, elle est d'une éternelle continuation*; {35a} but surely he is insisting upon one side of the truth only, to the neglect of another which is just as real, and just as important; he might have said, *Rien ne se continue, tout nait, tout se crée. La nature ne nous offre le spectacle d'aucune continuation. Elle est d'une éternelle création*; for change is no less patent a fact than continuity, and, indeed, the two stand or fall together. True, discontinuity, where development is normal, is on a very small scale, but this is only the difference between looking at distances on a small instead of a large map; we cannot have even the smallest change without a small partial corresponding discontinuity; on a small scale - too small, indeed, for us to cognise - these breaks in continuity, each one of which must, so far as our understanding goes, rank as a creation, are as essential a factor of the phenomena we see around us, as is the other factor that they shall normally be on too small a scale for us to find it out. Creations, then, there must be, but they must be so small that practically they are no creations. We must have a continuity in discontinuity, and a discontinuity in continuity; that is to say, we can only conceive the help of change at all by the help of flat contradiction in terms. It comes, therefore, to this, that if we are to think fluently and harmoniously upon any subject into which change enters (and there is no conceivable subject into which it does not), we must begin by flying in the face of every rule that professors of the art of thinking have drawn up for our instruction. These rules may be good enough as servants, but we have let them become the worst of masters, forgetting that philosophy is made for man, not man for philosophy. Logic has been the true Tower of Babel, which we have thought to build so that we might climb up into the heavens, and have no more miracle, but see God and live - nor has confusion of tongues failed to follow on our presumption. Truly St. Paul said well that the just shall live by faith; and the question "By what faith?" is a detail of minor moment, for there are as many faiths as species, whether of plants or animals, and each of them is in its own way both living and saving.

All, then, whether fusion or diffusion, whether of ideas or things, is miraculous. It is the two in one, and at the same time one in two, which is only two and two making five put before us in another shape; yet this fusion - so easy to think so long as it is not thought about, and so unthinkable if we try to think it - is, as it were, the matrix from which our more thinkable thought is taken; it is the cloud gathering in the unseen world from which the waters of life descend in an impalpable dew. Granted that all, whether fusion or diffusion, whether of ideas or things, is, if we dwell upon it and take it seriously, an outrage upon our understandings which common sense alone enables us to brook; granted that it carries with it a distinctly miraculous element which should vitiate the whole process *ab initio*, still, if we have faith we can so work these miracles as Orpheus-like to charm denizens of the unseen world into the seen again - provided we do not look back, and provided also we do not try to charm half a dozen Eurydices at a time. To think is to fuse and diffuse ideas, and to fuse and diffuse ideas is to feed. We can all feed, and by consequence within reasonable limits we can fuse ideas; or we can fuse ideas, and by consequence within reasonable limits we can feed; we know not which comes first, the food or the ideas, but we must not overtax our strength; the moment we do this we taste of death.

It is in the closest connection with this that we must chew our food fine before we can digest it, and that the same food given in large lumps will choke and kill which in small pieces feeds us; or, again, that that which is impotent as a pellet may be potent as a gas. Food is very thoughtful: through thought it comes, and back through thought it shall return; the process of its conversion and comprehension within our own system is mental as well as physical, and here, as everywhere else with mind and evolution, there must be a cross, but not too wide a cross - that is to say, there must be a miracle, but not upon a large scale. Granted that no one can draw a clear line and define the limits within which a miracle is healthy working and beyond which it is unwholesome, any more than he can prescribe the exact degree of fineness to which we must comminute our food; granted, again, that some can do more than others and that at all times all men sport, so to speak, and surpass themselves, still we know as a general rule near enough, and find that the strongest can do but very little at a time, and, to return to Mr. Spencer, the fusion of two such hitherto unassociated ideas as race and experience was a miracle beyond our strength.

Assuredly when Mr. Spencer wrote the passages he quoted in the letter to the *Athenæum* above referred to, we were not in the habit of thinking of any one as able to remember things that had happened before he had been born or thought of. This notion will still strike many of my non-readers as harsh and strained; no such discord, therefore, should have been taken unprepared, and when taken it should have been resolved with pomp and circumstance. Mr Spencer, however, though he took it continually, never either prepared it or resolved it at all, but by using the words "experience of the race" sprang this seeming paradox upon us, with the result that his words were barren. They were barren because they were incoherent; they were incoherent because they were approached and quitted too suddenly. While we were realising "experience" our minds excluded "race," inasmuch as experience was an idea we had been accustomed hitherto to connect only with the individual; while realising the idea "race," for the same reason, we as a matter of course excluded experience. We were required to fuse two ideas that were alien to one another, without having had those other ideas presented to us which would alone flux them. The absence of these - which indeed were not immediately ready to hand, or Mr. Spencer would have doubtless grasped them - made nonsense of the whole thing; we saw the ideas propped up as two cards one against the other, on one of Mr Spencer's pages, only to find that they had fallen asunder before we had turned over to the next, so we put down his book resentfully, as written by one who did not know what to do with his meaning even if he had one, or bore it meekly while he chastised us with scorpions, as Mr. Darwin had done with whips, according to our temperaments.

I may say, in passing, that the barrenness of incoherent ideas, and the sterility of widely distant species and genera of animals and plants, are one in principle - the sterility of hybrids being just as much due to inability to fuse widely unlike and unfamiliar ideas into a coherent whole, as barrenness of ideas is, and, indeed, resolving itself ultimately into neither more nor less than barrenness of ideas - that is to say, into inability to think at all, or at any rate to think as their neighbours do.

If Mr. Spencer had made it clear that the generations of any race are*bonâ fide* united by a common personality, and that in virtue of being so united each generation remembers (within, of course, the limits to which all memory is subject) what happened to it while still in the persons of its progenitors - then his order to Professor Hering and myself should be immediately obeyed; but this was just what was at once most wanted, and least done by Mr. Spencer. Even in the passages given above - passages collected by Mr. Spencer himself - this point is altogether ignored; make it clear as Professor Hering made it - put continued personality and memory in the foreground as Professor Hering did, instead of leaving them to be discovered "by implications," and then such expressions as "accumulated experiences" and "experience of the race" become luminous; till this had been done they were *Vox et præterea nihil.*

To sum up briefly. The passages quoted by Mr. Spencer from his "Principles of Psychology" can hardly be called clear, even now that Professor Hering and others have thrown light upon them. If, indeed, they had been clear Mr.

Spencer would probably have seen what they necesitated, and found the way of meeting the difficulties of the case which occurred to Professor Hering and myself. Till we wrote, very few writers had even suggested this. The idea that offspring was only "an elongation or branch proceeding from its parents" had scintillated in the ingenious brain of Dr. Erasmus Darwin, and in that of the designer of Jesse tree windows, but it had kindled no fire; it now turns out that Canon Kingsley had once called instinct inherited memory, {40a} but the idea, if born alive at all, died on the page on which it saw light: Professor Ray Lankester, again called attention to Professor Hering's address *(Nature,* July 13, 1876), but no discussion followed, and the matter dropped without having produced visible effect. As for offspring remembering in any legitimate sense of the words what it had done, and what had happened to it, before it was born, no such notion was understood to have been gravely mooted till very recently. I doubt whether Mr. Spencer and Mr. Romanes would accept this even now, when it is put thus undisguisedly; but this is what Professor Hering and I mean, and it is the only thing that should be meant, by those who speak of instinct as inherited memory. Mr Spencer cannot maintain that these two startling novelties went without saying "by implication" from the use of such expressions as "accumulated experiences" or "experience of the race."

CHAPTER III - MR. HERBERT SPENCER *(continued)*

Whether they ought to have gone or not, they did not go.

When "Life and Habit" was first published no one considered Mr. Spencer to be maintaining the phenomena of heredity to be in reality phenomena of memory. When, for example, Professor Ray Lankester first called attention to Professor Hering's address, he did not understand Mr. Spencer to be intending this. "Professor Hering," he wrote *(Nature,* July 13, 1876), "helps us to a comprehensive view of the nature of heredity and adaptation, by giving us the word 'memory,' conscious or unconscious, for the continuity of Mr. Spencer's polar forces or polarities of physiological units." He evidently found the prominence given to memory a help to him which he had not derived from reading Mr. Spencer's works.

When, again, he attacked me in the *Athenæum* (March 29, 1884), he spoke of my "tardy recognition" of the fact that Professor Hering had preceded me "in treating all manifestations of heredity as a form of memory." Professor Lankester's words could have no force if he held that any other writer, and much less so well known a writer as Mr. Spencer, had preceded me in putting forward the theory in question.

When Mr. Romanes reviewed "Unconscious Memory" in *Nature* (January 27, 1881) the notion of a "race-memory," to use his own words, was still so new to him that he declared it "simply absurd" to suppose that it could "possibly be fraught with any benefit to science," and with him too it was Professor Hering who had anticipated me in the matter, not Mr. Spencer.

In his "Mental Evolution in Animals" (p. 296) he said that Canon Kingsley, writing in 1867, was the first to advance the theory that instinct is inherited memory; he could not have said this if Mr. Spencer had been understood to have been upholding this view for the last thirty years.

Mr. A. R. Wallace reviewed "Life and Habit" in *Nature* (March 27, 1879), but he did not find the line I had taken a familiar one, as he surely must have done if it had followed easily by implication from Mr. Spencer's works. He called it "an ingenious and paradoxical explanation" which was evidently new to him. He concluded by saying that "it might yet afford a clue to some of the deepest mysteries of the organic world."

Professor Mivart, when he reviewed my books on Evolution in the *American Catholic Quarterly Review* (July 1881), said, "Mr Butler is not only perfectly logical and consistent in the startling consequences he deduces from his principles, but," &c. Professor Mivart could not have found my consequences startling if they had already been insisted upon for many years by one of the best-known writers of the day.

The reviewer of "Evolution Old and New" in the *Saturday Review* (March 31, 1879), of whom all I can venture to say is that he or she is a person whose name carries weight in matters connected with biology, though he (for brevity) was in the humour for seeing everything objectionable in me that could be seen, still saw no Mr. Spencer in me. He said - "Mr Butler's own particular contribution to the terminology of Evolution is the phrase two or three times repeated with some emphasis" (I repeated it not two or three times only, but whenever and wherever I could venture to do so without wearying the reader beyond endurance) "oneness of personality between parents and offspring." The writer proceeded to reprobate this in language upon which a Huxley could hardly improve, but as he declares himself unable to discover what it means, it may be presumed that the idea of continued personality between successive generations was new to him.

When Dr. Francis Darwin called on me a day or two before "Life and Habit" went to the press, he said the theory which had pleased him more than any he had seen for some time was one which referred all life to memory;{44a} he doubtless intended "which referred all the phenomena of heredity to memory." He then mentioned Professor Ray Lankester's article in *Nature*, of which I had not heard, but he said nothing about Mr. Spencer, and spoke of the idea as one which had been quite new to him.

The above names comprise (excluding Mr. Spencer himself) perhaps those of the best-known writers on evolution that can be mentioned as now before the public; it is curious that Mr Spencer should be the only one of them to see any substantial resemblance between the "Principles of Psychology" and Professor Hering's address and "Life and Habit."

I ought, perhaps, to say that Mr. Romanes, writing to the *Athenæum* (March 8, 1884), took a different view of the value of the theory of inherited memory to the one he took in 1881.

In 1881 he said it was "simply absurd" to suppose it could "possibly be fraught with any benefit to science" or "reveal any truth of profound significance;" in 1884 he said of the same theory, that "it formed the backbone of a the previous literature upon instinct" by Darwin, Spencer, Lewes, Fiske, and Spalding, "not to mention their numerous followers, and is by all of them elaborately stated as clearly as any theory can be stated in words."

Few except Mr. Romanes will say this. I grant it ought to "have formed the backbone," &c., and ought "to have been elaborately stated," &c., but when I wrote "Life and Habit" neither Mr Romanes nor any one else understood it to have been even glanced at by more than a very few, and as for having been "elaborately stated," it had been stated by Professor Hering as elaborately as it could be stated within the limits of an address of only twenty-two pages, but with this exception it had never been stated at all. It is not too much to say that "Life and Habit," when it first came out, was considered so startling a paradox that people would not believe in my desire to be taken seriously, or at any rate were able to pretend that they thought I was not writing seriously.

Mr. Romanes knows this just as well as all must do who keep an eye on evolution; he himself, indeed, had said (*Nature,* January 27, 1881) that so long as I "aimed only at entertaining" my "readers by such works as 'Erewhon' and 'Life and Habit'" (as though these books were of kindred character) I was in my proper sphere. It would be doing too little credit to Mr. Romanes' intelligence to suppose him not to have known when he said this that "Life and Habit" was written as seriously as my subsequent books on evolution, but it suited him at the moment to join those who professed to consider it another book of paradoxes such as, I suppose, "Erewhon" had been, so he classed the two together. He could not have done this unless enough people thought, or said they thought, the books akin, to give colour to his doing so.

One alone of all my reviewers has, to my knowledge, brought Mr. Spencer against me. This was a writer in the *St. James's Gazette* (December 2, 1880). I challenged him in a letter which appeared (December 8, 1880), and said, "I would ask your reviewer to be kind enough to refer your readers to those passages of Mr. Spencer's "Principles of Psychology" which in any direct intelligible way refer the phenomena of instinct and heredity generally, to memory on the part of offspring of the action it *bonâ fide* took in the persons of its forefathers." The reviewer made no reply, and I concluded, as I have since found correctly, that he could not find the passages.

True, in his "Principles of Psychology" (vol. ii. p. 195) Mr. Spencer says that we have only to expand the doctrine that all intelligence is acquired through experience "so as to make it include with the experience of each individual the experiences of all ancestral individuals," &c. This is all very good, but it is much the same as saying, "We have only got to stand on our heads and we shall be able to do so and so." We did not see our way to standing on our heads, and Mr. Spencer did not help us; we had been accustomed, as I am afraid I must have said *usque ad nauseam* already, to lose sight of the physical connection existing between parents and offspring; we understood from the marriage service that husband and wife were in a sense one flesh, but not that parents and children were so also; and without this conception of the matter, which in its way is just as true as the more commonly received one, we could not extend the experience of parents to offspring. It was not in the bond or *nexus* of our ideas to consider experience as appertaining to more than a single individual in the common acceptance of the term; these two ideas were so closely bound together that wherever the one went the other went perforce. Here, indeed, in the very passage of Mr. Spencer's just referred to, the race is throughout regarded as "a series of individuals" - without an attempt to call attention to that other view, in virtue of which we are able to extend to many an idea we had been accustomed to confine to one.

In his chapter on Memory, Mr. Spencer certainly approaches the Heringian view. He says, "On the one hand, Instinct may be regarded as a kind of organised memory; on the other, Memory may be regarded as a kind of incipient instinct" ("Principles of Psychology," ed. 2, vol. i. p. 445). Here the ball has fallen into his hands, but if he had got firm hold of it he could not have written, "Instinct *may be* regarded as *a kind of*, &c.;" to us there is neither "may be regarded as" nor "kind of" about it; we require, "Instinct is inherited memory," with an explanation making it intelligible how memory can come to be inherited at all. I do not like, again, calling memory "a kind of incipient instinct;" as Mr. Spencer puts them the words have a pleasant antithesis, but "instinct is inherited memory" covers all the ground, and to say that memory is inherited instinct is surplusage.

Nor does he stick to it long when he says that "instinct is a kind of organised memory," for two pages later he says that memory, to be memory at all, must be tolerably conscious or deliberate; he, therefore (vol. i. p. 447), denies that there can be such a thing as unconscious memory; but without this it is impossible for us to see instinct as the "kind of organised memory" which he has just been calling it, inasmuch as instinct is notably undeliberate and unreflecting.

A few pages farther on (vol. i. p. 452) he finds himself driven to unconscious memory after all, and says that "conscious memory passes into unconscious or organic memory." Having admitted unconscious memory, he declares (vol. i. p. 450) that "as fast as those connections among psychical states, which we form in memory, grow by constant repetition automatic - they *cease to be part of memory*" or, in other words, he again denies that there can be an unconscious memory.

Mr. Spencer doubtless saw that he was involved in contradiction in terms, and having always understood that contradictions in terms were very dreadful things - which, of course, under some circumstances they are - thought it well so to express himself that his readers should be more likely to push on than dwell on what was before them at the moment. I should be the last to complain of him merely on the ground that he could not escape contradiction in terms: who can? When facts conflict, contradict one another, melt into one another as the colours of the spectrum so insensibly that none can say where one begins and the other ends, contradictions in terms become first fruits of thought and speech. They are the basis of intellectual consciousness, in the same way that a physical obstacle is the basis of physical sensation. No opposition, no sensation, applies as much to the psychical as to the physical kingdom, as soon as these two have got well above the horizon of our thoughts and can be seen as two. No contradiction, no consciousness; no cross, no crown; contradictions are the very small deadlocks without which there is no going; going is our sense of a succession of small impediments or deadlocks; it is a succession of cutting Gordian knots, which on a small scale please or pain as the case may be; on a larger, give an ecstasy of pleasure, or shock to the extreme of endurance; and on a still larger, kill whether they be on the right side or the wrong. Nature, as I said in "Life and Habit," hates that any principle should breed hermaphroditically, but will give to each an helpmeet for it which shall cross it and be the undoing of it; and in the undoing, do; and in the doing, undo, and so *ad infinitum*. Cross-fertilisation is just as necessary for continued fertility of ideas as for that of organic life, and the attempt to frown this or that down merely on the ground that it involves contradiction in terms, without at the same time showing that the contradiction is on a larger scale than healthy thought can stomach, argues either small sense or small sincerity on the part of those who make it. The contradictions employed by Mr. Spencer are objectionable, not on the ground of their being contradictions at all, but on the ground of their being blinked, and used unintelligently.

But though it is not possible for any one to get a clear conception of Mr. Spencer's meaning, we may say with more confidence what it was that he did not mean. He did not mean to make memory the keystone of his system; he has none of that sense of the unifying, binding force of memory which Professor Hering has so well expressed, nor does he show any signs of perceiving the far-reaching consequences that ensue if the phenomena of heredity are considered as phenomena of memory. Thus, when he is dealing with the phenomena of old age (vol. i. p. 538, ed. 2) he does not ascribe them to lapse and failure of memory, nor surmise the principle underlying longevity. He never mentions memory in connection with heredity without presently saying something which makes us involuntarily think of a man missing an easy catch at cricket; it is only rarely, however, that he connects the two at all. I have only been able to find the word "inherited" or any derivative of the verb "to inherit" in connection with memory once in all the 1300 long pages of the "Principles of Psychology." It occurs in vol ii. p. 200, 2d ed., where the words stand, "Memory, inherited or acquired." I submit that this was unintelligible when Mr. Spencer wrote it, for want of an explanation which he never gave; I submit, also, that he could not have left it unexplained, nor yet as an unrepeated expression not introduced till late in his work, if he had had any idea of its pregnancy.

At any rate, whether he intended to imply what he now implies that he intended to imply (for Mr. Spencer, like the late Mr. Darwin, is fond of qualifying phrases), I have shown that those most able and willing to understand him did not take him to mean what he now appears anxious to have it supposed that he meant. Surely, moreover, if he had meant it he would have spoken sooner, when he saw his meaning had been missed. I can, however, have no hesitation in saying that if I had known the "Principles of Psychology" earlier, as well as I know the work now, I should have used it largely.

It may be interesting, before we leave Mr. Spencer, to see whether he even now assigns to continued personality and memory the place assigned to it by Professor Hering and myself. I will therefore give the concluding words of the letter to the *Athenæum* already referred to, in which he tells us to stand aside. He writes "I still hold that inheritance of functionally produced modifications is the chief factor throughout the higher stages of organic evolution, bodily as well as mental (see 'Principles of Biology,' i. 166), while I recognise the truth that throughout the lower stages survival of the fittest is the chief factor, and in the lowest the almost exclusive factor."

This is the same confused and confusing utterance which Mr. Spencer has been giving us any time this thirty years. According to him the fact that variations can be inherited and accumulated has less to do with the first development of organic life, than the fact that if a square organism happens to get into a square hole, it will live longer and more happily than a square organism which happens to get into a round one; he declares "the survival of the fittest" - and this is nothing but the fact that those who "fit" best into their surroundings will live longest and most comfortably - to have more to do with the development of the amœba into, we will say, a mollusc than heredity itself. True, "inheritance of functionally produced modifications" is allowed to be the chief factor throughout the "higher stages of organic evolution," but it has very little to do in the lower; in these "the almost exclusive factor" is not heredity, or inheritance, but "survival of the fittest."

Of course we know that Mr. Spencer does not believe this; of course, also, all who are fairly well up in the history of the development theory will see why Mr. Spencer has attempted to draw this distinction between the "factors" of the development of the higher and lower forms of life; but no matter how or why Mr. Spencer has been led to say what he has, he has no business to have said it. What can we think of a writer who, after so many years of writing upon his subject, in a passage in which he should make his meaning doubly clear, inasmuch as he is claiming ground taken by other writers, declares that though hereditary use and disuse, or, to use his own words, "the inheritance of functionally produced modifications," is indeed very important in connection with the development of the higher forms of life, yet heredity itself has little or nothing to do with that of the lower? Variations, whether produced functionally or not, can only be perpetuated and accumulated because they can be inherited; - and this applies just as much to the lower as to the higher forms of life; the question which Professor Hering and I have tried to answer is "How comes it that anything can be inherited at all? In virtue of what power is it that offspring can repeat and improve upon the performances of their parents?" Our answer was, "Because in a very valid sense, though not perhaps in the most usually understood, there is continued personality and an abiding memory between successive generations." How does Mr. Spencer's confession of faith touch this? If any meaning can be extracted from his words, he is no more supporting this view now than he was when he wrote the passages he has adduced to show that he was supporting it thirty years ago; but after all no coherent meaning can be got out of Mr. Spencer's letter - except, of course, that Professor Hering and myself are to stand aside. I have abundantly shown that I am very ready to do this in favour of Professor Hering, but see no reason for admitting Mr. Spencer's claim to have been among the forestallers of "Life and Habit."

CHAPTER IV {52a} - Mr. Romanes' "Mental Evolution in Animals"

Without raising the unprofitable question how Mr. Romanes, in spite of the indifference with which he treated the theory of Inherited Memory in 1881, came, in 1883, to be sufficiently imbued with a sense of its importance, I still cannot afford to dispense with the weight of his authority, and in this chapter will show how closely he not infrequently approaches the Heringian position.

Thus, he says that the analogies between the memory with which we are familiar in daily life and hereditary memory "are so numerous and precise" as to justify us in considering them to be of essentially the same kind. {52b}

Again, he says that although the memory of milk shown by new-born infants is "at all events in large part hereditary it is none the less memory" of a certain kind. {52c}

Two lines lower down he writes of "hereditary memory or instinct," thereby implying that instinct is "hereditary memory." "It makes no essential difference," he says, "whether the past sensation was actually experienced by the individual itself, or bequeathed it, so to speak, by its ancestors. {52d} For it makes no essential difference whether the nervous changes . . . were occasioned during the life-time of the individual or during that of the species, and afterwards impressed by heredity on the individual."

Lower down on the same page he writes:-

"As showing how close is the connection between hereditary memory and instinct," &c.

And on the following page:-

"And this shows how closely the phenomena of hereditary memory are related to those of individual memory: at thi stage . . . it is practically impossible to disentangle the effects of hereditary memory from those of the individual."

Again:-

"Another point which we have here to consider is the part which heredity has played in forming the perceptive faculty of the individual prior to its own experience. We have already seen that heredity plays an important part in forming memory of ancestral experiences, and thus it is that many animals come into the world with their power of perception already largely developed. The wealth of ready-formed information, and therefore of ready-made power of perception, with which many newly-born or newly-hatched animals are provided, is so great and so precise that it scarcely requires to be supplemented by the subsequent experience of the individual." {53a}

Again:-

"Instincts probably owe their origin and development to one or other of the two principles.

"I. The first mode of origin consists in natural selection or survival of the fittest, continuously preserving actions &c. &c.

"II. The second mode of origin is as follows:- By the effects of habit in successive generations, actions which were originally intelligent become as it were stereotyped into permanent instincts. Just as in the lifetime of the individual adjustive actions which were originally intelligent may by frequent repetition become automatic, so in the lifetime of species actions originally intelligent may by frequent repetition and heredity so write their effects on the nervous system that the latter is prepared, even before individual experience, to perform adjustive actions mechanically which in previous generations were performed intelligently. This mode of origin of instincts has been appropriately called (by Lewes - see "Problems of Life and Mind" {54a}) the 'lapsing of intelligence.'" {54b}

I may say in passing that in spite of the great stress laid by Mr. Romanes both in his "Mental Evolution in Animals" and in his letters to the *Athenæum* in March 1884, on Natural Selection as an originator and developer of instinct, he very soon afterwards let the Natural Selection part of the story go as completely without saying as I do myself, or a Mr. Darwin did during the later years of his life. Writing to *Nature,* April 10, 1884, he said: "To deny *that experience in the course of successive generations is the source of instinct* is not to meet by way of argument the enormous mass of evidence which goes to prove *that this is the case*." Here, then, instinct is referred, without reservation, to "experience in successive generations," and this is nonsense unless explained as Professor Hering and I explain it. Mr. Romanes' words, in fact, amount to an unqualified acceptance of the chapter "Instinct as Inherited Memory" given in "Life and Habit," of which Mr. Romanes in March 1884 wrote in terms which it is not necessary to repeat.

Later on:-

"That 'practice makes perfect' is a matter, as I have previously said, of daily observation. Whether we regard a juggler, a pianist, or a billiard-player, a child learning his lesson or an actor his part by frequently repeating it, or a thousand other illustrations of the same process, we see at once that there is truth in the cynical definition of a man as a 'bundle of habits.' And the same, of course, is true of animals." {55a}

From this Mr. Romanes goes on to show "that automatic actions and conscious habits may be inherited," {55b} and in the course of doing this contends that "instincts may be lost by disuse, and conversely that they may be acquired as instincts by the hereditary transmission of ancestral experience."

On another page Mr. Romanes says:-

"Let us now turn to the second of these two assumptions, viz., that some at least among migratory birds must possess, by inheritance alone, a very precise knowledge of the particular direction to be pursued. It is without question an astonishing fact that a young cuckoo should be prompted to leave its foster parents at a particular season of the year, and without any guide to show the course previously taken by its own parents, but this is a fact which must be met by any theory of instinct which aims at being complete. Now upon our own theory it can only be met by taking it to be due to inherited memory."

A little lower Mr. Romanes says: "Of what kind, then, is the inherited memory on which the young cuckoo (if not also other migratory birds) depends? We can only answer, of the same kind, whatever this may be, as that upon which the old bird depends." {55c}

I have given above most of the more marked passages which I have been able to find in Mr. Romanes' book which attribute instinct to memory, and which admit that there is no fundamental difference between the kind of memory with which we are all familiar and hereditary memory as transmitted from one generation to another.

But throughout his work there are passages which suggest, though less obviously, the same inference.

The passages I have quoted show that Mr. Romanes is upholding the same opinions as Professor Hering's and my own, but their effect and tendency is more plain here than in Mr Romanes' own book, where they are overlaid by nearly 400 long pages of matter which is not always easy of comprehension.

Moreover, at the same time that I claim the weight of Mr. Romanes' authority, I am bound to admit that I do not find his support satisfactory. The late Mr. Darwin himself - whose mantle seems to have fallen more especially and particularly on Mr. Romanes - could not contradict himself more hopelessly than Mr. Romanes often does. Indeed in one of the very passages I have quoted in order to show that Mr. Romanes accepts the phenomena of heredity as phenomena of memory, he speaks of "heredity as playing an important part*in forming memory* of ancestral experiences;" so that, whereas I want him to say that the phenomena of heredity are due to memory, he will have it that the memory is due to the heredity, which seems to me absurd.

Over and over again Mr. Romanes insists that it is heredity which does this or that. Thus it is "*heredity with natural selection which adapt* the anatomical plan of the ganglia." {56a} It is heredity which impresses nervous changes on the individual. {56b} "In the lifetime of species actions originally intelligent may by frequent repetition and heredity," &c.; {56c} but he nowhere tells us what heredity is any more than Messrs. Herbert Spencer, Darwin, and Lewes have done. This, however, is exactly what Professor Hering, whom I have unwittingly followed, does. He resolves all phenomena of heredity, whether in respect of body or mind, into phenomena of memory. He says in effect, "A man grows his body as he does, and a bird makes her nest as she does, because both man and bird remember having grown body and made nest as they now do, or very nearly so, on innumerable past occasions." He thus, as I have said on an earlier page, reduces life from an equation of say 100 unknown quantities to one of 99 only by showing that heredity and memory, two of the original 100 unknown quantities, are in reality part of one and the same thing.

That he is right Mr. Romanes seems to me to admit, though in a very unsatisfactory way.

What, for example, can be more unsatisfactory than the following? - Mr. Romanes says that the most fundamental principle of mental operation is that of memory, and that this "is the *conditio sine quâ non* of all mental life" (page 35).

I do not understand Mr. Romanes to hold that there is any living being which has no mind at all, and I do understand him to admit that development of body and mind are closely interdependent.

If, then, "the most fundamental principle" of mind is memory, it follows that memory enters also as a fundamental principle into development of body. For mind and body are so closely connected that nothing can enter largely into the one without correspondingly affecting the other.

On a later page Mr. Romanes speaks point-blank of the new-born child as "*embodying* the results of a great mass of *hereditary experience*" (p. 77), so that what he is driving at can be collected by those who take trouble, but is not seen until we call up from our own knowledge matter whose relevancy does not appear on the face of it, and until we connect passages many pages asunder, the first of which may easily be forgotten before we reach the second. There can be no doubt, however, that Mr. Romanes does in reality, like Professor Hering and myself, regard development, whether of mind or body, as due to memory, for it is now pretty generally seen to be nonsense to talk about "hereditary experience" or "hereditary memory" if anything else is intended.

I have said above that on page 113 of his recent work Mr. Romanes declares the analogies between the memory with which we are familiar in daily life, and hereditary memory, to be "so numerous and precise" as to justify us in considering them as of one and the same kind.

This is certainly his meaning, but, with the exception of the words within inverted commas, it is not his language. His own words are these:-

"Profound, however, as our ignorance unquestionably is concerning the physical substratum of memory, I think we are at least justified in regarding this substratum as the same both in ganglionic or organic, and in the conscious or psychological memory, seeing that the analogies between them are so numerous and precise. Consciousness is but an adjunct which arises when the physical processes, owing to infrequency of repetition, complexity of operation, or other causes, involve what I have before called ganglionic friction."

I submit that I have correctly translated Mr. Romanes' meaning, and also that we have a right to complain of his not saying what he has to say in words which will involve less "ganglionic friction" on the part of the reader.

Another example may be found on p. 43 of Mr. Romanes' book. "Lastly," he writes, "just as innumerable special mechanisms of muscular co-ordinations are found to be inherited, innumerable special associations of ideas are found to be the same, and in one case as in the other the strength of the organically imposed connection is found to bear a direct proportion to the frequency with which in the history of the species it has occurred."

Mr. Romanes is here intending what the reader will find insisted on on p. 51 of "Life and Habit;" but how difficult he has made what could have been said intelligibly enough, if there had been nothing but the reader's comfort to be considered. Unfortunately that seems to have been by no means the only thing of which Mr. Romanes was thinking, or why, after implying and even saying over and over again that instinct is inherited habit due to inherited memory, should he turn sharply round on p. 297 and praise Mr. Darwin for trying to snuff out "the well-known doctrine of inherited habit as advanced by Lamarck"? The answer is not far to seek. It is because Mr. Romanes did not merely want to tell us all about instinct, but wanted also, if I may use a homely metaphor, to hunt with the hounds and run with the hare at one and the same time.

I remember saying that if the late Mr. Darwin "had told us what the earlier evolutionists said, why they said it, wherein he differed from them, and in what way he proposed to set them straight, he would have taken a course at once more agreeable with usual practice, and more likely to remove misconception from his own mind and from those of his readers." {59a} This I have no doubt was one of the passages which made Mr. Romanes so angry with me. I can find no better words to apply to Mr. Romanes himself. He knows perfectly well what others have written about the connection between heredity and memory, and he knows no less well that so far as he is intelligible at all he is taking the same view that they have taken. If he had begun by saying what they had said, and had then improved on it, I for one should have been only too glad to be improved upon.

Mr. Romanes has spoiled his book just because this plain old-fashioned method of procedure was not good enough for him. One-half the obscurity which makes his meaning so hard to apprehend is due to exactly the same cause as that which has ruined so much of the late Mr. Darwin's work - I mean to a desire to appear to be differing altogether from others with whom he knew himself after all to be in substantial agreement. He adopts, but (probably quite unconsciously) in his anxiety to avoid appearing to adopt, he obscures what he is adopting.

Here, for example, is Mr. Romanes' definition of instinct:-

"Instinct is reflex action into which there is imported the element of consciousness. The term is therefore a generic one, comprising all those faculties of mind which are concerned in conscious and adaptive action, antecedent to individual experience, without necessary knowledge of the relation between means employed and ends attained, but similarly performed under similar and frequently recurring circumstances by all the individuals of the same species."

If Mr. Romanes would have been content to build frankly upon Professor Hering's foundation, the soundness of which he has elsewhere abundantly admitted, he might have said -

"Instinct is knowledge or habit acquired in past generations - the new generation remembering what happened to it before it parted company with the old. More briefly, Instinct is inherited memory." Then he might have added a rider -

"If a habit is acquired as a new one, during any given lifetime, it is not an instinct. If having been acquired in one lifetime it is transmitted to offspring, it is an instinct in the offspring, though it was not an instinct in the parent. If the habit is transmitted partially, it must be considered as partly instinctive and partly acquired."

This is easy; it tells people how they may test any action so as to know what they ought to call it; it leaves well alone by avoiding all such debatable matters as reflex action, consciousness, intelligence, purpose, knowledge of purpose, &c.; it both introduces the feature of inheritance which is the one mainly distinguishing instinctive from so-called intelligent actions, and shows the manner in which these last pass into the first, that is to say, by way of memory and habitual repetition; finally it points the fact that the new generation is not to be looked upon as a new thing, but (as Dr. Erasmus Darwin long since said {61a}) as "a branch or elongation" of the one immediately preceding it.

In Mr. Darwin's case it is hardly possible to exaggerate the waste of time, money and trouble that has been caused, by his not having been content to appear as descending with modification like other people from those who went before him. It will take years to get the evolution theory out of the mess in which Mr. Darwin has left it. He was heir to a discredited truth; he left behind him an accredited fallacy. Mr. Romanes, if he is not stopped in time, will get the theory connecting heredity and memory into just such another muddle as Mr. Darwin has got evolution, for surely the writer who can talk about *"heredity being able to work up* the faculty of homing into the instinct of migration," {61b} or of "the principle of (natural) selection combining with that of lapsing intelligence to the formation of a joint result," {61c} is little likely to depart from the usual methods of scientific procedure with advantage either to himself or any one else. Fortunately Mr. Romanes is not Mr. Darwin, and though he has certainly got Mr. Darwin's mantle, and got it very much too, it will not on Mr. Romanes' shoulders hide a good deal that people were not going to observe too closely while Mr. Darwin wore it.

I ought to say that the late Mr. Darwin appears himself eventually to have admitted the soundness of the theory connecting heredity and memory. Mr. Romanes quotes a letter written by Mr. Darwin in the last year of his life, in which he speaks of an intelligent action gradually becoming *"instinctive, i.e., memory transmitted from one generation to another."* {62a}

Briefly, the stages of Mr. Darwin's opinion upon the subject of hereditary memory are as follows:-

1859. "It would be *the most serious error* to suppose that the greater number of instincts have been acquired by habit in one generation and transmitted by inheritance to succeeding generations." {62b} And this more especially applies to the instincts of many ants.

1876. "It would be a *serious error* to suppose," &c., as before. {62c}

1881. "We should remember *what a mass of inherited knowledge* is crowded into the minute brain of a worker ant." {62d}

1881 or 1882. Speaking of a given habitual action Mr. Darwin writes: "It does not seem to me at all incredible that this action [and why this more than any other habitual action?] should then become instinctive:" i.e., *memory transmitted from one generation to another.* {62e}

And yet in 1839, or thereabouts, Mr. Darwin had pretty nearly grasped the conception from which until the last year or two of his life he so fatally strayed; for in his contribution to the volumes giving an account of the voyages of the *Adventure* and *Beagle,* he wrote: "Nature by making habit omnipotent and its effects hereditary, has fitted the Fuegian for the climate and productions of his country" (p. 237).

What is the secret of the long departure from the simple common-sense view of the matter which he took when he was a young man? I imagine simply what I have referred to in the preceding chapter, over-anxiety to appear to be differing from his grandfather, Dr. Erasmus Darwin, and Lamarck.

I believe I may say that Mr. Darwin before he died not only admitted the connection between memory and heredity, but came also to see that he must readmit that design in organism which he had so many years opposed. For in the preface to Hermann Muller's "Fertilisation of Flowers," {63a} which bears a date only a very few weeks prior to Mr. Darwin's death, I find him saying:- "Design in nature has for a long time deeply interested many men, and though the subject must now be looked at from a somewhat different point of view from what was formerly the case, it is not on that account rendered less interesting." This is mused forth as a general gnome, and may mean anything or nothing: the writer of the letterpress under the hieroglyph in Old Moore's Almanac could not be more guarded; but I think I know what it does mean.

I cannot, of course, be sure; Mr. Darwin did not probably intend that I should; but I assume with confidence that whether there is design in organism or no, there is at any rate design in this passage of Mr. Darwin's. This, we may be sure, is not a fortuitous variation; and, moreover, it is introduced for some reason which made Mr. Darwin think it worth while to go out of his way to introduce it. It has no fitness in its connection with Hermann Muller's book, for what little Hermann Müller says about teleology at all is to condemn it; why, then, should Mr. Darwin muse here of all places in the world about the interest attaching to design in organism? Neither has the passage any connection with the rest of the preface. There is not another word about design, and even here Mr. Darwin seems mainly anxious to face both ways, and pat design as it were on the head while not committing himself to any proposition which could be disputed.

The explanation is sufficiently obvious. Mr Darwin wanted to hedge. He saw that the design which his works had been mainly instrumental in pitchforking out of organisms no less manifestly designed than a burglar's jemmy is designed, had nevertheless found its way back again, and that though, as I insisted in "Evolution Old and New," and "Unconscious Memory," it must now be placed within the organism instead of outside it, as "was formerly the case," it was not on that account any the less - design, as well as interesting.

I should like to have seen Mr. Darwin say this more explicitly. Indeed I should have liked to have seen Mr. Darwin say anything at all about the meaning of which there could be no mistake, and without contradicting himself elsewhere; but this was not Mr. Darwin's manner.

In passing I will give another example of Mr Darwin's manner when he did not quite dare even to hedge. It is to be found in the preface which he wrote to Professor Weismann's "Studies in the Theory of Descent," published in 1881.

"Several distinguished naturalists," says Mr. Darwin, "maintain with much confidence that organic beings tend to vary and to rise in the scale, independently of the conditions to which they and their progenitors have been exposed whilst others maintain that all variation is due to such exposure, though the manner in which the environment acts is as yet quite unknown. At the present time there is hardly any question in biology of more importance than this of the nature and causes of variability; and the reader will find in the present work an able discussion on the whole subject, which will probably lead him to pause before he admits the existence of an innate tendency to perfectibility" - or towards *being able to be perfected.*

I could find no able discussion upon the whole subject in Professor Weismann's book. There was a little something here and there, but not much.

It may be expected that I should say something here about Mr. Romanes' latest contribution to biology - I mean his theory of physiological selection, of which the two first instalments have appeared in *Nature* just as these pages are leaving my hands, and many months since the foregoing, and most of the following chapters were written. I admit to feeling a certain sense of thankfulness that they did not appear earlier; as it is, my book is too far advanced to be capable of further embryonic change, and this must be my excuse for saying less about Mr. Romanes' theory than I might perhaps otherwise do. I cordially, however, agree with the *Times,* which says that "Mr. George Romanes appears to be the biological investigator on whom the mantle of Mr. Darwin has most conspicuously descended" (August 16, 1886). Mr. Romanes is just the person whom the late Mr. Darwin would select to carry on his work, and Mr. Darwin was just the kind of person towards whom Mr. Romanes would find himself instinctively attracted.

The *Times* continues - "The position which Mr. Romanes takes up is the result of his perception shared by many evolutionists, that the theory of natural selection is not really a theory of the origin of species. . . ." What, then becomes of Mr. Darwin's most famous work, which was written expressly to establish natural selection as the main means of organic modification? "The new factor which Mr. Romanes suggests," continues the *Times,* "is that at a certain stage of development of varieties in a state of nature a change takes place in their reproductive system: rendering those which differ in some particulars mutually infertile, and thus the formation of new permanent specie: takes place without the swamping effect of free intercrossing. . . . How his theory can be properly termed one o: selection he fails to make clear. If correct, it is a law or principle of operation rather than a process of selection. I has been objected to Mr. Romanes' theory that it is the re-statement of a fact. This objection is less important than the lack of facts in support of the theory." The *Times,* however, implies it as its opinion that the required facts will be forthcoming by and by, and that when they have been found Mr. Romanes' suggestion will constitute "the most important addition to the theory of evolution since the publication of the 'Origin of Species.'" Considering that th *Times* has just implied the main thesis of the "Origin of Species" to be one which does not stand examination, this i rather a doubtful compliment.

Neither Mr. Romanes nor the writer in the *Times* appears to perceive that the results which may or may not be supposed to ensue on choice depend upon what it is that is supposed to be chosen from; they do not appear to see that though the expression natural selection must be always more or less objectionable, as too highly charged with metaphor for purposes of science, there is nevertheless a natural selection which is open to no other objection than this, and which, when its metaphorical character is borne well in mind, may be used without serious risk of error, whereas natural selection from variations that are mainly fortuitous is chimerical as well as metaphorical. Both writers speak of natural selection as though there could not possibly be any selection in the course of nature, o: natural survival, of any but accidental variations. Thus Mr. Romanes says: {66a} "The swamping effect of free inter-crossing upon an individual variation constitutes perhaps the most formidable difficulty with which *the theory o) natural selection* is beset." And the writer of the article in the *Times* above referred to says: "In truth *the theory of natura selection* presents many facts and results which increase rather than diminish the difficulty of accounting for the existence of species." The assertion made in each case is true if the Charles-Darwinian selection from fortuitou: variations is intended, but it does not hold good if the selection is supposed to be made from variations under whick there lies a general principle of wide and abiding application. It is not likely that a man of Mr. Romanes' antecedent: should not be perfectly awake to considerations so obvious as the foregoing, and I am afraid I am inclined to consider his whole suggestion as only an attempt upon the part of the wearer of Mr. Darwin's mantle to carry on Mr Darwin's work in Mr. Darwin's spirit.

I have seen Professor Hering's theory adopted recently more unreservedly by Dr. Creighton in his "Illustrations of Unconscious Memory in Disease." {67a} Dr. Creighton avowedly bases his system on Professor Hering's address, and endorses it; it is with much pleasure that I have seen him lend the weight of his authority to the theory that eack cell and organ has an individual memory. In "Life and Habit" I expressed a hope that the opinions it upheld would be found useful by medical men, and am therefore the more glad to see that this has proved to be the case. I may perhaps be pardoned if I quote the passage in" Life and Habit" to which I am referring. It runs:-

'*Mutatis mutandis,* the above would seem to hold as truly about medicine as about politics. We cannot reason with our cells, for they know so much more" (of course I mean "about their own business") "than we do, that they cannot understand us; - but though we cannot reason with them, we can find out what they have been most accustomed to, and what, therefore, they are most likely to expect; we can see that they get this as far as it is in our power to give it them, and may then generally leave the rest to them, only bearing in mind that they will rebel equally against too sudden a change of treatment and no change at all" (p. 305).

Dr. Creighton insists chiefly on the importance of change, which - though I did not notice his saying so - he would doubtless see as a mode of cross-fertilisation, fraught in all respects with the same advantages as this, and requiring the same precautions against abuse; he would not, however, I am sure, deny that there could be no fertility of good results if too wide a cross were attempted, so that I may claim the weight of his authority as supporting both th theory of an unconscious memory in general, and the particular application of it to medicine which I had venture to suggest.

"Has the word 'memory,'" he asks, "a real application to unconscious organic phenomena, or do we use it outside its ancient limits only in a figure of speech?"

"If I had thought," he continues later, "that unconscious memory was no more than a metaphor, and the detailed application of it to these various forms of disease merely allegorical, I should still have judged it not unprofitable t represent a somewhat hackneyed class of maladies in the light of a parable. None of our faculties is more familiar t us in its workings than the memory, and there is hardly any force or power in nature which every one knows so well as the force of habit. To say that a neurotic subject is like a person with a retentive memory, or that a diathesis gradually acquired is like an over-mastering habit, is at all events to make comparisons with things that we all understand.

"For reasons given chiefly in the first chapter, I conclude that retentiveness, with reproduction, is a single undivided faculty throughout the whole of our life, whether mental or bodily, conscious or unconscious; and I claim the description of a certain class of maladies according to the phraseology of memory and habit as a real description an not a figurative." (p. 2.)

As a natural consequence of the foregoing he regards "alterative action" as "habit-breaking action."

As regards the organism's being guided throughout its development to maturity by an unconscious memory, Dr. Creighton says that "Professor Bain calls reproduction the acme of organic complication." "I should prefer to say," he adds, "the acme of organic implication; for the reason that the sperm and germ elements are perfectly simple having nothing in their form or structure to show for the marvellous potentialities within them.

"I now come to the application of these considerations to the doctrine of unconscious memory. If generation is th acme of organic implicitness, what is its correlative in nature, what is the acme of organic explicitness? Obviousl the fine flower of consciousness. Generation is implicit memory, consciousness is explicit memory; generation is potential memory, consciousness is actual memory."

I am not sure that I understand the preceding paragraph as clearly as I should wish, but having quoted enough to perhaps induce the reader to turn to Dr. Creighton's book, I will proceed to the subject indicated in my title.

CHAPTER V - Statement of the Question at Issue

Of the two points referred to in the opening sentence of this book - I mean the connection between heredity and memory, and the reintroduction of design into organic modification - the second is both the more important and the one which stands most in need of support. The substantial identity between heredity and memory is becoming generally admitted; as regards my second point, however, I cannot flatter myself that I have made much way against the formidable array of writers on the neo-Darwinian side; I shall therefore devote the rest of my book as far a possible to this subject only. Natural selection (meaning by these words the preservation in the ordinary course of nature of favourable variations that are supposed to be mainly matters of pure good luck and in no way arising ou of function) has been, to use an Americanism than which I can find nothing apter, the biggest biological boom of the last quarter of a century; it is not, therefore, to be wondered at that Professor Ray Lankester, Mr. Romanes, Mr. Grant Allen, and others, should show some impatience at seeing its value as prime means of modification called in question. Within the last few months, indeed, Mr. Grant Allen {70a} and Professor Ray Lankester {70b} in England, and Dr. Ernst Krause {70c} in Germany, have spoken and written warmly in support of the theory of natural selection, and in opposition to the views taken by myself; if they are not to be left in possession of the field the sooner they are met the better.

Stripped of detail the point at issue is this; - whether luck or cunning is the fitter to be insisted on as the main means of organic development. Erasmus Darwin and Lamarck answered this question in favour of cunning. They settled i in favour of intelligent perception of the situation - within, of course, ever narrower and narrower limits as organisı retreats farther backwards from ourselves - and persistent effort to turn it to account. They made this the soul of all development whether of mind or body.

And they made it, like all other souls, liable to aberration both for better and worse. They held that some organisms show more ready wit and *savoir faire* than others; that some give more proofs of genius and have more frequent happy thoughts than others, and that some have even gone through waters of misery which they have used as wells.

The sheet anchor both of Erasmus Darwin and Lamarck is in good sense and thrift; still they are aware that money has been sometimes made by "striking oil," and ere now been transmitted to descendants in spite of the haphazard way in which it was originally acquired. No speculation, no commerce; "nothing venture, nothing have," is as true for the development of organic wealth as for that of any other kind, and neither Erasmus Darwin nor Lamarcl hesitated about admitting that highly picturesque and romantic incidents of developmental venture do from time tc time occur in the race histories even of the dullest and most dead-level organisms under the name of "sports;" but they would hold that even these occur most often and most happily to those that have persevered in well-doing for some generations. Unto the organism that hath is given, and from the organism that hath not is taken away; so that even "sports" prove to be only a little off thrift, which still remains the sheet anchor of the early evolutionists. They believe, in fact, that more organic wealth has been made by saving than in any other way. The race is not in the long run to the phenomenally swift nor the battle to the phenomenally strong, but to the good average all-round organism that is alike shy of Radical crotchets and old world obstructiveness. *Festina,* but *festina lente* - perhaps as involving so completely the contradiction in terms which must underlie all modification - is the motto they would assign to organism, and *Chi va piano va lontano,* they hold to be a maxim as old, if not as the hills (and they have a hankering even after these), at any rate as the amœba.

To repeat in other words. All enduring forms establish a *modus vivendi* with their surroundings. They can do this because both they and the surroundings are plastic within certain undefined but somewhat narrow limits. They are plastic because they can to some extent change their habits, and changed habit, if persisted in, involves corresponding change, however slight, in the organs employed; but their plasticity depends in great measure upon their failure to perceive that they are moulding themselves. If a change is so great that they are seriously incommoded by its novelty, they are not likely to acquiesce in it kindly enough to grow to it, but they will make no difficulty about the miracle involved in accommodating themselves to a difference of only two or three per cent. {72a}

As long as no change exceeds this percentage, and as long, also, as fresh change does not supervene till the preceding one is well established, there seems no limit to the amount of modification which may be accumulated in the course of generations - provided, of course, always, that the modification continues to be in conformity with the instinctive habits and physical development of the organism in their collective capacity. Where the change is too great, or where an organ has been modified cumulatively in some one direction, until it has reached a development too seriously out of harmony with the habits of the organism taken collectively, then the organism holds itself excused from further effort, throws up the whole concern, and takes refuge in the liquidation and reconstruction of death. It is only on the relinquishing of further effort that this death ensues; as long as effort endures, organisms go on from change to change, altering and being altered - that is to say, either killing themselves piecemeal in deference to the surroundings or killing the surroundings piecemeal to suit themselves. There is a ceaseless higgling and haggling, or rather a life-and-death struggle between these two things as long as life lasts, and one or other or both have in no small part to re-enter into the womb from whence they came and be born again in some form which shall give greater satisfaction.

All change is *pro tanto* death or *pro tanto* birth. Change is the common substratum which underlies both life and death; life and death are not two distinct things absolutely antagonistic to one another; in the highest life there is still much death, and in the most complete death there is still not a little life. *La vie,* says Claud Bernard, {73a} *c'est la mort:* he might have added, and perhaps did, *et la mort ce n'est que la vie transformée.* Life and death are the extreme modes of something which is partly both and wholly neither; this something is common, ordinary change; solve any change and the mystery of life and death will be revealed; show why and how anything becomes ever anything other in any respect than what it is at any given moment, and there will be little secret left in any other change. One is not in its ultimate essence more miraculous that another; it may be more striking - a greater *congeries* of shocks, it may be more credible or more incredible, but not more miraculous; all change is *quâ* us absolutely incomprehensible and miraculous; the smallest change baffles the greatest intellect if its essence, as apart from its phenomena, be inquired into.

But however this may be, all organic change is either a growth or a dissolution, or a combination of the two. Growth is the coming together of elements with *quasi* similar characteristics. I understand it is believed to be the coming together of matter in certain states of motion with other matter in states so nearly similar that the rhythms of the one coalesce with and hence reinforce the rhythms pre-existing in the other - making, rather than marring and undoing them. Life and growth are an attuning, death and decay are an untuning; both involve a succession of greater or smaller attunings and untunings; organic life is "the diapason closing full in man"; it is the fulness of a tone that varies in pitch, quality, and in the harmonics to which it gives rise; it ranges through every degree of complexity from the endless combinations of life-and-death within life-and-death which we find in the mammalia, to the comparative simplicity of the amœba. Death, again, like life, ranges through every degree of complexity. All pleasant changes are recreative; they are *pro tanto* births; all unpleasant changes are wearing, and, as such, *pro tanto* deaths, but we can no more exhaust either wholly of the other, than we can exhaust all the air out of a receiver pleasure and pain lurk within one another, as life in death, and death in life, or as rest and unrest in one another.

There is no greater mystery in life than in death. We talk as though the riddle of life only need engage us; this is not so; death is just as great a miracle as life; the one is two and two making five, the other is five splitting into two and two. Solve either, and we have solved the other; they should be studied not apart, for they are never parted, but together, and they will tell more tales of one another than either will tell about itself. If there is one thing which advancing knowledge makes clearer than another, it is that death is swallowed up in life, and life in death; so that if the last enemy that shall be subdued is death, then indeed is our salvation nearer than what we thought, for in strictness there is neither life nor death, nor thought nor thing, except as figures of speech, and as the approximations which strike us for the time as most convenient. There is neither perfect life nor perfect death, but a being ever with the Lord only, in the eternal φορα, or going to and fro and heat and fray of the universe. When we were young we thought the one certain thing was that we should one day come to die; now we know the one certain thing to be that we shall never wholly do so. *Non omnis moriar,* says Horace, and "I die daily," says St. Paul, as though a life beyond the grave, and a death on this side of it, were each some strange thing which happened to them alone of all men; but who dies absolutely once for all, and for ever at the hour that is commonly called that of death and who does not die daily and hourly? Does any man in continuing to live from day to day or moment to moment, do more than continue in a changed body, with changed feelings, ideas, and aims, so that he lives from moment to moment only in virtue of a simultaneous dying from moment to moment also? Does any man in dying do more than, on a larger and more complete scale, what he has been doing on a small one, as the most essential factor of his life, from the day that he became "he" at all? When the note of life is struck the harmonics of death are sounded and so, again, to strike death is to arouse the infinite harmonics of life that rise forthwith as incense curling upwards from a censer. If in the midst of life we are in death, so also in the midst of death we are in life, and whether we live or whether we die, whether we like it and know anything about it or no, still we do it to the Lord - living always, dying always, and in the Lord always, the unjust and the just alike, for God is no respecter of persons.

Consciousness and change, so far as we can watch them, are as functionally interdependent as mind and matter, or condition and substance, are - for the condition of every substance may be considered as the expression and outcome of its mind. Where there is consciousness there is change; where there is no change there is no consciousness; may we not suspect that there is no change without a *pro tanto* consciousness however simple and unspecialised? Change and motion are one, so that we have substance, feeling, change (or motion), as the ultimate three-in-one of our thoughts, and may suspect all change, and all feeling, attendant or consequent, however limited, to be the interaction of those states which for want of better terms we call mind and matter. Action may be regarded as a kind of middle term between mind and matter; it is the throe of thought and thing, the quivering clash and union of body and soul commonplace enough in practice; miraculous, as violating every canon on which thought and reason are founded, if we theorise about it, put it under the microscope, and vivisect it. It is here, if anywhere, that body or substance is guilty of the contradiction in terms of combining with that which is without material substance and cannot therefore, be conceived by us as passing in and out with matter, till the two become a body ensouled and a soul embodied.

All body is more or less ensouled. As it gets farther and farther from ourselves, indeed, we sympathise less with it; nothing, we say to ourselves, can have intelligence unless we understand all about it - as though intelligence in all except ourselves meant the power of being understood rather than of understanding. We are intelligent, and no intelligence, so different from our own as to baffle our powers of comprehension deserves to be called intelligence at all. The more a thing resembles ourselves, the more it thinks as we do - and thus by implication tells us that we are right, the more intelligent we think it; and the less it thinks as we do, the greater fool it must be; if a substance does not succeed in making it clear that it understands our business, we conclude that it cannot have any business of its own, much less understand it, or indeed understand anything at all. But letting this pass, so far as we are concerned, χρηματων παντων μετρον ανθρωπος; we are body ensouled, and soul embodied, ourselves, nor is it possible for us to think seriously of anything so unlike ourselves as to consist either of soul without body, or body without soul. Unmattered condition, therefore, is as inconceivable by us as unconditioned matter; and we must hold that all body with which we can be conceivably concerned is more or less ensouled, and all soul, in like manner, more or less embodied. Strike either body or soul - that is to say, effect either a physical or a mental change, and the harmonics of the other sound. So long as body is minded in a certain way - so long, that is to say, as it feels, knows, remembers, concludes, and forecasts one set of things - it will be in one form; if it assumes a new one, otherwise than by external violence, no matter how slight the change may be, it is only through having changed its mind, through having forgotten and died to some trains of thought, and having been correspondingly born anew by the adoption of new ones. What it will adopt depends upon which of the various courses open to it it considers most to its advantage.

What it will think to its advantage depends mainly on the past habits of its race. Its past and now invisible lives will influence its desires more powerfully than anything it may itself be able to add to the sum of its likes and dislikes nevertheless, over and above preconceived opinion and the habits to which all are slaves, there is a small salary, or, as it were, agency commission, which each may have for himself, and spend according to his fancy; from this, indeed, income-tax must be deducted; still there remains a little margin of individual taste, and here, high up on this narrow, inaccessible ledge of our souls, from year to year a breed of not unprolific variations build where reason cannot reach them to despoil them; for *de gustibus non est disputandum.*

Here we are as far as we can go. Fancy, which sometimes sways so much and is swayed by so little, and which sometimes, again, is so hard to sway, and moves so little when it is swayed; whose ways have a method of their own, but are not as our ways - fancy, lies on the extreme borderland of the realm within which the writs of our thoughts run, and extends into that unseen world wherein they have no jurisdiction. Fancy is as the mist upon the horizon which blends earth and sky; where, however, it approaches nearest to the earth and can be reckoned with, it is seen as melting into desire, and this as giving birth to design and effort. As the net result and outcome of these last, living forms grow gradually but persistently into physical conformity with their own intentions, and become outward and visible signs of the inward and spiritual faiths, or wants of faith, that have been most within them. They thus very gradually, but none the less effectually, design themselves.

In effect, therefore, Erasmus Darwin and Lamarck introduce uniformity into the moral and spiritual worlds as it was already beginning to be introduced into the physical. According to both these writers development has ever been a matter of the same energy, effort, good sense, and perseverance, as tend to advancement of life now among ourselves. In essence it is neither more nor less than this, as the rain-drop which denuded an ancient formation is of the same kind as that which is denuding a modern one, though its effect may vary in geometrical ratio with the effect it has produced already. As we are extending reason to the lower animals, so we must extend a system of moral government by rewards and punishments no less surely; and if we admit that to some considerable extent man is man, and master of his fate, we should admit also that all organic forms which are saved at all have been in proportionate degree masters of their fate too, and have worked out, not only their own salvation, but their salvation according, in no small measure, to their own goodwill and pleasure, at times with a light heart, and at times in fear and trembling. I do not say that Erasmus Darwin and Lamarck saw all the foregoing as clearly as it is easy to see it now; what I have said, however, is only the natural development of their system.

CHAPTER VI - Statement of the Question at Issue *(continued)*

So much for the older view; and now for the more modern opinion. According to Messrs. Darwin and Wallace, and ostensibly, I am afraid I should add, a great majority of our most prominent biologists, the view taken by Erasmus Darwin and Lamarck is not a sound one. Some organisms, indeed, are so admirably adapted to their surroundings, and some organs discharge their functions with so much appearance of provision, that we are apt to think they must owe their development to sense of need and consequent contrivance, but this opinion is fantastic; the appearance of design is delusive; what we are tempted to see as an accumulated outcome of desire and cunning, we should regard as mainly an accumulated outcome of good luck.

Let us take the eye as a somewhat crucial example. It is a seeing-machine, or thing to see with. So is a telescope; the telescope in its highest development is a secular accumulation of cunning, sometimes small, sometimes great sometimes applied to this detail of the instrument, and sometimes to that. It is an admirable example of design nevertheless, as I said in "Evolution Old and New," he who made the first rude telescope had probably no idea of any more perfect form of the instrument than the one he had himself invented. Indeed, if he had, he would have carried his idea out in practice. He would have been unable to conceive such an instrument as Lord Rosse's; the design, therefore, at present evidenced by the telescope was not design all on the part of one and the same person. Nor yet was it unmixed with chance; many a detail has been doubtless due to an accident or coincidence which was forthwith seized and made the best of. Luck there always has been and always will be, until all brains are opened, and all connections made known, but luck turned to account becomes design; there is, indeed, if things are driven home, little other design than this. The telescope, therefore, is an instrument designed in all its parts for the purpose of seeing, and, take it all round, designed with singular skill.

Looking at the eye, we are at first tempted to think that it must be the telescope over again, only more so; we are tempted to see it as something which has grown up little by little from small beginnings, as the result of effort well applied and handed down from generation to generation, till, in the vastly greater time during which the eye has been developing as compared with the telescope, a vastly more astonishing result has been arrived at. We may indeed be tempted to think this, but, according to Mr. Darwin, we should be wrong. Design had a great deal to do with the telescope, but it had nothing or hardly anything whatever to do with the eye. The telescope owes its development to cunning, the eye to luck, which, it would seem, is so far more cunning than cunning that one does not quite understand why there should be any cunning at all. The main means of developing the eye was, according to Mr. Darwin, not use as varying circumstances might direct with consequent slow increase of power and an occasional happy flight of genius, but natural selection. Natural selection, according to him, though not the sole, is still the most important means of its development and modification. {81a} What, then, is natural selection?

Mr. Darwin has told us this on the title-page of the "Origin of Species." He there defines it as "The Preservation of Favoured Races;" "Favoured" is "Fortunate," and "Fortunate" "Lucky;" it is plain, therefore, that with Mr. Darwin natural selection comes to "The Preservation of Lucky Races," and that he regarded luck as the most important feature in connection with the development even of so apparently purposive an organ as the eye, and as the one therefore, on which it was most proper to insist. And what is luck but absence of intention or design? What, then can Mr. Darwin's title-page amount to when written out plainly, but to an assertion that the main means of modification has been the preservation of races whose variations have been unintentional, that is to say, not connected with effort or intention, devoid of mind or meaning, fortuitous, spontaneous, accidental, or whatever kindred word is least disagreeable to the reader? It is impossible to conceive any more complete denial of mind as having had anything to do with organic development, than is involved in the title-page of the "Origin of Species" when its doubtless carefully considered words are studied - nor, let me add, is it possible to conceive a title-page more likely to make the reader's attention rest much on the main doctrine of evolution, and little, to use the words now most in vogue concerning it, on Mr. Darwin's own "distinctive feature."

It should be remembered that the full title of the "Origin of Species" is, "On the origin of species by means of natural selection, or the preservation of favoured races in the struggle for life." The significance of the expansion of the title escaped the greater number of Mr. Darwin's readers. Perhaps it ought not to have done so, but we certainly failed to catch it. The very words themselves escaped us - and yet there they were all the time if we had only chosen to look. We thought the book was called "On the Origin of Species," and so it was on the outside; so it was also on the inside fly-leaf; so it was on the title-page itself as long as the most prominent type was used; the expanded title was only given once, and then in smaller type; so the three big "Origins of Species" carried us with them to the exclusion of the rest.

The short and working title, "On the Origin of Species," in effect claims descent with modification generally; the expanded and technically true title only claims the discovery that luck is the main means of organic modification, and this is a very different matter. The book ought to have been entitled, "On Natural Selection, or the preservation of favoured races in the struggle for life, as the main means of the origin of species;" this should have been the expanded title, and the short title should have been "On Natural Selection." The title would not then have involved an important difference between its working and its technical forms, and it would have better fulfilled the object of a title, which is, of course, to give, as far as may be, the essence of a book in a nutshell. We learn on the authority of Mr. Darwin himself {83a} that the "Origin of Species" was originally intended to bear the title "Natural Selection;" nor is it easy to see why the change should have been made if an accurate expression of the contents of the book was the only thing which Mr. Darwin was considering. It is curious that, writing the later chapters of "Life and Habit" in great haste, I should have accidentally referred to the "Origin of Species" as "Natural Selection;" it seems hard to believe that there was no intention in my thus unconsciously reverting to Mr. Darwin's own original title, but there certainly was none, and I did not then know what the original title had been.

If we had scrutinised Mr. Darwin's title-page as closely as we should certainly scrutinise anything written by Mr. Darwin now, we should have seen that the title did not technically claim the theory of descent; practically, however, it so turned out that we unhesitatingly gave that theory to the author, being, as I have said, carried away by the three large "Origins of Species" (which we understood as much the same thing as descent with modification), and finding, as I shall show in a later chapter, that descent was ubiquitously claimed throughout the work, either expressly or by implication, as Mr. Darwin's theory. It is not easy to see how any one with ordinary instincts could hesitate to believe that Mr. Darwin was entitled to claim what he claimed with so much insistance. If *ars est celare artem* Mr. Darwin must be allowed to have been a consummate artist, for it took us years to understand the ins and outs of what had been done.

I may say in passing that we never see the "Origin of Species" spoken of as "On the Origin of Species, &c.," or as "The Origin of Species, &c." (the word "on" being dropped in the latest editions). The distinctive feature of the book lies, according to its admirers, in the "&c.," but they never give it. To avoid pedantry I shall continue to speak of the "Origin of Species."

At any rate it will be admitted that Mr. Darwin did not make his title-page express his meaning so clearly that his readers could readily catch the point of difference between himself and his grandfather and Lamarck; nevertheles the point just touched upon involves the only essential difference between the systems of Mr. Charles Darwin and those of his three most important predecessors. All four writers agree that animals and plants descend with modification; all agree that the fittest alone survive; all agree about the important consequences of the geometrica ratio of increase; Mr. Charles Darwin has said more about these last two points than his predecessors did, but all three were alike cognisant of the facts and attached the same importance to them, and would have been astonished at its being supposed possible that they disputed them. The fittest alone survive; yes - but the fittest from among what? Here comes the point of divergence; the fittest from among organisms whose variations arise mainly through use and disuse? In other words, from variations that are mainly functional? Or from among organisms whose variations are in the main matters of luck? From variations into which a moral and intellectual system of paymen according to results has largely entered? Or from variations which have been thrown for with dice? From variations among which, though cards tell, yet play tells as much or more? Or from those in which cards are everything and play goes for so little as to be not worth taking into account? Is "the survival of the fittest" to be taken as meaning "the survival of the luckiest" or "the survival of those who know best how to turn fortune to account"? Is luck th only element of fitness, or is not cunning even more indispensable?

Mr. Darwin has a habit, borrowed, perhaps, *mutatis mutandis,* from the framers of our collects, of every now and the adding the words "through natural selection," as though this squared everything, and descent with modification thus became his theory at once. This is not the case. Buffon, Erasmus Darwin, and Lamarck believed in natural selection to the full as much as any follower of Mr. Charles Darwin can do. They did not use the actual words, but the idea underlying them is the essence of their system. Mr. Patrick Matthew epitomised their doctrine more tersely, perhaps, than was done by any other of the pre-Charles-Darwinian evolutionists, in the following passage which appeared in 1831, and which I have already quoted in "Evolution Old and New" (pp. 320, 323). The passage runs:-

"The self-regulating adaptive disposition of organised life may, in part, be traced to the extreme fecundity of nature who, as before stated, has in all the varieties of her offspring a prolific power much beyond (in many cases a thousandfold) what is necessary to fill up the vacancies caused by senile decay. As the field of existence is limited and preoccupied, it is only the hardier, more robust, better suited to circumstance individuals, who are able to struggle forward to maturity, these inhabiting only the situations to which they have superior adaptation and greater power of occupancy than any other kind; the weaker and less circumstance-suited being prematurely destroyed. This principle is in constant action; it regulates the colour, the figure, the capacities, and instincts; those individuals in each species whose colour and covering are best suited to concealment or protection from enemies, or defence from inclemencies or vicissitudes of climate, whose figure is best accommodated to health, strength, defence, and support whose capacities and instincts can best regulate the physical energies to self-advantage according to circumstances - in such immense waste of primary and youthful life those only come forward to maturity from*the strict ordeal by which nature tests their adaptation to her standard of perfection*and fitness to continue their kind by reproduction." {86a} A little lower down Mr. Matthew speaks of animals under domestication *"not having undergone selection by the law of nature, of which we have spoken,* and hence being unable to maintain their ground without culture and protection."

The distinction between Darwinism and Neo-Darwinism is generally believed to lie in the adoption of a theory of natural selection by the younger Darwin and its non-adoption by the elder. This is true in so far as that the elder Darwin does not use the words "natural selection," while the younger does, but it is not true otherwise. Both writers agree that offspring tends to inherit modifications that have been effected, from whatever cause, in parents; both hold that the best adapted to their surroundings live longest and leave most offspring; both, therefore, hold that favourable modifications will tend to be preserved and intensified in the course of many generations, and that this leads to divergence of type; but these opinions involve a theory of natural selection or quasi-selection, whethe the words "natural selection" are used or not; indeed it is impossible to include wild species in any theory of descent with modification without implying a quasi-selective power on the part of nature; but even with Mr. Charles Darwin the power is only quasi-selective; there is no conscious choice, and hence there is nothing that can in strictness be called selection.

It is indeed true that the younger Darwin gave the words "natural selection" the importance which of late years they have assumed; he probably adopted them unconsciously from the passage of Mr. Matthew's quoted above, but he ultimately said, {87a} "In the literal sense of the word *(sic)* no doubt natural selection is a false term," as personifying a fact, making it exercise the conscious choice without which there can be no selection, and generally crediting it with the discharge of functions which can only be ascribed legitimately to living and reasoning beings. Granted, however, that while Mr. Charles Darwin adopted the expression natural selection and admitted it to be a bad one, his grandfather did not use it at all; still Mr. Darwin did not mean the natural selection which Mr. Matthew and those whose opinions he was epitomising meant. Mr. Darwin meant the selection to be made from variations into which purpose enters to only a small extent comparatively. The difference, therefore, between the older evolutionists and their successor does not lie in the acceptance by the more recent writer of a quasi-selective power in nature which his predecessors denied, but in the background - hidden behind the words natural selection, which have served to cloak it - in the views which the old and the new writers severally took of the variations from among which they are alike agreed that a selection or quasi-selection is made.

It now appears that there is not one natural selection, and one survival of the fittest only, but two natural selections, and two survivals of the fittest, the one of which may be objected to as an expression more fit for religious and general literature than for science, but may still be admitted as sound in intention, while the other, inasmuch as it supposes accident to be the main purveyor of variations, has no correspondence with the actual course of things; for if the variations are matters of chance or hazard unconnected with any principle of constant application, they will not occur steadily enough, throughout a sufficient number of successive generations, nor to a sufficient number of individuals for many generations together at the same time and place, to admit of the fixing and permanency of modification at all. The one theory of natural selection, therefore, may, and indeed will, explain the facts that surround us, whereas the other will not. Mr. Charles Darwin's contribution to the theory of evolution was not, as is commonly supposed, "natural selection," but the hypothesis that natural selection from variations that are in the main fortuitous could accumulate and result in specific and generic differences.

In the foregoing paragraph I have given the point of difference between Mr. Charles Darwin and his predecessors. Why, I wonder, have neither he nor any of his exponents put this difference before us in such plain words that we should readily apprehend it? Erasmus Darwin and Lamarck were understood by all who wished to understand them; why is it that the misunderstanding of Mr. Darwin's "distinctive feature" should have been so long and obstinate? Why is it that, no matter how much writers like Mr. Grant Allen and Professor Ray Lankester may say about "Mr. Darwin's master-key," nor how many more like hyperboles they brandish, they never put a succinct *résumé* of Mr. Darwin's theory side by side with a similar *résumé* of his grandfather's and Lamarck's? Neither Mr. Darwin himself, not any of those to whose advocacy his reputation is mainly due, have done this. Professor Huxley is the man of all others who foisted Mr. Darwin most upon us, but in his famous lecture on the coming of age of the "Origin of Species" he did not explain to his hearers wherein the Neo-Darwinian theory of evolution differed from the old; and why not? Surely, because no sooner is this made clear than we perceive that the idea underlying the old evolutionists is more in accord with instinctive feelings that we have cherished too long to be able now to disregard them than the central idea which underlies the "Origin of Species."

What should we think of one who maintained that the steam-engine and telescope were not developed mainly through design and effort (letting the indisputably existing element of luck go without saying), but to the fact that in any telescope or steam-engine "happened to be made ever such a little more conveniently for man's purposes than another," &c., &c.?

Let us suppose a notorious burglar found in possession of a jemmy; it is admitted on all hands that he will use it as soon as he gets a chance; there is no doubt about this; how perverted should we not consider the ingenuity of one who tried to persuade us we were wrong in thinking that the burglar compassed the possession of the jemmy by means involving ideas, however vague in the first instance, of applying it to its subsequent function.

If any one could be found so blind to obvious inferences as to accept natural selection, "or the preservation of favoured machines," as the main means of mechanical modification, we might suppose him to argue much as follows:- "I can quite understand," he would exclaim, "how any one who reflects upon the originally simple form of the earliest jemmies, and observes the developments they have since attained in the hands of our most accomplished housebreakers, might at first be tempted to believe that the present form of the instrument has been arrived at by long-continued improvement in the hands of an almost infinite succession of thieves; but may not this inference be somewhat too hastily drawn? Have we any right to assume that burglars work by means analogous to those employed by other people? If any thief happened to pick up any crowbar which happened to be ever such a little better suited to his purpose than the one he had been in the habit of using hitherto, he would at once seize and carefully preserve it. If it got worn out or broken he would begin searching for a crowbar as like as possible to the one that he had lost; and when, with advancing skill, and in default of being able to find the exact thing he wanted, he took at length to making a jemmy for himself, he would imitate the latest and most perfect adaptation, which would thus be most likely to be preserved in the struggle of competitive forms. Let this process go on for countless generations, among countless burglars of all nations, and may we not suppose that a jemmy would be in time arrived at, as superior to any that could have been designed as the effect of the Niagara Falls is superior to the puny efforts of the landscape gardener?"

For the moment I will pass over the obvious retort that there is no sufficient parallelism between bodily organs and mechanical inventions to make a denial of design in the one involve in equity a denial of it in the other also, and tha therefore the preceding paragraph has no force. A man is not bound to deny design in machines wherein it can be clearly seen because he denies it in living organs where at best it is a matter of inference. This retort is plausible, but in the course of the two next following chapters but one it will be shown to be without force; for the moment, however, beyond thus calling attention to it, I must pass it by.

I do not mean to say that Mr. Darwin ever wrote anything which made the utility of his contention as apparent as it is made by what I have above put into the mouth of his supposed follower. Mr. Darwin was the Gladstone of biology, and so old a scientific hand was not going to make things unnecessarily clear unless it suited his convenience. Then, indeed, he was like the man in "The Hunting of the Snark," who said, "I told you once, I told you twice, what I tell you three times is true." That what I have supposed said, however, above about the jemmy is no exaggeration of Mr. Darwin's attitude as regards design in organism will appear from the passage about the eye already referred to, which it may perhaps be as well to quote in full. Mr. Darwin says:-

"It is scarcely possible to avoid comparing the eye to a telescope. We know that this instrument has been perfected by the long-continued efforts of the highest human intellects, and we naturally infer that the eye has been formed by a somewhat analogous process. But may not this inference be presumptuous? Have we any right to assume that the Creator works by intellectual powers like those of men? If we must compare the eye to an optical instrument, we ought in imagination to take a thick layer of transparent tissue, with a nerve sensitive to light beneath, and then suppose every part of this layer to be continually changing slowly in density, so as to separate into layers of different densities and thicknesses, placed at different distances from each other, and with the surfaces of each layer slowly changing in form. Further, we must suppose that there is a power always intently watching each slight accidental alteration in the transparent layers, and carefully selecting each alteration which, under varied circumstances, may in any way, or in any degree, tend to produce a distincter image. We must suppose each new state of the instrument to be multiplied by the million, and each to be preserved till a better be produced, and then the old ones to be destroyed. In living bodies variation will cause the slight alterations, generation will multiply them almost infinitely, and natural selection will pick out with unerring skill each improvement. Let this process go on for millions on millions of years, and during each year on millions of individuals of many kinds; and may we not believe that a living optical instrument might thus be formed as superior to one of glass as the works of the Creator are to those of man?" {92a}

Mr. Darwin does not in this passage deny design, or cunning, point blank; he was not given to denying things point blank, nor is it immediately apparent that he is denying design at all, for he does not emphasize and call attention to the fact that the *variations* on whose accumulation he relies for his ultimate specific difference are accidental, and, to use his own words, in the passage last quoted, caused by *variation*. He does, indeed, in his earlier editions, call the variations "accidental," and accidental they remained for ten years, but in 1869 the word "accidental" was taken out. Mr. Darwin probably felt that the variations had been accidental as long as was desirable; and though they would, of course, in reality remain as accidental as ever, still, there could be no use in crying "accidental variations" further. If the reader wants to know whether they were accidental or no, he had better find out for himself. Mr. Darwin was a master of what may be called scientific chiaroscuro, and owes his reputation in no small measure to the judgment with which he kept his meaning dark when a less practised hand would have thrown light upon it. There can, however, be no question that Mr. Darwin, though not denying purposiveness point blank, was trying to refer the development of the eye to the accumulation of small accidental improvements, which were not as a rule due to effort and design in any way analogous to those attendant on the development of the telescope.

Though Mr. Darwin, if he was to have any point of difference from his grandfather, was bound to make his variations accidental, yet, to do him justice, he did not like it. Even in the earlier editions of the "Origin of Species," where the "alterations" in the passage last quoted are called "accidental" in express terms, the word does not fall, so to speak, on a strong beat of the bar, and is apt to pass unnoticed. Besides, Mr. Darwin does not say point blank "we may believe," or "we ought to believe;" he only says "may we not believe?" The reader should always be on his guard when Mr. Darwin asks one of these bland and child-like questions, and he is fond of asking them; but however this may be, it is plain, as I pointed out in "Evolution Old and New" {93a} that the only "skill," that is to say the only thing that can possibly involve design, is "the unerring skill" of natural selection.

In the same paragraph Mr. Darwin has already said: "Further, we must suppose that there is a power represented by natural selection or the survival of the fittest always intently watching each slight alteration, &c." Mr. Darwin probably said "a power represented by natural selection" instead of "natural selection" only, because he saw that to talk too frequently about the fact that the most lucky live longest as "intently watching" something was greater nonsense than it would be prudent even for him to write, so he fogged it by making the intent watching done by "a power represented by" a fact, instead of by the fact itself. As the sentence stands it is just as great nonsense as it would have been if "the survival of the fittest" had been allowed to do the watching instead of "the power represented by" the survival of the fittest, but the nonsense is harder to dig up, and the reader is more likely to pass it over.

This passage gave Mr. Darwin no less trouble than it must have given to many of his readers. In the original edition of the "Origin of Species" it stood, "Further, we must suppose that there is a power always intently watching each slight accidental variation." I suppose it was felt that if this was allowed to stand, it might be fairly asked what natural selection was doing all this time? If the power was able to do everything that was necessary now, why not always? and why any natural selection at all? This clearly would not do, so in 1861 the power was allowed, by the help of brackets, actually to become natural selection, and remained so till 1869, when Mr. Darwin could stand it no longer, and, doubtless for the reason given above, altered the passage to "a power represented by natural selection," at the same time cutting out the word "accidental."

It may perhaps make the workings of Mr. Darwin's mind clearer to the reader if I give the various readings of this passage as taken from the three most important editions of the "Origin of Species."

In 1859 it stood, "Further, we must suppose that there is a power always intently watching each slight accidental alteration," &c.

In 1861 it stood, "Further, we must suppose that there is a power (natural selection) always intently watching each slight accidental alteration," &c.

And in 1869, "Further, we must suppose that there is a power represented by natural selection or the survival of the fittest always intently watching each slight alteration," &c. {94a}

The hesitating feeble gait of one who fears a pitfall at every step, so easily recognisable in the "numerous, successive, slight alterations" in the foregoing passage, may be traced in many another page of the "Origin of Species" by those who will be at the trouble of comparing the several editions. It is only when this is done, and the working of Mr Darwin's mind can be seen as though it were the twitchings of a dog's nose, that any idea can be formed of the difficulty in which he found himself involved by his initial blunder of thinking he had got a distinctive feature which entitled him to claim the theory of evolution as an original idea of his own. He found his natural selection hang round his neck like a millstone. There is hardly a page in the "Origin of Species" in which traces of the struggle going on in Mr. Darwin's mind are not discernible, with a result alike exasperating and pitiable. I can only repeat what I said in "Evolution Old and New," namely, that I find the task of extracting a well-defined meaning out of Mr. Darwin's words comparable only to that of trying to act on the advice of a lawyer who has obscured the main issue as much as he can, and whose chief aim has been to leave as many loopholes as possible for himself to escape by, if things should go wrong hereafter. Or, again, to that of one who has to construe an Act of Parliament which was originally drawn with a view to throwing as much dust as possible in the eyes of those who would oppose the measure, and which, having been found utterly unworkable in practice, has had clauses repealed up and down it till it is now in an inextricable tangle of confusion and contradiction.

The more Mr. Darwin's work is studied, and more especially the more his different editions are compared, the more impossible is it to avoid a suspicion of *arrière pensée* as pervading it whenever the "distinctive feature" is on the *tapis*. It is right to say, however, that no such suspicion attaches to Mr. A. R. Wallace, Mr. Darwin's fellow discoverer of natural selection. It is impossible to doubt that Mr. Wallace believed he had made a real and important improvement upon the Lamarckian system, and, as a natural consequence, unlike Mr. Darwin, he began by telling us what Lamarck had said. He did not, I admit, say quite all that I should have been glad to have seen him say, nor use exactly the words I should myself have chosen, but he said enough to make it impossible to doubt his good faith and his desire that we should understand that with him, as with Mr. Darwin, variations are mainly accidental, not functional. Thus, in his memorable paper communicated to the Linnean Society in 1858 he said, in a passage which I have quoted in "Unconscious Memory":

"The hypothesis of Lamarck - that progressive changes in speciesof their own organs, and thus modify their structures and habits - has been repeatedly and easily refuted by all writers on the subject of varieties and species; . . but the view here developed renders such an hypothesis quite unnecessary. . . . The powerful retractile talons of the falcon and cat tribes have not been produced or increased by the volition of those animals; . . . neither did the giraffe acquire its long neck by desiring to reach the foliage of the more lofty shrubs, and constantly stretching its neck for this purpose, but because any varieties which occurred among its antitypes with a longer neck than usual *at once secured a fresh range of pasture over the same ground as their shorter-necked companions, and on the first scarcity of food were thus enabled to outlive them*" (italics in original). {96a}

"Which occurred" is obviously "which happened to occur, by some chance or accident entirely unconnected with use and disuse;" and though the word "accidental" is never used, there can be no doubt about Mr. Wallace's desire to make the reader catch the fact that with him accident, and not, as with Erasmus Darwin and Lamarck, sustained effort, is the main purveyor of the variations whose accumulation amounts ultimately to specific difference. It is a pity, however, that instead of contenting himself like a theologian with saying that his opponent had been refuted over and over again, he did not refer to any particular and tolerably successful attempt to refute the theory that modifications in organic structure are mainly functional. I am fairly well acquainted with the literature of evolution and have never met with any such attempt. But let this pass; as with Mr. Darwin, so with Mr. Wallace, and so indeed with all who accept Mr. Charles Darwin's natural selection as the main means of modification, the central idea is luck, while the central idea of the Erasmus-Darwinian system is cunning.

I have given the opinions of these contending parties in their extreme development; but they both admit abatements which bring them somewhat nearer to one another. Design, as even its most strenuous upholders will admit, is a difficult word to deal with; it is, like all our ideas, substantial enough until we try to grasp it - and then, like all our ideas, it mockingly eludes us; it is like life or death - a rope of many strands; there is design within design, and design within undesign; there is undesign within design (as when a man shuffles cards designing that there shall be no design in their arrangement), and undesign within undesign; when we speak of cunning or design in connection with organism we do not mean cunning, all cunning, and nothing but cunning, so that there shall be no place for luck; we do not mean that conscious attention and forethought shall have been bestowed upon the minutest details of action and nothing been left to work itself out departmentally according to precedent, or as it otherwise best may according to the chapter of accidents.

So, again, when Mr. Darwin and his followers deny design and effort to have been the main purveyors of the variations whose accumulation results in specific difference, they do not entirely exclude the action of use and disuse - and this at once opens the door for cunning; nevertheless, according to Erasmus Darwin and Lamarck, the human eye and the long neck of the giraffe are alike due to the accumulation of variations that are mainly functional, and hence practical; according to Charles Darwin they are alike due to the accumulation of variations that are accidental, fortuitous, spontaneous, that is to say, mainly cannot be reduced to any known general principle. According to Charles Darwin "the preservation of favoured," or lucky, "races" is by far the most important means of modification; according to Erasmus Darwin effort *non sibi res sed se rebus subjungere* is unquestionably the most potent means; roughly, therefore, there is no better or fairer way of putting the matter, than to say that Charles Darwin is the apostle of luck, and his grandfather, and Lamarck, of cunning.

It should be observed also that the distinction between the organism and its surroundings - on which both systems are founded - is one that cannot be so universally drawn as we find it convenient to allege. There is a debatable ground of considerable extent on which *res* and *me*, ego and non ego, luck and cunning, necessity and freewill, meet and pass into one another as night and day, or life and death. No one can draw a sharp line between ego and non ego, nor indeed any sharp line between any classes of phenomena. Every part of the ego is non ego *quâ* organ or tool in use, and much of the non ego runs up into the ego and is inseparably united with it; still there is enough that it is obviously most convenient to call ego, and enough that it is no less obviously most convenient to call non ego, as there is enough obvious day and obvious night, or obvious luck and obvious cunning, to make us think it advisable to keep separate accounts for each.

I will say more on this head in a following chapter; in this present one my business should be confined to pointing out as clearly and succinctly as I can the issue between the two great main contending opinions concerning organic development that obtain among those who accept the theory of descent at all; nor do I believe that this can be done more effectually and accurately than by saying, as above, that Mr. Charles Darwin (whose name, by the way, was "Charles Robert," and not, as would appear from the title-pages of his books, "Charles" only), Mr. A. R. Wallace, and their supporters are the apostles of luck, while Erasmus Darwin and Lamarck, followed, more or less timidly, by the Geoffroys and by Mr. Herbert Spencer, and very timidly indeed by the Duke of Argyll, preach cunning as the most important means of organic modification.

NOTE. - It appears from "Samuel Butler: A Memoir" (II, 29) that Butler wrote to his father (Dec. 1885) about a passage in Horace (near the beginning of the First Epistle of the First Book) -

Nunc in Aristippi furtim praecepta relabor,
Et mihi res, non me rebus subjungere conor.

On the preceding page he is adapting the second of these two verses to his own purposes. - H. F. J.

CHAPTER VII - *(Intercalated)* Mr. Spencer's "The Factors of Organic Evolution"

Since the foregoing and several of the succeeding chapters were written, Mr. Herbert Spencer has made his position at once more clear and more widely understood by his articles "The Factors of Organic Evolution" which appeared in the *Nineteenth Century* for April and May, 1886. The present appears the fittest place in which to intercalate remarks concerning them.

Mr. Spencer asks whether those are right who regard Mr. Charles Darwin's theory of natural selection as by itself sufficient to account for organic evolution.

"On critically examining the evidence" (modern writers never examine evidence, they always "critically," or "carefully," or "patiently," examine it), he writes, we shall find reason to think that it by no means explains all that has to be explained. Omitting for the present any consideration of a factor which may be considered primordial, it may be contended that one of the factors alleged by Erasmus Darwin and Lamarck must be recognised as a co-operator. Unless that increase of a part resulting from extra activity, and that decrease of it resulting from inactivity, are transmissible to descendants, we are without a key to many phenomena of organic evolution. *Utterly inadequate to explain the major part of the facts as is the hypothesis of the inheritance of functionally produced modifications*, yet there is a minor part of the facts very extensive though less, which must be ascribed to this cause." (Italics mine.)

Mr. Spencer does not here say expressly that Erasmus Darwin and Lamarck considered inheritance of functionally produced modifications to be the sole explanation of the facts of organic life; modern writers on evolution for the most part avoid saying anything expressly; this nevertheless is the conclusion which the reader naturally draws - and was doubtless intended to draw - from Mr. Spencer's words. He gathers that these writers put forward an "utterly inadequate" theory, which cannot for a moment be entertained in the form in which they left it, but which, nevertheless, contains contributions to the formation of a just opinion which of late years have been too much neglected.

This inference would be, as Mr. Spencer ought to know, a mistaken one. Erasmus Darwin, who was the first to depend mainly on functionally produced modifications, attributes, if not as much importance to variations induced either by what we must call chance, or by causes having no connection with use and disuse, as Mr. Spencer does, still so nearly as much that there is little to choose between them. Mr. Spencer's words show that he attributes, if not half, still not far off half the modification that has actually been produced, to use and disuse. Erasmus Darwin does not say whether he considers use and disuse to have brought about more than half or less than half; he only says that animal and vegetable modification is "in part produced" by the exertions of the animals and vegetables themselves; the impression I have derived is, that just as Mr. Spencer considers rather less than half to be due to use and disuse, so Erasmus Darwin considers decidedly more than half - so much more, in fact, than half as to make function unquestionably the factor most proper to be insisted on if only one can be given. Further than this he did not go. I will quote enough of Dr. Erasmus Darwin's own words to put his position beyond doubt. He writes:-

"Thirdly, when we enumerate the great changes produced in the species of animals before their nativity, as, for example, when the offspring reproduces the effects produced upon the parent by accident mules; or the changes produced probably by exuberance of nourishment supplied to the foetus, as in monstrous births with additional limbs; many of these enormities are propagated and continued as a variety at least, if not as a new species of animal. I have seen a breed of cats with an additional claw on every foot; of poultry also with an additional claw and with wings to their feet; and of others without rumps. Mr. Buffon" (who, by the way, surely, was no more "Mr. Buffon" than Lord Salisbury is "Mr. Salisbury") "mentions a breed of dogs without tails which are common at Rome established of cutting their tails close off." {102a}

Here not one of the causes of variation adduced is connected with use and disuse, or effort, volition, and purpose the manner, moreover, in which they are brought forward is not that of one who shows signs of recalcitrancy about admitting other causes of modification as well as use and disuse; indeed, a little lower down he almost appears to assign the subordinate place to functionally produced modifications, for he says - "Fifthly, from their first rudiments or primordium to the termination of their lives, all animals undergo perpetual transformations;*which are in part produced* by their own exertions in consequence of their desires and aversions, of their pleasures and their pains, or of irritations or of associations; and many of these acquired forms or propensities are transmitted to their posterity."

I have quoted enough to show that Dr. Erasmus Darwin would have protested against the supposition that functionally produced modifications were an adequate explanation of all the phenomena of organic modification. He declares accident and the chances and changes of this mortal life to be potent and frequent causes of variations which, being not infrequently inherited, result in the formation of varieties and even species, but considers these causes if taken alone as no less insufficient to account for observable facts than the theory of functionally produced modifications would be if not supplemented by inheritance of so-called fortuitous, or spontaneous variations. The difference between Dr. Erasmus Darwin and Mr. Spencer does not consist in the denial by the first, that a variety which happens, no matter how accidentally, to have varied in a way that enables it to comply more fully and readily with the conditions of its existence, is likely to live longer and leave more offspring than one less favoured; nor in the denial by the second of the inheritance and accumulation of functionally produced modifications; but in the amount of stress which they respectively lay on the relative importance of the two great factors of organic evolution the existence of which they are alike ready to admit.

With Erasmus Darwin there is indeed luck, and luck has had a great deal to do with organic modification, but no amount of luck would have done unless cunning had known how to take advantage of it; whereas if cunning be given, a very little luck at a time will accumulate in the course of ages and become a mighty heap. Cunning, therefore, is the factor on which, having regard to the usage of language and the necessity for simplifying facts, he thinks it most proper to insist. Surely this is as near as may be the opinion which common consent ascribes to Mr. Spencer himself. It is certainly the one which, in supporting Erasmus Darwin's system as against his grandson's, I have always intended to support. With Charles Darwin, on the other hand, there is indeed cunning, effort, and consequent use and disuse; nor does he deny that these have produced some, and sometimes even an important, effect in modifying species, but he assigns by far the most important *rôle* in the whole scheme to natural selection, which, as I have already shown, must, with him, be regarded as a synonym for luck pure and simple. This, for reasons well shown by Mr. Spencer in the articles under consideration, is so untenable that it seems only possible to account for its having been advanced at all by supposing Mr. Darwin's judgment to have been perverted by some one or more of the many causes that might tend to warp them. What the chief of those causes may have been I shall presently point out.

Buffon erred rather on the side of ignoring functionally produced modifications than of insisting on them. The main agency with him is the direct action of the environment upon the organism. This, no doubt, is a flaw in Buffon's immortal work, but it is one which Erasmus Darwin and Lamarck easily corrected; nor can we doubt that Buffon would have readily accepted their amendment if it had been suggested to him. Buffon did infinitely more in the way of discovering and establishing the theory of descent with modification than any one has ever done either before or since. He was too much occupied with proving the fact of evolution at all, to dwell as fully as might have been wished upon the details of the process whereby the amœba had become man, but we have already seen that he regarded inherited mutilation as the cause of establishing a new breed of dogs, and this is at any rate not laying much stress on functionally produced modifications. Again, when writing of the dog, he speaks of variations arising "*by some chance* common enough with nature," {104a} and clearly does not contemplate function as the sole cause of modification. Practically, though I grant I should be less able to quote passages in support of my opinion than I quite like, I do not doubt that his position was much the same as that of his successors, Erasmus Darwin and Lamarck.

Lamarck is more vulnerable than either Erasmus Darwin or Buffon on the score of unwillingness to assign its full share to mere chance, but I do not for a moment believe his comparative reticence to have been caused by failure to see that the chapter of accidents is a fateful one. He saw that the cunning or functional side had been too much lost sight of, and therefore insisted on it, but he did not mean to say that there is no such thing as luck. "Let us suppose," he says, "that a grass growing in a low-lying meadow, gets carried *by some accident* to the brow of a neighbouring hill, where the soil is still damp enough for the plant to be able to exist." {105a} Or again - "With sufficient time, favourable conditions of life, successive changes in the condition of the globe, and the power of new surroundings and habits to modify the organs of living bodies, all animal and vegetable forms have been imperceptibly rendered such as we now see them." {105b} Who can doubt that accident is here regarded as a potent factor of evolution, as well as the design that is involved in the supposition that modification is, in the main, functionally induced? Again he writes, "As regards the circumstances that give rise to variation, the principal are climatic changes, different temperatures of any of a creature's environments, differences of abode, of habit, of the most frequent actions, and lastly of the means of obtaining food, self-defence, reproduction," &c. {105c} I will not dwell on the small inconsistencies which may be found in the passages quoted above; the reader will doubtless see them, and will also doubtless see that in spite of them there can be no doubt that Lamarck, while believing modification to be effected mainly by the survival in the struggle for existence of modifications which had been induced functionally, would not have hesitated to admit the survival of favourable variations due to mere accident as also a potent factor in inducing the results we see around us.

For the rest, Mr. Spencer's articles have relieved me from the necessity of going into the evidence which proves that such structures as a giraffe's neck, for example, cannot possibly have been produced by the accumulation of variations which had their origin mainly in accident. There is no occasion to add anything to what Mr. Spencer has said on this score, and I am satisfied that those who do not find his argument convince them would not be convinced by anything I might say; I shall, therefore, omit what I had written on this subject, and confine myself to giving the substance of Mr. Spencer's most telling argument against Mr. Darwin's theory that accidental variations, if favourable, would accumulate and result in seemingly adaptive structures. Mr. Spencer well shows that luck or chance is insufficient as a motive-power, or helm, of evolution; but luck is only absence of design; if, then, absence of design is found to fail, it follows that there must have been design somewhere, nor can the design be more conveniently placed than in association with function.

Mr. Spencer contends that where life is so simple as to consist practically in the discharge of only one function, or where circumstances are such that some one function is supremely important (a state of things, by the way, more easily found in hypothesis than in nature - at least as continuing without modification for many successive seasons), then accidental variations, if favourable, would indeed accumulate and result in modification, without the aid of the transmission of functionally produced modification. This is true; it is also true, however, that only a very small number of species in comparison with those we see around us could thus arise, and that we should never have got plants and animals as embodiments of the two great fundamental principles on which it is alone possible that life can be conducted, {107a} and species of plants and animals as embodiments of the details involved in carrying out these two main principles.

If the earliest organism could have only varied favourably in one direction, the one possible favourable accidental variation would have accumulated so long as the organism continued to exist at all, inasmuch as this would be preserved whenever it happened to occur, while every other would be lost in the struggle of competitive forms; but even in the lowest forms of life there is more than one condition in respect of which the organism must be supposed sensitive, and there are as many directions in which variations may be favourable as there are conditions of the environment that affect the organism. We cannot conceive of a living form as having a power of adaptation limited to one direction only; the elasticity which admits of a not being "extreme to mark that which is done amiss" in one direction will commonly admit of it in as many directions as there are possible favourable modes of variation; the number of these, as has been just said, depends upon the number of the conditions of the environment that affect the organism, and these last, though in the long run and over considerable intervals of time tolerably constant, are over shorter intervals liable to frequent and great changes; so that there is nothing in Mr. Charles Darwin's system of modification through the natural survival of the lucky, to prevent gain in one direction one year from being lost irretrievably in the next, through the greater success of some in no way correlated variation, the fortunate possessors of which alone survive. This, in its turn, is as likely as not to disappear shortly through the arising of some difficulty in some entirely new direction, and so on; nor, if function be regarded as of small effect in determining organism, is there anything to ensure either that, even if ground be lost for a season or two in any one direction, it shall be recovered presently on resumption by the organism of the habits that called it into existence, or that it shall appear synchronously in a sufficient number of individuals to ensure its not being soon lost through gamogenesis.

How is progress ever to be made if races keep reversing, Penelope-like, in one generation all that they have been achieving in the preceding? And how, on Mr. Darwin's system, of which the accumulation of strokes of luck is the greatly preponderating feature, is a hoard ever to be got together and conserved, no matter how often luck may have thrown good things in an organism's way? Luck, or absence of design, may be sometimes almost said to throw good things in our way, or at any rate we may occasionally get more through having made no design than any design we should have been likely to have formed would have given us; but luck does not hoard these good things for our use and make our wills for us, nor does it keep providing us with the same good gifts again and again, and no matter how often we reject them.

I had better, perhaps, give Mr. Spencer's own words as quoted by himself in his article in the *Nineteenth Century* for April, 1886. He there wrote as follows, quoting from § 166 of his "Principles of Biology," which appeared in 1864:-

"Where the life is comparatively simple, or where surrounding circumstances render some one function supremely important, the survival of the fittest" (which means here the survival of the luckiest) "may readily bring about the appropriate structural change, without any aid from the transmission of functionally-acquired modifications" (into which effort and design have entered). "But in proportion as the life grows complex - in proportion as a healthy existence cannot be secured by a large endowment of some one power, but demands many powers; in the same proportion do there arise obstacles to the increase of any particular power, by 'the preservation of favoured races in the struggle for life'" (that is to say, through mere survival of the luckiest). "As fast as the faculties are multiplied, so fast does it become possible for the several members of a species to have various kinds of superiority over one another. While one saves its life by higher speed, another does the like by clearer vision, another by keener scent, another by quicker hearing, another by greater strength, another by unusual power of enduring cold or hunger, another by special sagacity, another by special timidity, another by special courage; and others by other bodily and mental attributes. Now it is unquestionably true that, other things equal, each of these attributes, giving its possessor an equal extra chance of life, is likely to be transmitted to posterity. But there seems no reason to believe it will be increased in subsequent generations by natural selection. That it may be thus increased, the animals not possessing more than average endowments of it must be more frequently killed off than individuals highly endowed with it; and this can only happen when the attribute is one of greater importance, for the time being, than most of the other attributes.

If those members of the species which have but ordinary shares of it, nevertheless survive by virtue of other superiorities which they severally possess, then it is not easy to see how this particular attribute can be developed by natural selection in subsequent generations." (For if some other superiority is a greater source of luck, then natural selection, or survival of the luckiest, will ensure that this other superiority be preserved at the expense of the one acquired in the earlier generation.) "The probability seems rather to be, that by gamogenesis, this extra endowment will, on the average, be diminished in posterity - just serving in the long run to compensate the deficient endowments of other individuals, whose special powers lie in other directions; and so to keep up the normal structure of the species. The working out of the process is here somewhat difficult to follow" (there is no difficulty as soon as it is perceived that Mr. Darwin's natural selection invariably means, or ought to mean, the survival of the luckiest, and that seasons and what they bring with them, though fairly constant on an average, yet individually vary so greatly that what is luck in one season is disaster in another); "but it appears to me that as fast as the number of bodily and mental faculties increases, and as fast as the maintenance of life comes to depend less on the amount of any one, and more on the combined action of all, so fast does the production of specialities of character by natural selection alone become difficult. Particularly does this seem to be so with a species so multitudinous in powers as mankind; and above all does it seem to be so with such of the human powers as have but minor shares in aiding the struggle for life - the aesthetic faculties, for example.

"Dwelling for a moment on this last illustration of the class of difficulties described, let us ask how we are to interpret the development of the musical faculty; how came there that endowment of musical faculty which characterises modern Europeans at large, as compared with their remote ancestors? The monotonous chants of low savages cannot be said to show any melodic inspiration; and it is not evident that an individual savage who had a little more musical perception than the rest would derive any such advantage in the maintenance of life as would secure the spread of his superiority by inheritance of the variation," &c.

It should be observed that the passage given in the last paragraph but one appeared in 1864, only five years after the first edition of the "Origin of Species," but, crushing as it is, Mr. Darwin never answered it. He treated it as nonexistent - and this, doubtless from a business standpoint, was the best thing he could do. How far such a course was consistent with that single-hearted devotion to the interests of science for which Mr. Darwin developed such an abnormal reputation, is a point which I must leave to his many admirers to determine.

CHAPTER VIII - Property, Common Sense, and Protoplasm

One would think the issue stated in the three preceding chapters was decided in the stating. This, as I have already implied, is probably the reason why those who have a vested interest in Mr. Darwin's philosophical reputation have avoided stating it.

It may be said that, seeing the result is a joint one, inasmuch as both "res" and "me," or both luck and cunning, enter so largely into development, neither factor can claim pre-eminence to the exclusion of the other. But life is short and business long, and if we are to get the one into the other we must suppress details, and leave our words pregnant, as painters leave their touches when painting from nature. If one factor concerns us greatly more than the other, we should emphasize it, and let the other go without saying, by force of association. There is no fear of it being lost sight of; association is one of the few really liberal things in nature; by liberal, I mean precipitate and inaccurate; the power of words, as of pictures, and indeed the power to carry on life at all, vests in the fact that association does not stick to the letter of its bond, but will take the half for the whole without even looking closely at the coin given to make sure that it is not counterfeit. Through the haste and high pressure of business, errors arise continually, and these errors give us the shocks of which our consciousness is compounded. Our whole conscious life, therefore, grows out of memory and out of the power of association, in virtue of which not only does the right half pass for the whole, but the wrong half not infrequently passes current for it also, without being challenged and found out till, as it were, the accounts come to be balanced, and it is found that they will not do so.

Variations are an organism's way of getting over an unexpected discrepancy between its resources as shown by the fly-leaves of its own cheques and the universe's passbook; the universe is generally right, or would be upheld as right if the matter were to come before the not too incorruptible courts of nature, and in nine cases out of ten the organism has made the error in its own favour, so that it must now pay or die. It can only pay by altering its mode of life, and how long is it likely to be before a new departure in its mode of life comes out in its own person and in those of its family? Granted it will at first come out in their appearance only, but there can be no change in appearance without some slight corresponding organic modification. In practice there is usually compromise in these matters. The universe, if it does not give an organism short shrift and eat it at once, will commonly abate something of its claim; it gets tricked out of an additional moiety by the organism; the organism really does pay something by way of changed habits; this results in variation, in virtue of which the accounts are cooked, cobbled and passed by a series of those miracles of inconsistency which was call compromises, and after this they cannot be reopened - not till next time.

Surely of the two factors which go to the making up of development, cunning is the one more proper to be insisted on as determining the physical and psychical well or ill being, and hence, ere long, the future form of the organism. We can hardly open a newspaper without seeing some sign of this; take, for example, the following extract from a letter in the *Times* of the day on which I am writing (February 8, 1886) - "You may pass along a road which divides a settlement of Irish Celts from one of Germans. They all came to the country equally without money, and have had to fight their way in the forest, but the difference in their condition is very remarkable; on the German side there is comfort, thrift, peace, but on the other side the spectacle is very different." Few will deny that slight organic differences, corresponding to these differences of habit, are already perceptible; no Darwinian will deny that these differences are likely to be inherited, and, in the absence of intermarriage between the two colonies, to result in still more typical difference than that which exists at present. According to Mr. Darwin, the improved type of the more successful race would not be due mainly to transmitted perseverance in well-doing, but to the fact that if any member of the German colony "happened" to be born "ever so slightly," &c. Of course this last is true to a certain extent also; if any member of the German colony does "happen to be born," &c., then he will stand a better chance of surviving, and, if he marries a wife like himself, of transmitting his good qualities; but how about the happening How is it that this is of such frequent occurrence in the one colony, and is so rare in the other? *Fortes creantur fortibus et bonis*. True, but how and why? Through the race being favoured? In one sense, doubtless, it is true that no man can have anything except it be given him from above, but it must be from an above into the composition of which he himself largely enters. God gives us all things; but we are a part of God, and that part of Him, moreover, whose department it more especially is to look after ourselves. It cannot be through luck, for luck is blind, and does not pick out the same people year after year and generation after generation; shall we not rather say, then, that it is because mind, or cunning, is a great factor in the achievement of physical results, and because there is an abiding memory between successive generations, in virtue of which the cunning of an earlier one enures to the benefit of its successors?

It is one of the commonplaces of biology that the nature of the organism (which is mainly determined by ancestral antecedents) is greatly more important in determining its future than the conditions of its environment, provided, of course, that these are not too cruelly abnormal, so that good seed will do better on rather poor soil, than bad seed on rather good soil; this alone should be enough to show that cunning, or individual effort, is more important in determining organic results than luck is, and therefore that if either is to be insisted on to the exclusion of the other it should be cunning, not luck. Which is more correctly said to be the main means of the development of capital

Luck? or Cunning? Of course there must be something to be developed - and luck, that is to say, the unknowable and unforeseeable, enters everywhere; but is it more convenient with our oldest and best-established ideas to say that luck is the main means of the development of capital, or that cunning is so? Can there be a moment's hesitation in admitting that if capital is found to have been developed largely, continuously, by many people, in many ways, over a long period of time, it can only have been by means of continued application, energy, effort, industry, and good sense? Granted there has been luck too; of course there has, but we let it go without saying, whereas we cannot let the skill or cunning go without saying, inasmuch as we feel the cunning to have been the essence of the whole matter.

Granted, again, that there is no test more fallacious on a small scale than that of immediate success. As applied to any particular individual, it breaks down completely. It is unfortunately no rare thing to see the good man striving against fate, and the fool born with a silver spoon in his mouth. Still on a large scale no test can be conceivably more reliable; a blockhead may succeed for a time, but a succession of many generations of blockheads does not go on steadily gaining ground, adding field to field and farm to farm, and becoming year by year more capable and prosperous. Given time - of which there is no scant in the matter of organic development - and cunning will do more with ill luck than folly with good. People do not hold six trumps every hand for a dozen games of whist running, if they do not keep a card or two up their sleeves. Cunning, if it can keep its head above water at all, will beat mere luck unaided by cunning, no matter what start luck may have had, if the race be a fairly long one. Growth is a kind of success which does indeed come to some organisms with less effort than to others, but it cannot be maintained and improved upon without pains and effort. A foolish organism and its fortuitous variation will be soon parted, for, as a general rule, unless the variation has so much connection with the organism's past habits and ways of thought as to be in no proper sense of the word "fortuitous," the organism will not know what to do with it when it has got it, no matter how favourable it may be, and it is little likely to be handed down to descendants. Indeed the kind of people who get on best in the world - and what test to a Darwinian can be comparable to this? - commonly do insist on cunning rather than on luck, sometimes perhaps even unduly; speaking, at least, from experience, I have generally found myself more or less of a failure with those Darwinians to whom I have endeavoured to excuse my shortcomings on the score of luck.

It may be said that the contention that the nature of the organism does more towards determining its future than the conditions of its immediate environment do, is only another way of saying that the accidents which have happened to an organism in the persons of its ancestors throughout all time are more irresistible by it for good or ill than any of the more ordinary chances and changes of its own immediate life. I do not deny this; but these ancestral accidents were either turned to account, or neglected where they might have been taken advantage of; they thus passed either into skill, or want of skill; so that whichever way the fact is stated the result is the same; and if simplicity of statement be regarded, there is no more convenient way of putting the matter than to say that though luck is mighty, cunning is mightier still. Organism commonly shows its cunning by practising what Horace preached, and treating itself as more plastic than its surroundings; those indeed who have had the greatest the first to admit that they had gained their ends more by reputation as moulders of circumstances have ever been shaping their actions and themselves to suit events, than by trying to shape events to suit themselves and their actions. Modification, like charity, begins at home.

But however this may be, there can be no doubt that cunning is in the long run mightier than luck as regards the acquisition of property, and what applies to property applies to organism also. Property, as I have lately seen was said by Rosmini, is a kind of extension of the personality into the outside world. He might have said as truly that it is a kind of penetration of the outside world within the limits of the personality, or that it is at any rate a prophesying of, and essay after, the more living phase of matter in the direction of which it is tending. If approached from the dynamical or living side of the underlying substratum, it is the beginning of the comparatively stable equilibrium which we call brute matter; if from the statical side, that is to say, from that of brute matter, it is the beginning of that dynamical state which we associate with life; it is the last of ego and first of non ego, o*vice versâ,* as the case may be; it is the ground whereon the two meet and are neither wholly one nor wholly the other, but a whirling mass of contradictions such as attends all fusion.

What property is to a man's mind or soul that his body is also, only more so. The body is property carried to the bitter end, or property is the body carried to the bitter end, whichever the reader chooses; the expression "organic wealth" is not figurative; none other is so apt and accurate; so universally, indeed, is this recognised that the fact has found expression in our liturgy, which bids us pray for all those who are any wise afflicted "in mind, body, or estate;" no inference, therefore, can be more simple and legitimate than the one in accordance with which the laws that govern the development of wealth generally are supposed also to govern the particular form of health and wealth which comes most closely home to us - I mean that of our bodily implements or organs. What is the stomach but a living sack, or purse of untanned leather, wherein we keep our means of subsistence? Food is money made easy; it is petty cash in its handiest and most reduced form; it is our way of assimilating our possessions and making them indeed our own. What is the purse but a kind of abridged extra corporeal stomach wherein we keep the money which we convert by purchase into food, as we presently convert the food by digestion into flesh and blood? And what living form is there which is without a purse or stomach, even though it have to job it by the meal as the amœba does, and exchange it for some other article as soon as it has done eating? How marvellously does the analogy hold between the purse and the stomach alike as regards form and function; and I may say in passing that, as usual, the organ which is the more remote from protoplasm is at once more special, more an object of our consciousness, and less an object of its own.

Talk of ego and non ego meeting, and of the hopelessness of avoiding contradiction in terms - talk of this, and look in passing, at the amœba. It is itself *quâ* maker of the stomach and being fed; it is not itself *quâ* stomach and *quâ* its using itself as a mere tool or implement to feed itself with. It is active and passive, object and subject, *ego* and *non ego* - every kind of Irish bull, in fact, which a sound logician abhors - and it is only because it has persevered, as I said in "Life and Habit," in thus defying logic and arguing most virtuously in a most vicious circle, that it has come in the persons of some of its descendants to reason with sufficient soundness. And what the amœba is man is also; man is only a great many amœbas, most of them dreadfully narrow-minded, going up and down the country with their goods and chattels like gipsies in a caravan; he is only a great many amœbas that have had much time and money spent on their education, and received large bequests of organised intelligence from those that have gone before them.

The most incorporate tool - we will say an eye, or a tooth, or the closed fist when used to strike - has still something of the *non ego* about it in so far as it is used; those organs, again, that are the most completely separate from the body, as the locomotive engine, must still from time to time kiss the soil of the human body, and be handled and thus crossed with man again if they would remain in working order. They cannot be cut adrift from the most living form of matter (I mean most living from our point of view), and remain absolutely without connection with it for any length of time, any more than a seal can live without coming up sometimes to breathe; and in so far as they become linked on to living beings they live. Everything is living which is in close communion with, and interpermeated by, that something which we call mind or thought. Giordano Bruno saw this long ago when he made an interlocutor in one of his dialogues say that a man's hat and cloak are alive when he is wearing them. "Thy boots and spurs live," he exclaims, "when thy feet carry them; thy hat lives when thy head is within it; and so the stable lives when it contains the horse or mule, or even yourself;" nor is it easy to see how this is to be refuted except at a cost which no one in his senses will offer.

It may be said that the life of clothes in wear and implements in use is no true life, inasmuch as it differs from flesh and blood life in too many and important respects; that we have made up our minds about not letting life outside the body too decisively to allow the question to be reopened; that if this be tolerated we shall have societies for the prevention of cruelty to chairs and tables, or cutting clothes amiss, or wearing them to tatters, or whatever other absurdity may occur to idle and unkind people; the whole discussion, therefore, should be ordered out of court at once.

I admit that this is much the most sensible position to take, but it can only be taken by those who turn the deafest of deaf ears to the teachings of science, and tolerate no going even for a moment below the surface of things. People who take this line must know how to put their foot down firmly in the matter of closing a discussion. Some one may perhaps innocently say that some parts of the body are more living and vital than others, and those who stick to common sense may allow this, but if they do they must close the discussion on the spot; if they listen to another syllable they are lost; if they let the innocent interlocutor say so much as that a piece of well-nourished healthy brain is more living than the end of a finger-nail that wants cutting, or than the calcareous parts of a bone, the solvent will have been applied which will soon make an end of common sense ways of looking at the matter. Once even admit the use of the participle "dying," which involves degrees of death, and hence an entry of death in part into a living body, and common sense must either close the discussion at once, or ere long surrender at discretion.

Common sense can only carry weight in respect of matters with which every one is familiar, as forming part of the daily and hourly conduct of affairs; if we would keep our comfortable hard and fast lines, our rough and ready unspecialised ways of dealing with difficult questions, our impatience of what St. Paul calls "doubtful disputations," we must refuse to quit the ground on which the judgments of mankind have been so long and often given that they are not likely to be questioned. Common sense is not yet formulated in manners of science or philosophy, for only few consider them; few decisions, therefore, have been arrived at which all hold final. Science is, like love, "too young to know what conscience," or common sense, is. As soon as the world began to busy itself with evolution it said good-bye to common sense, and must get on with uncommon sense as best it can. The first lesson that uncommon sense will teach it is that contradiction in terms is the foundation of all sound reasoning - and, as an obvious consequence, compromise, the foundation of all sound practice. This, it follows easily, involves the corollary that as faith, to be of any value, must be based on reason, so reason, to be of any value, must be based on faith, and that neither can stand alone or dispense with the other, any more than culture or vulgarity can stand unalloyed with one another without much danger of mischance.

It may not perhaps be immediately apparent why the admission that a piece of healthy living brain is more living than the end of a finger-nail, is so dangerous to common sense ways of looking at life and death; I had better therefore, be more explicit. By this admission degrees of livingness are admitted within the body; this involves approaches to non-livingness. On this the question arises, "Which are the most living parts?" The answer to this was given a few years ago with a flourish of trumpets, and our biologists shouted with one voice, "Great is protoplasm. There is no life but protoplasm, and Huxley is its prophet." Read Huxley's "Physical Basis of Mind." Read Professor Mivart's article, "What are Living Beings?" in the *Contemporary Review,* July, 1879. Read Dr. Andrew Wilson's article in the *Gentleman's Magazine,* October, 1879. Remember Professor Allman's address to the British Association, 1879; ask, again, any medical man what is the most approved scientific attitude as regards the protoplasmic and non-protoplasmic parts of the body, and he will say that the thinly veiled conclusion arrived at by all of them is, that the protoplasmic parts are alone truly living, and that the non-protoplasmic are non-living.

It may suffice if I confine myself to Professor Allman's address to the British Association in 1879, as a representative utterance. Professor Allman said:-

"Protoplasm lies at the base of every vital phenomenon. It is, as Huxley has well expressed it, 'the physical basis of life;' wherever there is life from its lowest to its highest manifestation there is protoplasm; wherever there is protoplasm there is life." {122a}

To say wherever there is life there is protoplasm, is to say that there can be no life without protoplasm, and this is saying that where there is no protoplasm there is no life. But large parts of the body are non-protoplasmic; a bone is, indeed, permeated by protoplasm, but it is not protoplasm; it follows, therefore, that according to Professor Allman bone is not in any proper sense of words a living substance. From this it should follow, and doubtless does follow in Professor Allman's mind, that large tracts of the human body, if not the greater part by weight (as bones, skin, muscular tissues, &c.), are no more alive than a coat or pair of boots in wear is alive, except in so far as the bones, &c., are more closely and nakedly permeated by protoplasm than the coat or boots, and are thus brought into closer, directer, and more permanent communication with that which, if not life itself, still has more of the ear of life, and comes nearer to its royal person than anything else does. Indeed that this is Professor Allman's opinion appears from the passage on page 26 of the report, in which he says that in "protoplasm we find the only form of matter in which life can manifest itself."

According to this view the skin and other tissues are supposed to be made from dead protoplasm which living protoplasm turns to account as the British Museum authorities are believed to stuff their new specimens with the skins of old ones; the matter used by the living protoplasm for this purpose is held to be entirely foreign to protoplasm itself, and no more capable of acting in concert with it than bricks can understand and act in concert with the bricklayer. As the bricklayer is held to be living and the bricks non-living, so the bones and skin which protoplasm is supposed to construct are held non-living and the protoplasm alone living. Protoplasm, it is said, goes about masked behind the clothes or habits which it has fashioned. It has habited itself as animals and plants, and we have mistaken the garment for the wearer - as our dogs and cats doubtless think with Giordano Bruno that our boots live when we are wearing them, and that we keep spare paws in our bedrooms which lie by the wall and go to sleep when we have not got them on.

If, in answer to the assertion that the osseous parts of bone are non-living, it is said that they must be living, for they heal if broken, which no dead matter can do, it is answered that the broken pieces of bone do not grow together they are mended by the protoplasm which permeates the Haversian canals; the bones themselves are no more living merely because they are tenanted by something which really does live, than a house lives because men and women inhabit it; and if a bone is repaired, it no more repairs itself than a house can be said to have repaired itself becaus its owner has sent for the bricklayer and seen that what was wanted was done.

We do not know, it is said, by what means the structureless viscid substance which we call protoplasm can build for itself a solid bone; we do not understand how an amœba makes its test; no one understands how anything is done unless he can do it himself; and even then he probably does not know how he has done it. Set a man who has never painted, to watch Rembrandt paint the Burgomaster Six, and he will no more understand how Rembrandt can have done it, than we can understand how the amœba makes its test, or the protoplasm cements two broken ends of a piece of bone. *Ces choses se font mais ne s'expliquent pas.* So some denizen of another planet looking at our earth through a telescope which showed him much, but still not quite enough, and seeing the St. Gothard tunnel plumb on end so that he could not see the holes of entry and exit, would think the trains there a kind of caterpillar which went through the mountain by a pure effort of the will - that enabled them in some mysterious way to disregard material obstacles and dispense with material means. We know, of course, that it is not so, and that exemption from the toil attendant on material obstacles has been compounded for, in the ordinary way, by the single payment of a tunnel; and so with the cementing of a bone, our biologists say that the protoplasm, which is alone living, cements it much as a man might mend a piece of broken china, but that it works by methods and processes which elude us, even as the holes of the St. Gothard tunnel may be supposed to elude a denizen of another world.

The reader will already have seen that the toils are beginning to close round those who, while professing to be guided by common sense, still parley with even the most superficial probers beneath the surface; this, however, will appear more clearly in the following chapter. It will also appear how far-reaching were the consequences of the denial of design that was involved in Mr. Darwin's theory that luck is the main element in survival, and how largely this theory is responsible for the fatuous developments in connection alike with protoplasm and automatism which a few years ago seemed about to carry everything before them.

CHAPTER IX - Property, Common Sense, and Protoplasm *(continued)*

The position, then, stands thus. Common sense gave the inch of admitting some parts of the body to be less living than others, and philosophy took the ell of declaring the body to be almost all of it stone dead. This is serious; still if it were all, for a quiet life, we might put up with it. Unfortunately we know only too well that it will not be all. Our bodies, which seemed so living and now prove so dead, have served us such a trick that we can have no confidence in anything connected with them. As with skin and bones to-day, so with protoplasm to-morrow. Protoplasm is mainly oxygen, hydrogen, nitrogen, and carbon; if we do not keep a sharp look out, we shall have it going the way of the rest of the body, and being declared dead in respect, at any rate, of these inorganic components. Science has not, I believe, settled all the components of protoplasm, but this is neither here nor there; she has settled what it is in great part, and there is no trusting her not to settle the rest at any moment, even if she has not already done so. As soon as this has been done we shall be told that nine-tenths of the protoplasm of which we are composed must go the way of our non-protoplasmic parts, and that the only really living part of us is the something with a new name that runs the protoplasm that runs the flesh and bones that run the organs -

Why stop here? Why not add "which run the tools and properties which are as essential to our life and health as much that is actually incorporate with us?" The same breach which has let the non-living effect a lodgment within the body must, in all equity, let the organic character - bodiliness, so to speak - pass out beyond its limits and effect a lodgment in our temporary and extra-corporeal limbs. What, on the protoplasmic theory, the skin and bones are, that the hammer and spade are also; they differ in the degree of closeness and permanence with which they are associated with protoplasm, but both bones and hammers are alike non-living things which protoplasm uses for its own purposes and keeps closer or less close at hand as custom and convenience may determine.

According to this view, the non-protoplasmic parts of the body are tools of the first degree; they are not living, but they are in such close and constant contact with that which really lives, that an aroma of life attaches to them. Some of these, however, such as horns, hooves, and tusks, are so little permeated by protoplasm that they cannot rank much higher than the tools of the second degree, which come next to them in order.

These tools of the second degree are either picked up ready-made, or are manufactured directly by the body, as being torn or bitten into shape, or as stones picked up to throw at prey or at an enemy.

Tools of the third degree are made by the instrumentality of tools of the second and first degrees; as, for example chipped flint, arrow-heads, &c.

Tools of the fourth degree are made by those of the third, second, and first. They consist of the simpler compound instruments that yet require to be worked by hand, as hammers, spades, and even hand flour-mills.

Tools of the fifth degree are made by the help of those of the fourth, third, second, and first. They are compounded of many tools, worked, it may be, by steam or water and requiring no constant contact with the body.

But each one of these tools of the fifth degree was made in the first instance by the sole instrumentality of the four preceding kinds of tool. They must all be linked on to protoplasm, which is the one original tool-maker, but which can only make the tools that are more remote from itself by the help of those that are nearer, that is to say, it can only work when it has suitable tools to work with, and when it is allowed to use them in its own way. There can be no direct communication between protoplasm and a steam-engine; there may be and often is direct communication between machines of even the fifth order and those of the first, as when an engine-man turns a cock, or repairs something with his own hands if he has nothing better to work with. But put a hammer, for example, to a piece of protoplasm, and the protoplasm will no more know what to do with it than we should be able to saw a piece of wood in two without a saw. Even protoplasm from the hand of a carpenter who has been handling hammers all his life would be hopelessly put off its stroke if not allowed to work in its usual way but put bare up against a hammer it would make a slimy mess and then dry up; still there can be no doubt (so at least those who uphold protoplasm as the one living substance would say) that the closer a machine can be got to protoplasm and the more permanent the connection, the more living it appears to be, or at any rate the more does it appear to be endowed with spontaneous and reasoning energy, so long, of course, as the closeness is of a kind which protoplasm understands and is familiar with. This, they say, is why we do not like using any implement or tool with gloves on, for these impose a barrier between the tool and its true connection with protoplasm by means of the nervous system. For the same reason we put gloves on when we box so as to bar the connection.

That which we handle most unglovedly is our food, which we handle with our stomachs rather than with our hands. Our hands are so thickly encased with skin that protoplasm can hold but small conversation with what they contain, unless it be held for a long time in the closed fist, and even so the converse is impeded as in a strange language; the inside of our mouths is more naked, and our stomachs are more naked still; it is here that protoplasm brings its fullest powers of suasion to bear on those whom it would proselytise and receive as it were into its own communion - whom it would convert and bring into a condition of mind in which they shall see things as it sees them itself, and, as we commonly say, "agree with" it, instead of standing out stiffly for their own opinion. We call this digesting our food; more properly we should call it being digested by our food, which reads, marks, learns, and inwardly digests us, till it comes to understand us and encourage us by assuring us that we were perfectly right all the time, no matter what any one might have said, or say, to the contrary. Having thus recanted all its own past heresies, it sets to work to convert everything that comes near it and seems in the least likely to be converted. Eating is a mode of love; it is an effort after a closer union; so we say we love roast beef. A French lady told me once that she adored veal; and a nurse tells her child that she would like to eat it. Even he who caresses a dog or horse *pro tanto* both weds and eats it. Strange how close the analogy between love and hunger; in each case the effort is after closer union and possession; in each case the outcome is reproduction (for nutrition is the most complete of reproductions), and in each case there are *residua*. But to return.

I have shown above that one consequence of the attempt so vigorously made a few years ago to establish protoplasm as the one living substance, is the making it clear that the non-protoplasmic parts of the body and the simpler extra-corporeal tools or organs must run on all fours in the matter of livingness and non-livingness. If the protoplasmic parts of the body are held living in virtue of their being used by something that really lives, then so, though in a less degree, must tools and machines. If, on the other hand, tools and machines are held non-living inasmuch as they only owe what little appearance of life they may present when in actual use to something else that lives, and have no life of their own - so, though in a less degree, must the non-protoplasmic parts of the body. Allow an overflowing aroma of life to vivify the horny skin under the heel, and from this there will be a spilling which will vivify the boot in wear. Deny an aroma of life to the boot in wear, and it must ere long be denied to ninety-nine per cent. of the body; and if the body is not alive while it can walk and talk, what in the name of all that is unreasonable can be held to be so?

That the essential identity of bodily organs and tools is no ingenious paradoxical way of putting things is evident from the fact that we speak of bodily organs at all. Organ means tool. There is nothing which reveals our most genuine opinions to us so unerringly as our habitual and unguarded expressions, and in the case under consideration so completely do we instinctively recognise the underlying identity of tools and limbs, that scientific men use the word "organ" for any part of the body that discharges a function, practically to the exclusion of any other term. Of course, however, the above contention as to the essential identity of tools and organs does not involve a denial of their obvious superficial differences - differences so many and so great as to justify our classing them in distinct categories so long as we have regard to the daily purposes of life without looking at remoter ones.

If the above be admitted, we can reply to those who in an earlier chapter objected to our saying that if Mr. Darwin denied design in the eye he should deny it in the burglar's jemmy also. For if bodily and non-bodily organs are essentially one in kind, being each of them both living and non-living, and each of them only a higher development of principles already admitted and largely acted on in the other, then the method of procedure observable in the evolution of the organs whose history is within our ken should throw light upon the evolution of that whose history goes back into so dim a past that we can only know it by way of inference. In the absence of any show of reason to the contrary we should argue from the known to the unknown, and presume that even as our non-bodily organs originated and were developed through gradual accumulation of design, effort, and contrivance guided by experience, so also must our bodily organs have been, in spite of the fact that the contrivance has been, as it were, denuded of external evidences in the course of long time. This at least is the most obvious inference to draw; the burden of proof should rest not with those who uphold function as the most important means of organic modification, but with those who impugn it; it is hardly necessary, however, to say that Mr. Darwin never attempted to impugn by way of argument the conclusions either of his grandfather or of Lamarck. He waved them both aside in one or two short semi-contemptuous sentences, and said no more about them - not, at least, until late in life he wrote his "Erasmus Darwin," and even then his remarks were purely biographical; he did not say one syllable by way of refutation, or even of explanation.

I am free to confess that, overwhelming as is the evidence brought forward by Mr. Spencer in the articles already referred to, as showing that accidental variations, unguided by the helm of any main general principle which should as it were keep their heads straight, could never accumulate with the results supposed by Mr. Darwin; and overwhelming, again, as is the consideration that Mr. Spencer's most crushing argument was allowed by Mr. Darwin to go without reply, still the considerations arising from the discoveries of the last forty years or so in connection with protoplasm, seem to me almost more overwhelming still. This evidence proceeds on different lines from that adduced by Mr. Spencer, but it points to the same conclusion, namely, that though luck will avail much if backed by cunning and experience, it is unavailing for any permanent result without them. There is an irony which seems almost always to attend on those who maintain that protoplasm is the only living substance which ere long points their conclusions the opposite way to that which they desire - in the very last direction, indeed, in which they of all people in the world would willingly see them pointed.

It may be asked why I should have so strong an objection to seeing protoplasm as the only living substance, when I find this view so useful to me as tending to substantiate design - which I admit that I have as much and as seriously at heart as I can allow myself to have any matter which, after all, can so little affect daily conduct; I reply that it is no part of my business to inquire whether this or that makes for my pet theories or against them; my concern is to inquire whether or no it is borne out by facts, and I find the opinion that protoplasm is the one living substance unstable, inasmuch as it is an attempt to make a halt where no halt can be made. This is enough; but, furthermore, the fact that the protoplasmic parts of the body are *more* living than the non-protoplasmic - which I cannot deny, without denying that it is any longer convenient to think of life and death at all - will answer my purpose to the full as well or better.

I pointed out another consequence, which, again, was cruelly the reverse of what the promoters of the protoplasm movement might be supposed anxious to arrive at - in a series of articles which appeared in the *Examiner* during the summer of 1879, and showed that if protoplasm were held to be the sole seat of life, then this unity in the substance vivifying all, both animals and plants, must be held as uniting them into a single corporation or body - especially when their community of descent is borne in mind - more effectually than any merely superficial separation into individuals can be held to disunite them, and that thus protoplasm must be seen as the life of the world - as a vast body corporate, never dying till the earth itself shall pass away. This came practically to saying that protoplasm was God Almighty, who, of all the forms open to Him, had chosen this singularly unattractive one as the channel through which to make Himself manifest in the flesh by taking our nature upon Him, and animating us with His own Spirit. Our biologists, in fact, were fast nearing the conception of a God who was both personal and material, but who could not be made to square with pantheistic notions inasmuch as no provision was made for the inorganic world; and, indeed, they seem to have become alarmed at the grotesqueness of the position in which they must ere long have found themselves, for in the autumn of 1879 the boom collapsed, and thenceforth the leading reviews and magazines have known protoplasm no more. About the same time bathybius, which at one time bade fair to supplant it upon the throne of popularity, died suddenly, as I am told, at Norwich, under circumstances which did not transpire, nor has its name, so far as I am aware, been ever again mentioned.

So much for the conclusions in regard to the larger aspect of life taken as a whole which must follow from confining life to protoplasm; but there is another aspect - that, namely, which regards the individual. The inevitable consequences of confining life to the protoplasmic parts of the body were just as unexpected and unwelcome here as they had been with regard to life at large; for, as I have already pointed out, there is no drawing the line at protoplasm and resting at this point; nor yet at the next halting-point beyond; nor at the one beyond that. How often is this process to be repeated? and in what can it end but in the rehabilitation of the soul as an ethereal, spiritual, vital principle, apart from matter, which, nevertheless, it animates, vivifying the clay of our bodies? No one who has followed the course either of biology or psychology during this century, and more especially during the last five-and-twenty years, will tolerate the reintroduction of the soul as something apart from the substratum in which both feeling and action must be held to inhere. The notion of matter being ever changed except by other matter in another state is so shocking to the intellectual conscience that it may be dismissed without discussion; yet if bathybius had not been promptly dealt with, it must have become apparent even to the British public that there were indeed but few steps from protoplasm, as the only living substance, to vital principle. Our biologists therefore stifled bathybius, perhaps with justice, certainly with prudence, and left protoplasm to its fate.

Any one who reads Professor Allman's address above referred to with due care will see that he was uneasy about protoplasm, even at the time of its greatest popularity. Professor Allman never says outright that the non-protoplasmic parts of the body are no more alive than chairs and tables are. He said what involved this as an inevitable consequence, and there can be no doubt that this is what he wanted to convey, but he never insisted on it with the outspokenness and emphasis with which so startling a paradox should alone be offered us for acceptance; nor is it easy to believe that his reluctance to express his conclusion *totidem verbis* was not due to a sense that it might ere long prove more convenient not to have done so. When I advocated the theory of the livingness, or quasi-livingness of machines, in the chapters of "Erewhon" of which all else that I have written on biological subjects is development, I took care that people should see the position in its extreme form; the non-livingness of bodily organs is to the full as startling a paradox as the livingness of non-bodily ones, and we have a right to expect the fullest explicitness from those who advance it. Of course it must be borne in mind that a machine can only claim any appreciable even aroma of livingness so long as it is in actual use. In "Erewhon" I did not think it necessary to insist on this, and did not, indeed, yet fully know what I was driving at.

The same disposition to avoid committing themselves to the assertion that any part of the body is non-living may be observed in the writings of the other authorities upon protoplasm above referred to; I have searched all they said and cannot find a single passage in which they declare even the osseous parts of a bone to be non-living, though this conclusion was the *raison d'être* of all they were saying and followed as an obvious inference. The reader will probably agree with me in thinking that such reticence can only have been due to a feeling that the ground was one on which it behoved them to walk circumspectly; they probably felt, after a vague, ill-defined fashion, that the more they reduced the body to mechanism the more they laid it open to an opponent to raise mechanism to the body, but, however this may be, they dropped protoplasm, as I have said, in some haste with the autumn of 1879.

CHAPTER X - The Attempt to Eliminate Mind

What, it may be asked, were our biologists really aiming at? - for men like Professor Huxley do not serve protoplasm for nought. They wanted a good many things, some of them more righteous than others, but all intelligible. Among the more lawful of their desires was a craving after a monistic conception of the universe. We all desire this; who can turn his thoughts to these matters at all and not instinctively lean towards the old conception of one supreme and ultimate essence as the source from which all things proceed and have proceeded, both now and ever? The most striking and apparently most stable theory of the last quarter of a century had been Sir William Grove's theory of the conservation of energy; and yet wherein is there any substantial difference between this recent outcome of modern amateur, and hence most sincere, science - pointing as it does to an imperishable, and as such unchangeable, and as such, again, for ever unknowable underlying substance the modes of which alone change - wherein, except in mere verbal costume, does this differ from the conclusions arrived at by the psalmist?

"Of old," he exclaims, "hast Thou laid the foundation of the earth; and the heavens are the work of Thy hands. They shall perish, but Thou shalt endure; yea, all of them shall wax old like a garment; as a vesture shalt Thou change them and they shall be changed; but Thou art the same, and Thy years shall have no end." {135a}

I know not what theologians may think of this passage, but from a scientific point of view it is unassailable. So again, "O Lord," he exclaims, "Thou hast searched me out, and known me: Thou knowest my down-sitting and mine up-rising; Thou understandest my thoughts long before. Thou art about my path, and about my bed: and spiest out all my ways. For lo, there is not a word in my tongue but Thou, O Lord, knowest it altogether . . . Whither shall I go, then, from Thy Spirit? Or whither shall I go, then, from Thy presence? If I climb up into heaven Thou art there: if I go down to hell, Thou art there also. If I take the wings of the morning, and remain in the uttermost part of the sea, even there also shall Thy hand lead me and Thy right hand shall hold me. If I say, Peradventure the darkness shall cover me, then shall my night be turned to day. Yea, the darkness is no darkness with Thee, but . . . the darkness and light to Thee are both alike." {136a}

What convention or short cut can symbolise for us the results of laboured and complicated chains of reasoning or bring them more aptly and concisely home to us than the one supplied long since by the word God? What can approach more nearly to a rendering of that which cannot be rendered - the idea of an essence omnipresent in all things at all times everywhere in sky and earth and sea; ever changing, yet the same yesterday, to-day, and for ever; the ineffable contradiction in terms whose presence none can either ever enter, or ever escape? Or rather, what convention would have been more apt if it had not been lost sight of as a convention and come to be regarded as an idea in actual correspondence with a more or less knowable reality? A convention was converted into a fetish, and now that its worthlessness as a fetish is being generally felt, its great value as a hieroglyph or convention is in danger of being lost sight of. No doubt the psalmist was seeking for Sir William Grove's conception, if haply he might feel after it and find it, and assuredly it is not far from every one of us. But the course of true philosophy never did run smooth; no sooner have we fairly grasped the conception of a single eternal and for ever unknowable underlying substance, then we are faced by mind and matter. Long-standing ideas and current language alike lead us to see these as distinct things - mind being still commonly regarded as something that acts on body from without as the wind blows upon a leaf, and as no less an actual entity than the body. Neither body nor mind seems less essential to our existence than the other; not only do we feel this as regards our own existence, but we feel it also as pervading the whole world of life; everywhere we see body and mind working together towards results that must be ascribed equally to both; but they are two, not one; if, then, we are to have our monistic conception, it would seem as though one of these must yield to the other; which, therefore, is it to be?

This is a very old question. Some, from time immemorial, have tried to get rid of matter by reducing it to a mere concept of the mind, and their followers have arrived at conclusions that may be logically irrefragable, but are as far removed from common sense as they are in accord with logic; at any rate they have failed to satisfy, and matter is no nearer being got rid of now than it was when the discussion first began. Others, again, have tried materialism, have declared the causative action of both thought and feeling to be deceptive, and posit matter obeying fixed laws of which thought and feeling must be admitted as concomitants, but with which they have no causal connection. The same thing has happened to these men as to their opponents; they made out an excellent case on paper, but thought and feeling still remain the mainsprings of action that they have been always held to be. We still say, "I gave him £5 because I felt pleased with him, and thought he would like it;" or, "I knocked him down because I felt angry, and thought I would teach him better manners." Omnipresent life and mind with appearances of brute non-livingness - which appearances are deceptive; this is one view. Omnipresent non-livingness or mechanism with appearances as though the mechanism were guided and controlled by thought - which appearances are deceptive; this is the other. Between these two views the slaves of logic have oscillated for centuries, and to all appearance will continue to oscillate for centuries more.

People who think - as against those who feel and act - want hard and fast lines - without which, indeed, they cannot think at all; these lines are as it were steps cut on a slope of ice without which there would be no descending it. When we have begun to travel the downward path of thought, we ask ourselves questions about life and death, ego and non ego, object and subject, necessity and free will, and other kindred subjects. We want to know where we are, and in the hope of simplifying matters, strip, as it were, each subject to the skin, and finding that even this has not freed it from all extraneous matter, flay it alive in the hope that if we grub down deep enough we shall come upon it in its pure unalloyed state free from all inconvenient complication through intermixture with anything alien to itself. Then, indeed, we can docket it, and pigeon-hole it for what it is; but what can we do with it till we have got it pure? We want to account for things, which means that we want to know to which of the various accounts opened in our mental ledger we ought to carry them - and how can we do this if we admit a phenomenon to be neither one thing nor the other, but to belong to half-a-dozen different accounts in proportions which often cannot even approximately be determined? If we are to keep accounts we must keep them in reasonable compass; and if keeping them within reasonable compass involves something of a Procrustean arrangement, we may regret it, but cannot help it; having set up as thinkers we have got to think, and must adhere to the only conditions under which thought is possible; life, therefore, must be life, all life, and nothing but life, and so with death, free will, necessity, design, and everything else. This, at least, is how philosophers must think concerning them in theory; in practice, however, not even John Stuart Mill himself could eliminate all taint of its opposite from any one of these things, any more than

Lady Macbeth could clear her hand of blood; indeed, the more nearly we think we have succeeded the more certain are we to find ourselves ere long mocked and baffled; and this, I take it, is what our biologists began in the autumn of 1879 to discover had happened to themselves.

For some years they had been trying to get rid of feeling, consciousness, and mind generally, from active participation in the evolution of the universe. They admitted, indeed, that feeling and consciousness attend the working of the world's gear, as noise attends the working of a steam-engine, but they would not allow that consciousness produced more effect in the working of the world than noise on that of the steam-engine. Feeling and noise were alike accidental unessential adjuncts and nothing more. Incredible as it may seem to those who are happy enough not to know that this attempt is an old one, they were trying to reduce the world to the level of a piece of unerring though sentient mechanism. Men and animals must be allowed to feel and even to reflect; this much must be conceded, but granted that they do, still (so, at least, it was contended) it has no effect upon the result; it does not matter as far as this is concerned whether they feel and think or not; everything would go on exactly as it does and always has done, though neither man nor beast knew nor felt anything at all. It is only by maintaining things like this that people will get pensions out of the British public.

Some such position as this is a *sine quâ non* for the Neo-Darwinistic doctrine of natural selection, which, as Von Hartmann justly observes, involves an essentially mechanical mindless conception of the universe; to natural selection's door, therefore, the blame of the whole movement in favour of mechanism must be justly laid. It was natural that those who had been foremost in preaching mindless designless luck as the main means of organic modification, should lend themselves with alacrity to the task of getting rid of thought and feeling from all share in the direction and governance of the world. Professor Huxley, as usual, was among the foremost in this good work, and whether influenced by Hobbes, or Descartes, or Mr. Spalding, or even by the machine chapters in "Erewhon" which were still recent, I do not know, led off with his article "On the hypothesis that animals are automata" (which it may be observed is the exact converse of the hypothesis that automata are animated) in the *Fortnightly Review* for November 1874. Professor Huxley did not say outright that men and women were just as living and just as dead as their own watches, but this was what his article came to in substance. The conclusion arrived at was that animals were automata; true, they were probably sentient, still they were automata pure and simple, mere sentient pieces of exceedingly elaborate clockwork, and nothing more.

"Professor Huxley," says Mr. Romanes, in his Rede Lecture for 1885, {140a} "argues by way of perfectly logical deduction from this statement, that thought and feeling have nothing to do with determining action; they are merely the bye-products of cerebration, or, as he expresses it, the indices of changes which are going on in the brain. Under this view we are all what he terms conscious automata, or machines which happen, as it were by chance, to be conscious of some of their own movements. But the consciousness is altogether adventitious, and bears the same ineffectual relation to the activity of the brain as a steam whistle bears to the activity of a locomotive, or the striking of a clock to the time-keeping adjustments of the clockwork. Here, again, we meet with an echo of Hobbes, who opens his work on the commonwealth with these words:-

"'Nature, the art whereby God hath made and governs the world, is by the *art* of man, as in many other things, in this also imitated, that it can make an artificial animal. For seeing life is but a motion of limbs, the beginning whereof is in the principal part within; why may we not say that all automata (engines that move themselves by springs and wheels as doth a watch) have an artificial life? For what is the *heart* but a spring, and the *nerves* but so many *strings;* and the *joints* but so many *wheels* giving motion to the whole body, such as was intended by the artificer?'

"Now this theory of conscious automatism is not merely a legitimate outcome of the theory that nervous changes are the causes of mental changes, but it is logically the only possible outcome. Nor do I see any way in which this theory can be fought on grounds of physiology."

In passing, I may say the theory that living beings are conscious machines, can be fought just as much and just as little as the theory that machines are unconscious living beings; everything that goes to prove either of these propositions goes just as well to prove the other also. But I have perhaps already said as much as is necessary on this head; the main point with which I am concerned is the fact that Professor Huxley was trying to expel consciousness and sentience from any causative action in the working of the universe. In the following month appeared the late Professor Clifford's hardly less outspoken article, "Body and Mind," to the same effect, also in the *Fortnightly Review,* then edited by Mr. John Morley. Perhaps this view attained its frankest expression in an article by the late Mr. Spalding, which appeared in *Nature,* August 2, 1877; the following extracts will show that Mr. Spalding must be credited with not playing fast and loose with his own conclusions, and knew both how to think a thing out to its extreme consequences, and how to put those consequences clearly before his readers. Mr. Spalding said:-

"Against Mr. Lewes's proposition that the movements of living beings are prompted and guided by feeling, I urged that the amount and direction of every nervous discharge must depend solely on physical conditions. And I contended that to see this clearly is to see that when we speak of movement being guided by feeling, we use the language of a less advanced stage of enlightenment. This view has since occupied a good deal of attention. Under the name of automatism it has been advocated by Professor Huxley, and with firmer logic by Professor Clifford. In the minds of our savage ancestors feeling was the source of all movement . . . Using the word feeling in its ordinary sense . . . *we assert not only that no evidence can be given that feeling ever does guide or prompt action, but that the process of its doing so is inconceivable.* (Italics mine.) How can we picture to ourselves a state of consciousness putting in motion any particle of matter, large or small? Puss, while dozing before the fire, hears a light rustle in the corner, and darts towards the spot. What has happened? Certain sound-waves have reached the ear, a series of physical changes have taken place within the organism, special groups of muscles have been called into play, and the body of the cat has changed its position on the floor. Is it asserted that this chain of physical changes is not at all points complete and sufficient in itself?"

I have been led to turn to this article of Mr. Spalding's by Mr. Stewart Duncan, who, in his "Conscious Matter," {142a} quotes the latter part of the foregoing extract. Mr. Duncan goes on to quote passages from Professor Tyndall's utterances of about the same date which show that he too took much the same line - namely, that there is no causative connection between mental and physical processes; from this it is obvious he must have supposed that physical processes would go on just as well if there were no accompaniment of feeling and consciousness at all.

I have said enough to show that in the decade, roughly, between 1870 and 1880 the set of opinion among our leading biologists was strongly against mind, as having in any way influenced the development of animal and vegetable life, and it is not likely to be denied that the prominence which the mindless theory of natural selection had assumed in men's thoughts since 1860 was one of the chief reasons, if not the chief, for the turn opinion was taking. Our leading biologists had staked so heavily upon natural selection from among fortuitous variations that they would have been more than human if they had not caught at everything that seemed to give it colour and support. It was while this mechanical fit was upon them, and in the closest connection with it, that the protoplasm boom developed. It was doubtless felt that if the public could be got to dislodge life, consciousness, and mind from any considerable part of the body, it would be no hard matter to dislodge it, presently, from the remainder; on this the deceptiveness of mind as a causative agent, and the sufficiency of a purely automatic conception of the universe, as of something that will work if a penny be dropped into the box, would be proved to demonstration. It would be proved from the side of mind by considerations derivable from automatic and unconscious action where mind *ex hypothesi* was not, but where action went on as well or better without it than with it; it would be proved from the side of body by what they would doubtless call the "most careful and exhaustive" examination of the body itself by the aid of appliances more ample than had ever before been within the reach of man.

This was all very well, but for its success one thing was a *sine quâ non* - I mean the dislodgment must be thorough; the key must be got clean of even the smallest trace of blood, for unless this could be done all the argument went to the profit not of the mechanism, with which, for some reason or other, they were so much enamoured, but of the soul and design, the ideas which of all others were most distasteful to them. They shut their eyes to this for a long time, but in the end appear to have seen that if they were in search of an absolute living and absolute non-living, the path along which they were travelling would never lead them to it. They were driving life up into a corner, but they were not eliminating it, and, moreover, at the very moment of their thinking they had hedged it in and could throw their salt upon it, it flew mockingly over their heads and perched upon the place of all others where they were most scandalised to see it - I mean upon machines in use. So they retired sulkily to their tents baffled but not ashamed.

Some months subsequent to the completion of the foregoing chapter, and indeed just as this book is on the point of leaving my hands, there appears in *Nature* {144a} a letter from the Duke of Argyll, which shows that he too is impressed with the conviction expressed above - I mean that the real object our men of science have lately had in view has been the getting rid of mind from among the causes of evolution. The Duke says:-

"The violence with which false interpretations were put upon this theory (natural selection) and a function was assigned to it which it could never fulfil, will some day be recognised as one of the least creditable episodes in the history of science. With a curious perversity it was the weakest elements in the theory which were seized upon as the most valuable, particularly the part assigned to blind chance in the occurrence of variations. This was valued not for its scientific truth, - for it could pretend to none, - but because of its assumed bearing upon another field of thought and the weapon it afforded for expelling mind from the causes of evolution."

The Duke, speaking of Mr. Herbert Spencer's two articles in the *Nineteenth Century* for April and May, 1886, to which I have already called attention, continues:-

"In these two articles we have for the first time an avowed and definite declaration against some of the leading ideas on which the mechanical philosophy depends; and yet the caution, and almost timidity, with which a man so eminent approaches the announcement of conclusions of the most self-evident truth is a most curious proof of the reign of terror which has come to be established."

Against this I must protest; the Duke cannot seriously maintain that the main scope and purpose of Mr. Herbert Spencer's articles is new. Their substance has been before us in Mr. Spencer's own writings for some two-and-twenty years, in the course of which Mr. Spencer has been followed by Professor Mivart, the Rev. J. J. Murphy, the Duke of Argyll himself, and many other writers of less note. When the Duke talks about the establishment of scientific reign of terror, I confess I regard such an exaggeration with something like impatience. Any one who has known his own mind and has had the courage of his opinions has been able to say whatever he wanted to say with as little let or hindrance during the last twenty years, as during any other period in the history of literature. Of course if a man will keep blurting out unpopular truths without considering whose toes he may or may not be treading on he will make enemies some of whom will doubtless be able to give effect to their displeasure; but that is part of the game. It is hardly possible for any one to oppose the fallacy involved in the Charles-Darwinian theory of natural selection more persistently and unsparingly than I have done myself from the year 1877 onwards; naturally I have at times been very angrily attacked in consequence, and as a matter of business have made myself as unpleasant as I could in my rejoinders, but I cannot remember anything having been ever attempted against me which could cause fear in any ordinarily constituted person. If, then, the Duke of Argyll is right in saying that Mr. Spencer has shown a caution almost amounting to timidity in attacking Mr. Darwin's theory, either Mr. Spencer must be a singularly timid person, or there must be some cause for his timidity which is not immediately obvious. If terror reigns anywhere among scientific men, I should say it reigned among those who have staked imprudently on Mr. Darwin's reputation as a philosopher. I may add that the discovery of the Duke's impression that there exists a scientific reign of terror explains a good deal in his writings which it has not been easy to understand hitherto.

As regards the theory of natural selection, the Duke says:-

"From the first discussions which arose on this subject, I have ventured to maintain that . . . the phrase 'natural-selection' represented no true physical cause, still less the complete set of causes requisite to account for the orderly procession of organic forms in Nature; that in so far as it assumed variations to arise by accident it was not only essentially faulty and incomplete, but fundamentally erroneous; in short, that its only value lay in the convenience with which it groups under one form of words, highly charged with metaphor, an immense variety of causes, some purely mental, some purely vital, and others purely physical or mechanical."

CHAPTER XI - The Way of Escape

To sum up the conclusions hitherto arrived at. Our philosophers have made the mistake of forgetting that they cannot carry the rough-and-ready language of common sense into precincts within which politeness and philosophy are supreme. Common sense sees life and death as distinct states having nothing in common, and hence in all respects the antitheses of one another; so that with common sense there should be no degrees of livingness, but if a thing is alive at all it is as much alive as the most living of us, and if dead at all it is stone dead in every part of it. Our philosophers have exercised too little consideration in retaining this view of the matter. They say that an amœba is as much a living being as a man is, and do not allow that a well-grown, highly educated man in robust health is more living than an idiot cripple. They say he differs from the cripple in many important respects, but not in degree of livingness. Yet, as we have seen already, even common sense by using the word "dying" admits degrees of life; that is to say, it admits a more and a less; those, then, for whom the superficial aspects of things are insufficient should surely find no difficulty in admitting that the degrees are more numerous than is dreamed of in the somewhat limited philosophy which common sense alone knows. Livingness depends on range of power, versatility, wealth of body and mind - how often, indeed, do we not see people taking a new lease of life when they have come into money even at an advanced age; it varies as these vary, beginning with things that, though they have mind enough for an outsider to swear by, can hardly be said to have yet found it out themselves, and advancing to those that know their own minds as fully as anything in this world does so. The more a thing knows its own mind the more living it becomes, for life viewed both in the individual and in the general as the outcome of accumulated developments, is one long process of specialising consciousness and sensation; that is to say, of getting to know one's own mind more and more fully upon a greater and greater variety of subjects. On this I hope to touch more fully in another book; in the meantime I would repeat that the error of our philosophers consists in not having borne in mind that when they quitted the ground on which common sense can claim authority, they should have reconsidered everything that common sense had taught them.

The votaries of common sense make the same mistake as philosophers do, but they make it in another way. Philosophers try to make the language of common sense serve for purposes of philosophy, forgetting that they are in another world, in which another tongue is current; common sense people, on the other hand, every now and then attempt to deal with matters alien to the routine of daily life. The boundaries between the two kingdoms being very badly defined, it is only by giving them a wide berth and being so philosophical as almost to deny that there is any either life or death at all, or else so full of common sense as to refuse to see one part of the body as less living than another, that we can hope to steer clear of doubt, inconsistency, and contradiction in terms in almost every other word we utter. We cannot serve the God of philosophy and the Mammon of common sense at one and the same time, and yet it would almost seem as though the making the best that can be made of both these worlds were the whole duty of organism.

It is easy to understand how the error of philosophers arose, for, slaves of habit as we all are, we are more especially slaves when the habit is one that has not been found troublesome. There is no denying that it saves trouble to have things either one thing or the other, and indeed for all the common purposes of life if a thing is either alive or dead the small supplementary residue of the opposite state should be neglected as too small to be observable. If it is good to eat we have no difficulty in knowing when it is dead enough to be eaten; if not good to eat, but valuable for its skin, we know when it is dead enough to be skinned with impunity; if it is a man, we know when he has presented enough of the phenomena of death to allow of our burying him and administering his estate; in fact, I cannot call to mind any case in which the decision of the question whether man or beast is alive or dead is frequently found to be perplexing; hence we have become so accustomed to think there can be no admixture of the two states, that we have found it almost impossible to avoid carrying this crude view of life and death into domains of thought in which it has no application. There can be no doubt that when accuracy is required we should see life and death not as fundamentally opposed, but as supplementary to one another, without either's being ever able to exclude the other altogether; thus we should indeed see some things as more living than others, but we should see nothing as either unalloyedly living or unalloyedly non-living. If a thing is living, it is so living that it has one foot in the grave already; if dead, it is dead as a thing that has already re-entered into the womb of Nature. And within the residue of life that is in the dead there is an element of death; and within this there is an element of life, and so*ad infinitum* - again, as reflections in two mirrors that face one another.

In brief, there is nothing in life of which there are not germs, and, so to speak, harmonics in death, and nothing in death of which germs and harmonics may not be found in life. Each emphasizes what the other passes over most lightly - each carries to its extreme conceivable development that which in the other is only sketched in by a faint suggestion - but neither has any feature rigorously special to itself. Granted that death is a greater new departure in an organism's life, than any since that *congeries* of births and deaths to which the name embryonic stages is commonly given, still it is a new departure of the same essential character as any other - that is to say, though there be much new there is much, not to say more, old along with it. We shrink from it as from any other change to the unknown, and also perhaps from an instinctive sense that the fear of death is a *sine quâ non* for physical and moral progress, but the fear is like all else in life, a substantial thing which, if its foundations be dug about, is found to rest on a superstitious basis.

Where, and on what principle, are the dividing lines between living and non-living to be drawn? All attempts to draw them hitherto have ended in deadlock and disaster; of this M. Vianna De Lima, in his "Exposé Sommaire des Théories transformistes de Lamarck, Darwin, et Haeckel," {150a} says that all attempts to trace *une ligne de démarcation nette et profonde entre la matière vivante et la matière inerte*have broken down. {150b} *Il y a un reste de vie dans le cadavre,* says Diderot, {150c} speaking of the more gradual decay of the body after an easy natural death, than after a sudden and violent one; and so Buffon begins his first volume by saying that "we can descend, by almost imperceptible degrees, from the most perfect creature to the most formless matter - from the most highly organised matter to the most entirely inorganic substance." {150d}

Is the line to be so drawn as to admit any of the non-living within the body? If we answer "yes," then, as we have seen, moiety after moiety is filched from us, till we find ourselves left face to face with a tenuous quasi immaterial vital principle or soul as animating an alien body, with which it not only has no essential underlying community of substance, but with which it has no conceivable point in common to render a union between the two possible, or give the one a grip of any kind over the other; in fact, the doctrine of disembodied spirits, so instinctively rejected by all who need be listened to, comes back as it would seem, with a scientific *imprimatur;* if, on the other hand, we exclude the non-living from the body, then what are we to do with nails that want cutting, dying skin, or hair that is ready to fall off? Are they less living than brain? Answer "yes," and degrees are admitted, which we have already seen prove fatal; answer "no," and we must deny that one part of the body is more vital than another - and this is refusing to go as far even as common sense does; answer that these things are not very important, and we quit the ground of equity and high philosophy on which we have given ourselves such airs, and go back to common sense as unjust judges that will hear those widows only who importune us.

As with the non-living so also with the living. Are we to let it pass beyond the limits of the body, and allow a certain temporary overflow of livingness to ordain as it were machines in use? Then death will fare, if we once let life without the body, as life fares if we once let death within it. It becomes swallowed up in life, just as in the other case life was swallowed up in death. Are we to confine it to the body? If so, to the whole body, or to parts? And if to parts, to what parts, and why? The only way out of the difficulty is to rehabilitate contradiction in terms, and say that everything is both alive and dead at one and the same time - some things being much living and little dead, and others, again, much dead and little living. Having done this we have only got to settle what a thing is - when a thing is a thing pure and simple, and when it is only a *congeries* of things - and we shall doubtless then live very happily and very philosophically ever afterwards.

But here another difficulty faces us. Common sense does indeed know what is meant by a "thing" or "an individual," but philosophy cannot settle either of these two points. Professor Mivart made the question "What are Living Beings?" the subject of an article in one of our leading magazines only a very few years ago. He asked, but he did not answer. And so Professor Moseley was reported *(Times,* January 16, 1885) as having said that it was "almost impossible" to say what an individual was. Surely if it is only "almost" impossible for philosophy to determine this, Professor Moseley should have at any rate tried to do it; if, however, he had tried and failed, which from my own experience I should think most likely, he might have spared his "almost." "Almost" is a very dangerous word. I once heard a man say that an escape he had had from drowning was "almost" providential. The difficulty about defining an individual arises from the fact that we may look at "almost" everything from two different points of view. If we are in a common-sense humour for simplifying things, treating them broadly, and emphasizing resemblances rather than differences, we can find excellent reasons for ignoring recognised lines of demarcation, calling everything by a new name, and unifying up till we have united the two most distant stars in heaven as meeting and being linked together in the eyes and souls of men; if we are in this humour individuality after individuality disappears, and ere long, if we are consistent, nothing will remain but one universal whole, one true and only atom from which alone nothing can be cut off and thrown away on to something else; if, on the other hand, we are in a subtle philosophically accurate humour for straining at gnats and emphasizing differences rather than resemblances, we can draw distinctions, and give reasons for subdividing and subdividing, till, unless we violate what we choose to call our consistency somewhere, we shall find ourselves with as many names as atoms and possible combinations and permutations of atoms. The lines we draw, the moments we choose for cutting this or that off at this or that place and thenceforth the dubbing it by another name, are as arbitrary as the moments chosen by a South-Eastern Railway porter for leaving off beating doormats; in each case doubtless there is an approximate equity, but it is of a very rough and ready kind.

What else, however, can we do? We can only escape the Scylla of calling everything by one name, and recognising no individual existences of any kind, by falling into the Charybdis of having a name for everything, or by some piece of intellectual sharp practice like that of the shrewd but unprincipled Ulysses. If we were consistent honourable gentlemen, into Charybdis or on to Scylla we should go like lambs; every subterfuge by the help of which we escape our difficulty is but an arbitrary high-handed act of classification that turns a deaf ear to everything not robust enough to hold its own; nevertheless even the most scrupulous of philosophers pockets his consistency at a pinch and refuses to let the native hue of resolution be sicklied o'er with the pale cast of thought, nor yet fobbed by the rusty curb of logic. He is right, for assuredly the poor intellectual abuses of the time want countenancing now as much as ever, but so far as he countenances them, he should bear in mind that he is returning to the ground of common sense, and should not therefore hold himself too stiffly in the matter of logic.

As with life and death so with design and absence of design or luck. So also with union and disunion. There is never either absolute design rigorously pervading every detail, nor yet absolute absence of design pervading any detail rigorously, so, as between substances, there is neither absolute union and homogeneity, not absolute disunion and heterogeneity; there is always a little place left for repentance; that is to say, in theory we should admit that both design and chance, however well defined, each have an aroma, as it were, of the other. Who can think of a case in which his own design - about which he should know more than any other, and from which, indeed, all his ideas of design are derived - was so complete that there was no chance in any part of it? Who, again, can bring forward a case even of the purest chance or good luck into which no element of design had entered directly or indirectly at any juncture? This, nevertheless, does not involve our being unable ever to ascribe a result baldly either to luck or cunning. In some cases a decided preponderance of the action, whether seen as a whole or looked at in detail, is recognised at once as due to design, purpose, forethought, skill, and effort, and then we properly disregard the undesigned element; in others the details cannot without violence be connected with design, however much the position which rendered the main action possible may involve design - as, for example, there is no design in the way in which individual pieces of coal may hit one another when shot out of a sack, but there may be design in the sack's being brought to the particular place where it is emptied; in others design may be so hard to find that we rightly deny its existence, nevertheless in each case there will be an element of the opposite, and the residuary element would, if seen through a mental microscope, be found to contain a residuary element of *its* opposite, and this again of *its* opposite, and so on *ad infinitum,* as with mirrors standing face to face. This having been explained, and it being understood that when we speak of design in organism we do so with a mental reserve of *exceptis excipiendis,* there should be no hesitation in holding the various modifications of plants and animals to be in such preponderating measure due to function, that design, which underlies function, is the fittest idea with which to connect them in our minds.

We will now proceed to inquire how Mr. Darwin came to substitute, or try to substitute, the survival of the luckiest fittest, for the survival of the most cunning fittest, as held by Erasmus Darwin and Lamarck; or more briefly how he came to substitute luck for cunning.

CHAPTER XII - Why Darwin's Variations were Accidental

Some may perhaps deny that Mr. Darwin did this, and say he laid so much stress on use and disuse as virtually to make function his main factor of evolution.

If, indeed, we confine ourselves to isolated passages, we shall find little difficulty in making out a strong case to this effect. Certainly most people believe this to be Mr. Darwin's doctrine, and considering how long and fully he had the ear of the public, it is not likely they would think thus if Mr. Darwin had willed otherwise, nor could he have induced them to think as they do if he had not said a good deal that was capable of the construction so commonly put upon it; but it is hardly necessary, when addressing biologists, to insist on the fact that Mr. Darwin's distinctive doctrine is the denial of the comparative importance of function, or use and disuse, as a purveyor of variations, with some, but not very considerable, exceptions, chiefly in the cases of domesticated animals.

He did not, however, make his distinctive feature as distinct as he should have done. Sometimes he said one thing, and sometimes the directly opposite. Sometimes, for example, the conditions of existence "included natural selection" or the fact that the best adapted to their surroundings live longest and leave most offspring; {156a} sometimes "the principle of natural selection" "fully embraced" "the expression of conditions of existence."{156b} It would not be easy to find more unsatisfactory writing than this is, nor any more clearly indicating a mind ill at ease with itself. Sometimes "ants work *by inherited instincts* and inherited tools;" {157a} sometimes, again, it is surprising that the case of ants working by inherited instincts has not been brought as a demonstrative argument "against the well-known doctrine of *inherited habit,* as advanced by Lamarck." {157b} Sometimes the winglessness of beetles inhabiting ocean islands is "mainly due to natural selection," {157c} and though we might be tempted to ascribe the rudimentary condition of the wing to disuse, we are on no account to do so - though disuse was probably to some extent "combined with" natural selection; at other times "it is probable that disuse has been the main means of rendering the wings of beetles living on small exposed islands" rudimentary.{157d} We may remark in passing that if disuse, as Mr. Darwin admits on this occasion, is the main agent in rendering an organ rudimentary, use should have been the main agent in rendering it the opposite of rudimentary - that is to say, in bringing about its development. The ostensible *raison d'être,* however, of the "Origin of Species" is to maintain that this is not the case.

There is hardly an opinion on the subject of descent with modification which does not find support in some one passage or another of the "Origin of Species." If it were desired to show that there is no substantial difference between the doctrine of Erasmus Darwin and that of his grandson, it would be easy to make out a good case for this in spite of Mr. Darwin's calling his grandfather's views "erroneous," in the historical sketch prefixed to the later editions of the "Origin of Species." Passing over the passage already quoted on p. 62 of this book, in which Mr Darwin declares "habit omnipotent and its effects hereditary" - a sentence, by the way, than which none can be either more unfalteringly Lamarckian or less tainted with the vices of Mr. Darwin's later style - passing this over as having been written some twenty years before the "Origin of Species" - the last paragraph of the "Origin of Species" itse is purely Lamarckian and Erasmus-Darwinian. It declares the laws in accordance with which organic forms assumed their present shape to be - "Growth with reproduction; Variability from the indirect and direct action of the external conditions of life and from use and disuse, &c." {158a} Wherein does this differ from the confession of faith made by Erasmus Darwin and Lamarck? Where are the accidental fortuitous, spontaneous variations now? And if they are not found important enough to demand mention in this peroration and *stretto,* as it were, of the whole matter, in which special prominence should be given to the special feature of the work, where ought they to be made important?

Mr. Darwin immediately goes on: "A ratio of existence so high as to lead to a struggle for life, and as a consequence to natural selection, entailing divergence of character and the extinction of less improved forms;" so that natura selection turns up after all. Yes - in the letters that compose it, but not in the spirit; not in the special sense up to this time attached to it in the "Origin of Species." The expression as used here is one with which Erasmus Darwin would have found little fault, for it means not as elsewhere in Mr. Darwin's book and on his title-page the preservation of "favoured" or lucky varieties, but the preservation of varieties that have come to be varieties througl the causes assigned in the preceding two or three lines of Mr. Darwin's sentence; and these are mainly functional or Erasmus-Darwinian; for the indirect action of the conditions of life is mainly functional, and the direct action i admitted on all hands to be but small.

It now appears more plainly, as insisted upon on an earlier page, that there is not one natural selection and one survival of the fittest, but two, inasmuch as there are two classes of variations from which nature (supposing nc exception taken to her personification) can select. The bottles have the same labels, and they are of the same colour, but the one holds brandy, and the other toast and water. Nature can, by a figure of speech, be said to select from variations that are mainly functional or from variations that are mainly accidental; in the first case she will eventually get an accumulation of variation, and widely different types will come into existence; in the second, the variations will not occur with sufficient steadiness for accumulation to be possible. In the body of Mr. Darwin's book the variations are supposed to be mainly due to accident, and function, though not denied all efficacy, is declared to be the greatly subordinate factor; natural selection, therefore, has been hitherto throughout tantamount to luck; in the peroration the position is reversed *in toto;* the selection is now made from variations into which luck has entered so little that it may be neglected, the greatly preponderating factor being function; here, then, natural selection is tantamount to cunning. We are such slaves of words that, seeing the words "natural selection" employed - and forgetting that the results ensuing on natural selection will depend entirely on what it is that is selected from, so that the gist of the matter lies in this and not in the words "natural selection" - it escaped us that a change of front hac been made, and a conclusion entirely alien to the tenor of the whole book smuggled into the last paragraph as th one which it had been written to support; the book preached luck, the peroration cunning.

And there can be no doubt Mr. Darwin intended that the change of front should escape us; for it cannot be believed that he did not perfectly well know what he had done. Mr. Darwin edited and re-edited with such minuteness of revision that it may be said no detail escaped him provided it was small enough; it is incredible that he should have allowed this paragraph to remain from first to last unchanged (except for the introduction of the words "by the Creator," which are wanting in the first edition) if they did not convey the conception he most wished his readers to retain. Even if in his first edition he had failed to see that he was abandoning in his last paragraph all that it hac been his ostensible object most especially to support in the body of his book, he must have become aware of it lon before he revised the "Origin of Species" for the last time; still he never altered it, and never put us on our guard.

It was not Mr. Darwin's manner to put his reader on his guard; we might as well expect Mr. Gladstone to put us on our guard about the Irish land bills. Caveat *lector* seems to have been his motto. Mr. Spencer, in the articles already referred to, is at pains to show that Mr. Darwin's opinions in later life underwent a change in the direction of laying greater stress on functionally produced modifications, and points out that in the sixth edition of the "Origin o Species" Mr. Darwin says, "I think there can be no doubt that use in our domestic animals has strengthened and enlarged certain parts, and disuse diminished them;" whereas in his first edition he said, "I think there can be *little* doubt" of this. Mr. Spencer also quotes a passage from "The Descent of Man," in which Mr. Darwin said that *even in the first edition* of the "Origin of Species" he had attributed great effect to function, as though in the later ones he ha attributed still more; but if there was any considerable change of position, it should not have been left to b toilsomely collected by collation of editions, and comparison of passages far removed from one another in othe books. If his mind had undergone the modification supposed by Mr. Spencer, Mr. Darwin should have said so in a prominent passage of some later edition of the "Origin of Species." He should have said - "In my earlier editions underrated, as now seems probable, the effects of use and disuse as purveyors of the slight successive modification whose accumulation in the ordinary course of things results in specific difference, and I laid too much stress on the accumulation of merely accidental variations;" having said this, he should have summarised the reasons that had made him change his mind, and given a list of the most important cases in which he has seen fit to alter what he had originally written. If Mr. Darwin had dealt thus with us we should have readily condoned all the mistakes he would have been at all likely to have made, for we should have known him as one who was trying to help us, tidy us up, keep us straight, and enable us to use our judgments to the best advantage. The public will forgive many errors alike of taste and judgment, where it feels that a writer persistently desires this.

I can only remember a couple of sentences in the later editions of the "Origin of Species" in which Mr. Darwin directly admits a change of opinion as regards the main causes of organic modification. How shuffling the first o these is I have already shown in "Life and Habit," p. 260, and in "Evolution, Old and New," p. 359; I need not, therefore, say more here, especially as there has been no rejoinder to what I then said. Curiously enough the sentence does not bear out Mr. Spencer's contention that Mr. Darwin in his later years leaned more decidedly towards functionally produced modifications, for it runs: {161a} - "In the earlier editions of this work I underrated, as now seems probable, the frequency and importance of modifications due," not, as Mr. Spencer would have us believe, to use and disuse, but "to spontaneous variability," by which can only be intended, "to variations in no way connected with use and disuse," as not being assignable to any known cause of general application, and referable as far as we are concerned to accident only; so that he gives the natural survival of the luckiest, which is indeed his distinctive feature, if it deserve to be called a feature at all, greater prominence than ever. Nevertheless there is no change in his concluding paragraph, which still remains an embodiment of the views of Erasmus Darwin and Lamarck.

The other passage is on p. 421 of the edition of 1876. It stands: "I have now recapitulated the facts and considerations which have thoroughly" (why "thoroughly"?) "convinced me that species have been modified during a long course of descent. This has been effected chiefly through the natural selection of numerous, successive, slight favourable variations; aided in an important manner by the inherited effects of the use and disuse of parts; and in an unimportant manner, that is, in relation to adaptive structures, whether past or present, by the direct action of external conditions, and by variations which seem to us in our ignorance to arise spontaneously. It appears that I formerly underrated the frequency and value of these latter forms of variation as leading to permanent modification of structure independently of natural selection."

Here, again, it is not use and disuse which Mr. Darwin declares himself to have undervalued, but spontaneous variations. The sentence just given is one of the most confusing I ever read even in the works of Mr Darwin. It is the essence of his theory that the "numerous successive, slight, favourable variations," above referred to, should be fortuitous, accidental, spontaneous; it is evident, moreover, that they are intended in this passage to be accidental or spontaneous, although neither of these words is employed, inasmuch as use and disuse and the action of the conditions of existence, whether direct or indirect, are mentioned specially as separate causes which purvey only the minor part of the variations from among which nature selects. The words "that is, in relation to adaptive forms" should be omitted, as surplusage that draws the reader's attention from the point at issue; the sentence really amounts to this - that modification has been effected *chiefly through selection* in the ordinary course of nature*from among spontaneous variations, aided in an unimportant manner by variations which quâ us are spontaneous*. Nevertheless, though these spontaneous variations are still so trifling in effect that they only aid spontaneous variations in an unimportant manner, in his earlier editions Mr. Darwin thought them still less important than he does now.

This comes of tinkering. We do not know whether we are on our heads or our heels. We catch ourselves repeating "important," "unimportant," "unimportant," "important," like the King when addressing the jury in "Alice in Wonderland;" and yet this is the book of which Mr. Grant Allen {163a} says that it is "one of the greatest, and most learned, the most lucid, the most logical, the most crushing, the most conclusive, that the world has ever seen. Step by step, and principle by principle, it proved every point in its progress triumphantly before it went on to the next. So vast an array of facts so thoroughly in hand had never before been mustered and marshalled in favour of any biological theory." The book and the eulogy are well mated.

I see that in the paragraph following on the one just quoted, Mr. Allen says, that "to the world at large Darwinism and evolution became at once synonymous terms." Certainly it was no fault of Mr. Darwin's if they did not, but I will add more on this head presently; for the moment, returning to Mr. Darwin, it is hardly credible, but it is nevertheless true, that Mr Darwin begins the paragraph next following on the one on which I have just reflected so severely, with the words, "It can hardly be supposed that a false theory would explain in so satisfactory a manner as does the theory of natural selection, the several large classes of facts above specified." If Mr. Darwin found the large classes of facts "satisfactorily" explained by the survival of the luckiest irrespectively of the cunning which enable them to turn their luck to account, he must have been easily satisfied. Perhaps he was in the same frame of mind as when he said {164a} that "even an imperfect answer would be satisfactory," but surely this is being thankful for small mercies.

On the following page Mr. Darwin says:- "Although I am fully" (why "fully"?) "convinced of the truth of the views given in this volume under the form of an abstract, I by no means expect to convince experienced naturalists," &c. I have not quoted the whole of Mr. Darwin's sentence, but it implies that any experienced naturalist who remained unconvinced was an old-fashioned, prejudiced person. I confess that this is what I rather feel about the experienced naturalists who differ in only too great numbers from myself, but I did not expect to find so much of the old Adam remaining in Mr. Darwin; I did not expect to find him support me in the belief that naturalists are made of much the same stuff as other people, and, if they are wise, will look upon new theories with distrust until they find them becoming generally accepted. I am not sure that Mr. Darwin is not just a little bit flippant here.

Sometimes I ask myself whether it is possible that, not being convinced, I may be an experienced naturalist after all; at other times, when I read Mr. Darwin's works and those of his eulogists, I wonder whether there is not some other Mr. Darwin, some other "Origin of Species," some other Professors Huxley, Tyndal, and Ray Lankester, and whether in each case some malicious fiend has not palmed off a counterfeit upon me that differs *toto cœlo* from the original. I felt exactly the same when I read Goethe's "Wilhelm Meister"; I could not believe my eyes, which nevertheless told me that the dull diseased trash I was so toilsomely reading was a work which was commonly held to be one of the great literary masterpieces of the world. It seemed to me that there must be some other Goethe and some other Wilhelm Meister. Indeed I find myself so depressingly out of harmony with the prevailing not opinion only, but spirit - if, indeed, the Huxleys, Tyndals, Miss Buckleys, Ray Lankesters, and Romaneses express the prevailing spirit as accurately as they appear to do - that at times I find it difficult to believe I am not the victim of hallucination; nevertheless I know that either every canon, whether of criticism or honourable conduct, which I have learned to respect is an impudent swindle, suitable for the cloister only, and having no force or application in the outside world; or else that Mr. Darwin and his supporters are misleading the public to the full as much as the theologians of whom they speak at times so disapprovingly. They sin, moreover, with incomparably less excuse. Right as they doubtless are in much, and much as we doubtless owe them (so we owe much also to the theologians, and they also are right in much), they are giving way to a temper which cannot be indulged with impunity. I know the great power of academicism; I know how instinctively academicism everywhere must range itself on Mr. Darwin's side, and how askance it must look on those who write as I do; but I know also that there is a power before which even academicism must bow, and to this power I look not unhopefully for support.

As regards Mr. Spencer's contention that Mr. Darwin leaned more towards function as he grew older, I do not doubt that at the end of his life Mr. Darwin believed modification to be mainly due to function, but the passage quoted on page 62 written in 1839, coupled with the concluding paragraph of the "Origin of Species" written in 1859, and allowed to stand during seventeen years of revision, though so much else was altered - these passages, when their dates and surroundings are considered, suggest strongly that Mr. Darwin thought during all the forty years or so thus covered exactly as his grandfather and Lamarck had done, and indeed as all sensible people since Buffon wrote have done if they have accepted evolution at all.

Then why should he not have said so? What object could he have in writing an elaborate work to support a theory which he knew all the time to be untenable? The impropriety of such a course, unless the work was, like Buffon's, transparently ironical, could only be matched by its fatuousness, or indeed by the folly of one who should assign action so motiveless to any one out of a lunatic asylum.

This sounds well, but unfortunately we cannot forget that when Mr. Darwin wrote the "Origin of Species" he claimed to be the originator of the theory of descent with modification generally; that he did this without one word of reference either to Buffon or Erasmus Darwin until the first six thousand copies of his book had been sold, and then with as meagre, inadequate notice as can be well conceived. Lamarck was just named in the first editions of the "Origin of Species," but only to be told that Mr. Darwin had not got anything to give him, and he must go away; the author of the "Vestiges of Creation" was also just mentioned, but only in a sentence full of such gross misrepresentation that Mr. Darwin did not venture to stand by it, and expunged it in later editions, as usual, without calling attention to what he had done. It would have been in the highest degree imprudent, not to say impossible, for one so conscientious as Mr. Darwin to have taken the line he took in respect of descent with modification generally, if he were not provided with some ostensibly distinctive feature, in virtue of which, if people said anything he might claim to have advanced something different, and widely different, from the theory of evolution propounded by his illustrious predecessors; a distinctive theory of some sort, therefore, had got to be looked for - and if people look in this spirit they can generally find.

I imagine that Mr. Darwin, casting about for a substantial difference, and being unable to find one, committed the Gladstonian blunder of mistaking an unsubstantial for a substantial one. It was doubtless because he suspected it that he never took us fully into his confidence, nor in all probability allowed even to himself how deeply he distrusted it. Much, however, as he disliked the accumulation of accidental variations, he disliked not claiming the theory of descent with modification still more; and if he was to claim this, accidental his variations had got to be. Accidental they accordingly were, but in as obscure and perfunctory a fashion as Mr. Darwin could make them consistently with their being to hand as accidental variations should later developments make this convenient. Under these circumstances it was hardly to be expected that Mr. Darwin should help the reader to follow the workings of his mind - nor, again, that a book the writer of which was hampered as I have supposed should prove clear and easy reading.

The attitude of Mr. Darwin's mind, whatever it may have been in regard to the theory of descent with modification generally, goes so far to explain his attitude in respect to the theory of natural selection (which, it cannot be too often repeated, is only one of the conditions of existence advanced as the main means of modification by the earlier evolutionists), that it is worth while to settle the question once for all whether Mr. Darwin did or did not believe himself justified in claiming the theory of descent as an original discovery of his own. This will be a task of some little length, and may perhaps try the reader's patience, as it assuredly tried mine; if, however, he will read the two following chapters, he will probably be able to make up his mind upon much that will otherwise, if he thinks about it at all, continue to puzzle him.

CHAPTER XIII - Darwin's Claim to Descent with Modification

Mr. Allen, in his "Charles Darwin," {168a} says that "in the public mind Mr. Darwin is commonly regarded as the discoverer and founder of the evolution hypothesis," and on p. 177 he says that to most men Darwinism and evolution mean one and the same thing. Mr. Allen declares misconception on this matter to be "so extremely general" as to be "almost universal;" this is more true than creditable to Mr. Darwin.

Mr. Allen says {168b} that though Mr. Darwin gained "far wider general acceptance" for both the doctrine of descent in general, and for that of the descent of man from a simious or semi-simious ancestor in particular, "he laid no sort of claim to originality or proprietorship in either theory." This is not the case. No one can claim a theory more frequently and more effectually than Mr. Darwin claimed descent with modification, nor, as I have already said, is it likely that the misconception of which Mr. Allen complains would be general, if he had not so claimed it. The "Origin of Species" begins:-

"When on board H.M.S. *Beagle,* as naturalist, I was much struck with certain facts in the distribution of the inhabitants of South America, and in the geological relation of the present to the past inhabitants of that continent. These facts seemed to me to throw some light on the origin of species - that mystery of mysteries, as it has been called by one of our greatest philosophers. On my return home it occurred to me, in 1837, that something might perhaps be made out on this question by patiently accumulating and reflecting upon all sorts of facts which could possibly have any bearing on it. After five years' work I allowed myself to speculate upon the subject, and drew up some short notes; these I enlarged in 1844 {169a} into a sketch of the conclusions which then seemed to me probable. From that period to the present day I have steadily pursued the same object. I hope I may be excused these personal details, as I give them to show that I have not been hasty in coming to a decision."

This is bland, but peremptory. Mr. Darwin implies that the mere asking of the question how species has come about opened up a field into which speculation itself had hardly yet ventured to intrude. It was the mystery of mysteries; one of our greatest philosophers had said so; not one little feeble ray of light had ever yet been thrown upon it. Mr. Darwin knew all this, and was appalled at the greatness of the task that lay before him; still, after he had pondered on what he had seen in South America, it really did occur to him, that if he was very very patient, and went on reflecting for years and years longer, upon all sorts of facts, good, bad, and indifferent, which could possibly have any bearing on the subject - and what fact might not possibly have some bearing? - well, something, as against the nothing that had been made out hitherto, might by some faint far-away possibility be one day dimly seem. It was only what he had seen in South America that made all this occur to him. He had never seen anything about descent with modification in any book, nor heard any one talk about it as having been put forward by other people; if he had, he would, of course, have been the first to say so; he was not as other philosophers are; so the mountain went on for years and years gestating, but still there was no labour.

"My work," continues Mr. Darwin, "is now nearly finished; but as it will take me two or three years to complete it, and as my health is far from strong, I have been urged to publish this abstract. I have been more especially induced to do this, as Mr. Wallace, who is now studying the natural history of the Malay Archipelago, has arrived at almost exactly the same general conclusions that I have on the origin of species." Mr. Darwin was naturally anxious to forestall Mr. Wallace, and hurried up with his book. What reader, on finding descent with modification to be its most prominent feature, could doubt - especially if new to the subject, as the greater number of Mr. Darwin's readers in 1859 were - that this same descent with modification was the theory which Mr. Darwin and Mr. Wallace had jointly hit upon, and which Mr. Darwin was so anxious to show that he had not been hasty in adopting? When Mr. Darwin went on to say that his abstract would be very imperfect, and that he could not give references and authorities for his several statements, we did not suppose that such an apology could be meant to cover silence concerning writers who during their whole lives, or nearly so, had borne the burden and heat of the day in respect of descent with modification in its most extended application. "I much regret," says Mr. Darwin, "that want of space prevents my having the satisfaction of acknowledging the generous assistance I have received from very many naturalists, some of them personally unknown to me." This is like what the Royal Academicians say when they do not intend to hang our pictures; they can, however, generally find space for a picture if they want to hang it, and we assume with safety that there are no master-works by painters of the very highest rank for which no space has been available. Want of space will, indeed, prevent my quoting from more than one other paragraph of Mr. Darwin's introduction; this paragraph, however, should alone suffice to show how inaccurate Mr. Allen is in saying that Mr. Darwin "laid no sort of claim to originality or proprietorship" in the theory of descent with modification, and this is the point with which we are immediately concerned. Mr. Darwin says:-

"In considering the origin of species, it is quite conceivable that a naturalist, reflecting on the mutual affinities of organic beings, on their embryological relations, their geographical distribution, geological succession, and other such facts, might come to the conclusion that each species had not been independently created, but had descended like varieties from other species."

It will be observed that not only is no hint given here that descent with modification was a theory which, though unknown to the general public, had been occupying the attention of biologists for a hundred years and more, but it is distinctly implied that this was not the case. When Mr. Darwin said it was "conceivable that a naturalist might" arrive at the theory of descent, straightforward readers took him to mean that though this was conceivable, it had never, to Mr. Darwin's knowledge, been done. If we had a notion that we had already vaguely heard of the theory that men and the lower animals were descended from common ancestors, we must have been wrong; it was not this that we had heard of, but something else, which, though doubtless a little like it, was all wrong, whereas this was obviously going to be all right.

To follow the rest of the paragraph with the closeness that it merits would be a task at once so long and so unpleasant that I will omit further reference to any part of it except the last sentence. That sentence runs:-

"In the case of the mistletoe, which draws its nourishment from certain trees, which has seeds that must be transported by certain birds, and which has flowers with separate sexes absolutely requiring the agency of certain insects to bring pollen from one flower to the other, it is equally preposterous to account for the structure of this parasite, with its relations to several distinct organic beings, by the effects of the external conditions, or of habit, or of the volition of the plant itself."

Doubtless it would be preposterous to refer the structure of either woodpecker or mistletoe to the single agency of any one of these three causes; but neither Lamarck nor any other writer on evolution has, so far as I know, even contemplated this; the early evolutionists supposed organic modification to depend on the action and interaction of all three, and I venture to think that this will ere long be considered as, to say the least of it, not more preposterous than the assigning of the largely preponderating share in the production of such highly and variously correlated organisms as the mistletoe and woodpecker mainly to luck pure and simple, as is done by Mr. Charles Darwin's theory.

It will be observed that in the paragraph last quoted from, Mr. Darwin, *more suo,* is careful not to commit himself.

All he has said is, that it would be preposterous to do something the preposterousness of which cannot be reasonably disputed; the impression, however, is none the less effectually conveyed, that some one of the three assigned agencies, taken singly, was the only cause of modification ever yet proposed, if, indeed, any writer had even gone so far as this. We knew we did not know much about the matter ourselves, and that Mr. Darwin was a naturalist of long and high standing; we naturally, therefore, credited him with the same good faith as a writer that we knew in ourselves as readers; it never so much as crossed our minds to suppose that the head which he was holding up all dripping before our eyes as that of a fool, was not that of a fool who had actually lived and written but only of a figure of straw which had been dipped in a bucket of red paint. Naturally enough we concluded, sinc Mr. Darwin seemed to say so, that if his predecessors had nothing better to say for themselves than this, it would not be worth while to trouble about them further; especially as we did not know who they were, nor what they had written, and Mr. Darwin did not tell us. It would be better and less trouble to take the goods with which it was plain Mr. Darwin was going to provide us, and ask no questions. We have seen that even tolerably obvious conclusions were rather slow in occurring to poor simple-minded Mr. Darwin, and may be sure that it never once occurred to him that the British public would be likely to argue thus; he had no intention of playing the scientific confidence trick upon us. I dare say not, but unfortunately the result has closely resembled the one that would have ensued if Mr. Darwin had had such an intention.

The claim to originality made so distinctly in the opening sentences of the" Origin of Species"is repeated in a letter to Professor Haeckel, written October 8, 1864, and giving an account of the development of his belief in descen with modification. This letter, part of which is quoted by Mr. Allen, {173a} is given on p. 134 of the English translation of Professor Haeckel's "History of Creation," {173b} and runs as follows:-

"In South America three classes of facts were brought strongly before my mind. Firstly, the manner in which closely allied species replace species in going southward. Secondly, the close affinity of the species inhabiting the islands near South America to those proper to the continent. This struck me profoundly, especially the difference of the species in the adjoining islets in the Galapagos Archipelago. Thirdly, the relation of the living Edentata and Rodentia to the extinct species. I shall never forget my astonishment when I dug out a gigantic piece of armour like that of the living armadillo.

"Reflecting on these facts, and collecting analogous ones, it seemed to me probable that allied species were descended from a common ancestor. But during several years I could not conceive how each form could have been modified so as to become admirably adapted to its place in nature. I began, therefore, to study domesticated animals and cultivated plants, and after a time perceived that man's power of selecting and breeding from certain individuals was the most powerful of all means in the production of new races. Having attended to the habits of animals an their relations to the surrounding conditions, I was able to realise the severe struggle for existence to which all organisms are subjected, and my geological observations had allowed me to appreciate to a certain extent the duration of past geological periods. Therefore, when I happened to read Malthus on population, the idea of natura selection flashed on me. Of all minor points, the last which I appreciated was the importance and cause of th principle of divergence."

This is all very naïve, and accords perfectly with the introductory paragraphs of the "Origin of Species;" it gives u the same picture of a solitary thinker, a poor, lonely, friendless student of nature, who had never so much as heard o Buffon, Erasmus Darwin, or Lamarck. Unfortunately, however, we cannot forget the description of the influences which, according to Mr. Grant Allen, did in reality surround Mr. Darwin's youth, and certainly they are more what we should have expected than those suggested rather than expressly stated by Mr. Darwin. "Everywhere around him," says Mr. Allen, {174a} "in his childhood and youth these great but formless" (why "formless"?) "evolutionar ideas were brewing and fermenting. The scientific society of his elders and of the contemporaries among whom h grew up was permeated with the leaven of Laplace and Lamarck, of Hutton and of Herschel. Inquiry was especial everywhere rife as to the origin and nature of specific distinctions among plants and animals. Those who believed in the doctrine of Buffon and of the 'Zoonomia,' and those who disbelieved in it, alike, were profoundly interested an agitated in soul by the far-reaching implications of that fundamental problem. On every side evolutionism, in it crude form." (I suppose Mr. Allen could not help saying "in its crude form," but descent with modification in 1809 meant, to all intents and purposes, and was understood to mean, what it means now, or ought to mean, to most people.) "The universal stir," says Mr. Allen on the following page, "and deep prying into evolutionary questions which everywhere existed among scientific men in his early days was naturally communicated to a lad born of a scientific family and inheriting directly in blood and bone the biological tastes and tendencies of Erasmus Darwin."

I confess to thinking that Mr. Allen's account of the influences which surrounded Mr. Darwin's youth, if tainted with picturesqueness, is still substantially correct. On an earlier page he had written:- "It is impossible to take up any scientific memoirs or treatises of the first half of our own century without seeing at a glance how every mind of hig original scientific importance was permeated and disturbed by the fundamental questions aroused, but not fully answered, by Buffon, Lamarck, and Erasmus Darwin. In Lyell's letters, and in Agassiz's lectures, in the 'Botanic Journal' and in the 'Philosophical Transactions,' in treatises on Madeira beetles and the Australian flora, we find everywhere the thoughts of men profoundly influenced in a thousand directions by this universal evolutionary solvent and leaven.

"And while the world of thought was thus seething and moving restlessly before the wave of ideas set in motion by these various independent philosophers, another group of causes in another field was rendering smooth the path beforehand for the future champion of the amended evolutionism. Geology on the one hand and astronomy on the other were making men's minds gradually familiar with the conception of slow natural development, as opposed to immediate and miraculous creation.

. . .

"The influence of these novel conceptions upon the growth and spread of evolutionary ideas was far-reaching and twofold. In the first place, the discovery of a definite succession of nearly related organic forms following one another with evident closeness through the various ages, inevitably suggested to every inquiring observer the possibility of their direct descent one from the other. In the second place, the discovery that geological formations were not really separated each from its predecessor by violent revolutions, but were the result of gradual and ordinary changes, discredited the old idea of frequent fresh creations after each catastrophe, and familiarised the minds of men of science with the alternative notion of slow and natural evolutionary processes. The past was seen in effect to be the parent of the present; the present was recognised as the child of the past."

This is certainly not Mr. Darwin's own account of the matter. Probably the truth will lie somewhere between the two extreme views: and on the one hand, the world of thought was not seething quite so badly as Mr. Allen represents it, while on the other, though "three classes of fact," &c., were undoubtedly "brought strongly before" Mr. Darwin's "mind in South America," yet some of them had perhaps already been brought before it at an earlier time, which he did not happen to remember at the moment of writing his letter to Professor Haeckel and the opening paragraph of the "Origin of Species."

CHAPTER XIV - Darwin and Descent with Modification *(continued)*

I have said enough to show that Mr. Darwin claimed I to have been the originator of the theory of descent with modification as distinctly as any writer usually claims any theory; but it will probably save the reader trouble in the end if I bring together a good many, though not, probably, all (for I much disliked the task, and discharged it perfunctorily), of the passages in the "Origin of Species" in which the theory of descent with modification in it widest sense is claimed expressly or by implication. I shall quote from the original edition, which, it should be remembered, consisted of the very unusually large number of four thousand copies, and from which no importan deviation was made either by addition or otherwise until a second edition of two thousand further copies had been sold; the "Historical Sketch," &c., being first given with the third edition. The italics, which I have employed so as to catch the reader's eye, are mine, not Mr. Darwin's. Mr. Darwin writes:-

"Although much remains obscure, and will long remain obscure, *I can entertain no doubt, after the most deliberate study and dispassionate judgment of which I am capable, that the view which most naturalists entertain, and which I formerly entertained - namely that each species has been independently created - is erroneous.* I am fully convinced that species are not immutable, but that those belonging to what are called the same genera are lineal descendants of some other and generally extinct species, in the same manner as the acknowledged varieties of any one species are the descendants of that species. Furthermore, I am convinced that natural selection" (or the preservation of fortunate races) "has been the main but not exclusive means of modification" (p. 6).

It is not here expressly stated that the theory of the mutability of species is Mr. Darwin's own; this, nevertheless, is the inference which the great majority of his readers were likely to draw, and did draw, from Mr. Darwin's words.

Again:-

"It is not that all large genera are now varying much, and are thus increasing in the number of their species, or that no small genera are now multiplying and increasing; for if this had been so it would have been fatal to *my theory;* inasmuch as geology," &c. (p. 56).

The words "my theory" stand in all the editions. Again:-

"This relation has a clear meaning *on my view* of the subject; I look upon all the species of any genus as having as certainly descended from the same progenitor, as have the two sexes of any one of the species" (p. 157).

"My view" here, especially in the absence of reference to any other writer as having held the same opinion, implies as its most natural interpretation that descent pure and simple is Mr. Darwin's view. Substitute "the theory of descent" for "my view," and we do not feel that we are misinterpreting the author's meaning. The words "my view" remain in all editions.

Again:-

"Long before having arrived at this part of my work, a crowd of difficulties will have occurred to the reader. Some of them are so grave that to this day I can never reflect on them without being staggered; but to the best of my belief the greater number are only apparent, and those that are real are not, I think, *fatal to my theory.*

"These difficulties and objections may be classed under the following heads:- Firstly, if species have descended from other species by insensibly fine gradations, why do we not everywhere see?" &c. (p. 171).

We infer from this that "my theory" is the theory "that species have descended from other species by insensibly fine gradations" - that is to say, that it is the theory of descent with modification; for the theory that is being objected to is obviously the theory of descent *in toto,* and not a mere detail in connection with that theory.

The words "my theory" were altered in 1872, with the sixth edition of the "Origin of species," into "the theory;" but I am chiefly concerned with the first edition of the work, my object being to show that Mr. Darwin was led into his false position as regards natural selection by a desire to claim the theory of descent with modification; if he claimed it in the first edition, this is enough to give colour to the view which I take; but it must be remembered that descent with modification remained, by the passage just quoted "my theory," for thirteen years, and even when in 1869 and 1872, for a reason that I can only guess at, "my theory" became generally "the theory," this did not make it become any one else's theory. It is hard to say whose or what it became, if the words are to be construed technically; practically, however, with all ingenuous readers, "the theory" remained as much Mr. Darwin's theory as though the words "my theory" had been retained, and Mr. Darwin cannot be supposed so simple-minded as not to have known this would be the case. Moreover, it appears, from the next page but one to the one last quoted, that Mr. Darwin claimed the theory of descent with modification generally, even to the last, for we there read, "*By my theory* these allied species have descended from a common parent," and the "my" has been allowed, for some reason not quite obvious, to survive the general massacre of Mr. Darwin's "my's" which occurred in 1869 and 1872.

Again:-

"He who believes that each being has been created as we now see it, must occasionally have felt surprise when he has met," &c. (p. 185).

Here the argument evidently lies between descent and independent acts of creation. This appears from the paragraph immediately following, which begins, "He who believes in separate and innumerable acts of creation," &c. We therefore understand descent to be the theory so frequently spoken of by Mr. Darwin as "my."

Again:-

"He who will go thus far, if he find on finishing this treatise that large bodies of facts, otherwise inexplicable, can be explained *by the theory of descent,* ought not to hesitate to go farther, and to admit that a structure even as perfect as an eagle's eye might be formed *by natural selection,* although in this case he does not know any of the transitional grades" (p. 188).

The natural inference from this is that descent and natural selection are one and the same thing.

Again:-

"If it could be demonstrated that any complex organ existed which could not possibly have been formed by numerous, successive, slight modifications, *my theory* would absolutely break down. But I can find out no such case. No doubt many organs exist of which we do not know the transitional grades, more especially if we look to much isolated species, round which, according to my *theory,* there has been much extinction" (p. 189).

This makes "my theory" to be "the theory that complex organs have arisen by numerous, successive, slight modifications;" that is to say, to be the theory of descent with modification. The first of the two "my theory's" in the passage last quoted has been allowed to stand. The second became "the theory" in 1872. It is obvious, therefore, that "the theory" means "my theory;" it is not so obvious why the change should have been made at all, nor why the one "my theory" should have been taken and the other left, but I will return to this question.

Again, Mr. Darwin writes:-

"Although we must be extremely cautious in concluding that any gradations, yet, undoubtedly grave cases of difficulty occur, some of which will be discussed in my future work" (p. 192).

This, as usual, implies descent with modification to be the theory that Mr. Darwin is trying to make good.

Again:-

"I have been astonished how rarely an organ can be named towards which no transitional variety is known to lead . . . Why, *on the theory of creation,* should this be so? Why should not nature have taken a leap from structure to structure? *On the theory of natural selection* we can clearly understand why she should not; for natural selection can act only by taking advantage of slight successive variations; she can never take a leap, but must advance by the slowest and shortest steps" (p. 194).

Here "the theory of natural selection" is opposed to "the theory of creation;" we took it, therefore, to be another way of saying "the theory of descent with modification."

Again:-

"We have in this chapter discussed some of the difficulties and objections which may be urged against *my theory.* Many of them are very grave, but I think that in the discussion light has been thrown on several facts which, *on the theory of independent acts of creation,* are utterly obscure" (p. 203).

Here we have, on the one hand, "my theory," on the other, "independent acts of creation." The natural antithesis to independent acts of creation is descent, and we assumed with reason that Mr. Darwin was claiming this when he spoke of "my theory." "My theory" became "the theory" in 1869.

Again:-

"On the theory of natural selection we can clearly understand the full meaning of that old canon in natural history '*Natura non facit saltum.*' This canon, if we look only to the present inhabitants of the world is not strictly correct, but if we include all those of past times, it must *by my theory* be strictly true" (p. 206).

Here the natural interpretation of "by my theory" is "by the theory of descent with modification;" the words "on the theory of natural selection," with which the sentence opens, lead us to suppose that Mr. Darwin regarded natural selection and descent as convertible terms. "My theory" was altered to "this theory" in 1872. Six lines lower down we read, "*On my theory* unity of type is explained by unity of descent." The "my" here has been allowed to stand.

Again:-

"Again, as in the case of corporeal structure, and conformably with *my theory,* the instinct of each species is good for itself, but has never," &c. (p. 210).

Who was to see that "my theory" did not include descent with modification? The "my" here has been allowed to stand.

Again:-

"The fact that instincts . . . are liable to make mistakes; - that no instinct has been produced for the exclusive good of other animals, but that each animal takes advantage of the instincts of others; - that the canon of natural history '*Natura non facit saltum*,' is applicable to instincts as well as to corporeal structure, and is plainly explicable on the foregoing views, but is otherwise inexplicable, - *all tend to corroborate the theory of natural selection*" (p. 243).

We feel that it is the theory of evolution, or descent with modification, that is here corroborated, and that it is this which Mr. Darwin is mainly trying to establish; the sentence should have ended "all tend to corroborate the theory of descent with modification;" the substitution of "natural selection" for descent tends to make us think that these conceptions are identical. That they are so regarded, or at any rate that it is the theory of descent in full which Mr Darwin has in his mind, appears from the immediately succeeding paragraph, which begins "*This theory*," and continues six lines lower, "For instance, we can understand, on the *principle of inheritance*, how it is that," &c.

Again:-

"In the first place, it should always be borne in mind what sort of intermediate forms must, *on my theory*, formerly have existed" (p. 280).

"My theory" became "the theory" in 1869. No reader who read in good faith could doubt that the theory of descent with modification was being here intended.

"It is just possible *by my theory*, that one of two living forms might have descended from the other; for instance, a horse from a tapir; but in this case *direct* intermediate links will have existed between them" (p. 281).

"My theory" became "the theory" in 1869.

Again:-

"*By the theory of natural selection* all living species have been connected with the parent species of each genus," &c. We took this to mean, "By the theory of descent with modification all living species," &c. (p. 281).

Again:-

"Some experienced conchologists are now sinking many of the very fine species of D'Orbigny and others into the rank of varieties; and on this view we do find the kind of evidence of change which *on my theory* we ought to find" (p. 297).

"My theory" became "the theory" in 1869.

In the fourth edition (1866), in a passage which is not in either of the two first editions, we read (p. 359), "So that here again we have undoubted evidence of change in the direction required by *my theory*." "My theory" became "the theory" in 1869; the theory of descent with modification is unquestionably intended.

Again:-

"Geological research has done scarcely anything in breaking down the distinction between species, by connecting them together by numerous, fine, intermediate varieties; and this not having been effected, is probably the gravest and most obvious of all the many objections which may be urged against *my views*" (p. 299).

We naturally took "my views" to mean descent with modification. The "my" has been allowed to stand.

Again:-

"If, then, there be some degree of truth in these remarks, we have no right to expect to find in our geological formations an infinite number of those transitional forms which *on my theory* assuredly have connected all the past and present species of the same group in one long and branching chain of life . . . But I do not pretend that I should ever have suspected how poor was the record in the best preserved geological sections, had not the absence of innumerable transitional links between the species which lived at the commencement and at the close of each formation pressed so hardly *on my theory*" (pp. 301, 302).

Substitute "descent with modification" for "my theory" and the meaning does not suffer. The first of the two "my theories" in the passage last quoted was altered in 1869 into "our theory;" the second has been allowed to stand.

Again:-

"The abrupt manner in which whole groups of species suddenly appear in some formations, has been urged by several palæontologists . . . as a fatal objection *to the belief in the transmutation of species* If numerous species, belonging to the same genera or families, have really started into life all at once, the fact would be fatal *to the theory of descent with slow modification through natural selection*" (p. 302).

Here "the belief in the transmutation of species," or descent with modification, is treated as synonymous with "the theory of descent with slow modification through natural selection; "but it has nowhere been explained that there are two widely different "theories of descent with slow modification through natural selection," the one of which may be true enough for all practical purposes, while the other is seen to be absurd as soon as it is examined closely. The theory of descent with modification is not properly convertible with either of these two views, for descent with modification deals with the question whether species are transmutable or no, and dispute as to the respective merits of the two natural selections deals with the question how it comes to be transmuted; nevertheless, the words "the theory of descent with slow modification through the ordinary course of things" (which is what "descent with modification through natural selection" comes to) may be considered as expressing the facts with practical accuracy, if the ordinary course of nature is supposed to be that modification is mainly consequent on the discharge of some correlated function, and that modification, if favourable, will tend to accumulate so long as the given function continues important to the wellbeing of the organism; the words, however, have no correspondence with reality if they are supposed to imply that variations which are mainly matters of pure chance and unconnected in any way with function will accumulate and result in specific difference, no matter how much each one of them may be preserved in the generation in which it appears. In the one case, therefore, the expression natural selection may be loosely used as a synonym for descent with modification, and in the other it may not. Unfortunately with Mr. Charles Darwin the variations are mainly accidental. The words "through natural selection," therefore, in the passage last quoted carry no weight, for it is the wrong natural selection that is, or ought to be, intended; practically, however, they derived a weight from Mr. Darwin's name to which they had no title of their own, and we understood that "the theory of descent with slow modification" through the kind of natural selection ostensibly intended by Mr. Darwin was a quasi-synonymous expression for the transmutation of species. We understood - so far as we understood anything beyond that we were to believe in descent with modification - that natural selection was Mr. Darwin's theory; we therefore concluded, since Mr. Darwin seemed to say so, that the theory of the transmutation of species generally was so also. At any rate we felt as regards the passage last quoted that the theory of descent with modification was the point of attack and defence, and we supposed it to be the theory so often referred to by Mr. Darwin as "my."

Again:-

"Some of the most ancient Silurian animals, as the Nautilus, Lingula, &c., do not differ much from the living species; and it cannot *on my theory* be supposed that these old species were the progenitors," &c. (p. 306) . . . "Consequently *if my theory be true,* it is indisputable," &c. (p. 307).

Here the two "my theories" have been altered, the first into "our theory," and the second into "the theory," both in 1869; but, as usual, the thing that remains with the reader is the theory of descent, and it remains morally and practically as much claimed when called "the theory" - as during the many years throughout which the more open "my" distinctly claimed it.

Again:-

"All the most eminent palæontologists, namely, Cuvier, Owen, Agassiz, Barrande, E. Forbes, &c., and all our greatest geologists, as Lyell, Murchison, Sedgwick, &c., have unanimously, often vehemently, maintained *the immutability of species*.. . . I feel how rash it is to differ from these great authorities . . . Those who think the natural geological record in any degree perfect, and who do not attach much weight to the facts and arguments of other kinds brought forward in this volume, will undoubtedly at once *reject my theory*" (p. 310).

What is "my theory" here, if not that of the mutability of species, or the theory of descent with modification? "My theory" became "the theory" in 1869.

Again:-

"Let us now see whether the several facts and rules relating to the geological succession of organic beings, better accord with the common view of the immutability of species, or with that of their *slow and gradual modification, through descent and natural selection*" (p. 312).

The words "natural selection" are indeed here, but they might as well be omitted for all the effect they produce. The argument is felt to be about the two opposed theories of descent, and independent creative efforts.

Again:-

"These several facts accord well with *my theory*" (p. 314). That "my theory" is the theory of descent is the conclusion most naturally drawn from the context. "My theory" became "our theory" in 1869.

Again:-

"This gradual increase in the number of the species of a group is strictly conformable *with my theory;* for the process of modification and the production of a number of allied forms must be slow and gradual, . . . like the branching of a great tree from a single stem, till the group becomes large" (p. 314).

"My theory" became "the theory" in 1869. We took "my theory" to be the theory of descent; that Mr. Darwin treats this as synonymous with the theory of natural selection appears from the next paragraph, on the third line of which we read, "On *the theory of natural selection* the extinction of old forms," &c.

Again:-

"*The theory of natural selection* is grounded on the belief that each new variety and ultimately each new species, is produced and maintained by having some advantage over those with which it comes into competition; and the consequent extinction of less favoured forms almost inevitably follows" (p. 320). Sense and consistency cannot be made of this passage. Substitute "The theory of the preservation of favoured races in the struggle for life" for "The theory of natural selection" (to do this is only taking Mr. Darwin's own synonym for natural selection) and see what the passage comes to. "The preservation of favoured races" is not a theory, it is a commonly observed fact; it is not "grounded on the belief that each new variety," &c., it is one of the ultimate and most elementary principles in the world of life. When we try to take the passage seriously and think it out, we soon give it up, and pass on, substituting "the theory of descent" for "the theory of natural selection," and concluding that in some way these two things must be identical.

Again:-

"The manner in which single species and whole groups of species become extinct accords well with *the theory of natural selection*" (p. 322).

Again:-

"This great fact of the parallel succession of the forms of life throughout the world, is explicable *on the theory of natural selection*" (p. 325).

Again:-

"Let us now look to the mutual affinities of extinct and living species. They all fall into one grand natural system; and this is at once explained *on the principle of descent*" (p. 329).

Putting the three preceding passages together, we naturally inferred that "the theory of natural selection" and "the principle of descent" were the same things. We knew Mr. Darwin claimed the first, and therefore unhesitatingly gave him the second at the same time.

Again:-

"Let us see how far these several facts and inferences accord with *the theory of descent with modification*" (p. 331)

Again:-

"Thus, *on the theory of descent with modification,*the main facts with regard to the mutual affinities of the extinct forms o: life to each other and to living forms, seem to me explained in a satisfactory manner. And they are wholly inexplicable *on any other view*" (p. 333).

The words "seem to me" involve a claim in the absence of so much as a hint in any part of the book concerning indebtedness to earlier writers.

Again:-

"*On the theory of descent,* the full meaning of the fossil remains," &c. (p. 336).

In the following paragraph we read:-

"But in one particular sense the more recent forms must, *on my theory,* be higher than the more ancient."

Again:-

"Agassiz insists that ancient animals resemble to a certain extent the embryos of recent animals of the same classes or that the geological succession of extinct forms is in some degree parallel to the embryological development o recent forms. . . . This doctrine of Agassiz accords well with *the theory of natural selection*" (p. 338).

"The theory of natural selection" became "our theory" in 1869. The opinion of Agassiz accords excellently with th theory of descent with modification, but it is not easy to see how it bears upon the fact that lucky races are preservec in the struggle for life - which, according to Mr. Darwin's title-page, is what is meant by natural selection.

Again:-

"*On the theory of descent with modification,*the great law of the long-enduring but not immutable succession of the sam types within the same areas, is at once explained" (p. 340).

Again:-

"It must not be forgotten that, *on my theory,* all the species of the same genus have descended from some one species" (p. 341).

"My theory" became "our theory" in 1869.

Again:-

"He who rejects these views on the nature of the geological record, will rightly reject *my whole theory*" (p. 342).

"My" became "our" in 1869.

Again:-

"Passing from these difficulties, the other great leading facts in palæontology agree admirably with *the theory of descen with modification through variation and natural selection*" (p. 343).

Again:-

The succession of the same types of structure within the same areas during the later geological periods*ceases to be mysterious,* and *is simply explained by inheritance* (p. 345).

I suppose inheritance was not when Mr. Darwin wrote considered mysterious. The last few words have been altered to "and is intelligible on the principle of inheritance." It seems as though Mr. Darwin did not like saying that inheritance was not mysterious, but had no objection to implying that it was intelligible.

The next paragraph begins - "If, then, the geological record be as imperfect as I believe it to be, . . . the main objections *to the theory of natural selection*are greatly diminished or disappear. On the other hand, all the chief laws of palæontology plainly generation."

Here again the claim to the theory of descent with modification is unmistakable; it cannot, moreover, but occur to us that if species "have beenas good a claim to be the main means of originating species as natural selection has. It is hardly necessary to point out that ordinary generation involves descent with modification, for all known offspring differ from their parents, so far, at any rate, as that practised judges can generally tell them apart.

Again:-

"We see in these facts some deep organic bond, prevailing throughout space and time, over the same areas of land and water, and independent of their physical condition. The naturalist must feel little curiosity who is not led to inquire what this bond is.

"This bond, *on my theory, is simply inheritance,* that cause which alone," &c. (p. 350).

This passage was altered in 1869 to "The bond is simply inheritance." The paragraph concludes, "*On this principle of inheritance with modification,* we can understand how it is that sections of genera . . . are confined to the same areas," &c.

Again:-

"He who rejects it rejects the *vera causa of ordinary* generation," &c. (p. 352).

We naturally ask, Why call natural selection the "main means of modification," if "ordinary generation" is a*vera causa*?

Again:-

"In discussing this subject, we shall be enabled at the same time to consider a point equally important for us, namely, whether the several distinct species of a genus, *which on my theory have all descended from a common ancestor,* can have migrated (undergoing modification during some part of their migration) from the area inhabited by their progenitor" (p. 354).

The words "on my theory" became "on our theory" in 1869.

Again:-

"With those organic beings which never intercross (if such exist) *the species, on my theory, must have descended from a succession of improved varieties,*" &c. (p. 355).

The words "on my theory" were cut out in 1869.

Again:-

"A slow southern migration of a marine fauna will account, *on the theory of modification,*for many closely allied forms," &c. (p. 372).

Again:-

"But the existence of several quite distinct species, belonging to genera exclusively confined to the southern hemisphere, is, *on my theory of descent with modification,* a far more remarkable case of difficulty" (p. 381).

"My" became "the" in 1866 with the fourth edition. This was the most categorical claim to the theory of descen with modification in the "Origin of Species." The "my" here is the only one that was taken out before 1869. I suppose Mr. Darwin thought that with the removal of this "my" he had ceased to claim the theory of descent with modification. Nothing, however, could be gained by calling the reader's attention to what had been done, so nothing was said about it.

Again:-

"Some species of fresh-water shells have a very wide range,*and allied species, which, on my theory, are descended from a single source,* prevail throughout the world" (p. 385).

"My theory" became "our theory" in 1869.

Again:-

"In the following remarks I shall not confine myself to the mere question of dispersal, but shall consider some other facts which bear upon the truth of *the two theories of independent creation and of descent with modification*" (p. 389). What can be plainer than that the theory which Mr. Darwin espouses, and has so frequently called "my," is descent with modification?

Again:-

"But as these animals and their spawn are known to be immediately killed by sea-water, *on my view,* we can see that there would be great difficulty in their transportal across the sea, and therefore why they do not exist on any oceanic island. But why, *on the theory of creation,* they should not have been created there, it would be very difficult to explain" (p. 393).

"On my view" was cut out in 1869.

On the following page we read - "On my view this question can easily be answered." "On my view" is retained in the latest edition.

Again:-

"Yet there must be, *on my view,* some unknown but highly efficient means for their transportation" (p. 397).

"On my view" became "according to our view" in 1869.

Again:-

"I believe this grand fact can receive no sort of explanation *on the ordinary view of independent creation,* whereas, *on the view here maintained,* it is obvious that the Galapagos Islands would be likely to receive colonists . . . from America, and the Cape de Verde Islands from Africa; and that such colonists would be liable to modification; the principle of inheritance still betraying their original birth-place" (p. 399).

Again:-

"With respect to the distinct species of the same genus which, *on my theory,* must have spread from one parent source, if we make the same allowances as before," &c.

"On my theory" became "on our theory" in 1869.

Again:-

"*On my theory* these several relations throughout time and space are intelligible; . . . the forms within each class have been connected by the same bond of ordinary generation; . . . in both cases the laws of variation have been the same and modifications have been accumulated by the same power of natural selection" (p. 410).

"On my theory" became "according to our theory" in 1869, and natural selection is no longer a power, but has become a means.

Again:-

"*I believe that something more is included,* and that propinquity of descent - the only known cause of the similarity o organic beings - is the bond, hidden as it is by various degrees of modification, which is partially revealed to us by our classification" (p. 418).

Again:-

"*Thus, on the view which I hold,* the natural system is genealogical in its arrangement, like a pedigree" (p. 422).

"On the view which I hold" was cut out in 1872.

Again:-

"We may feel almost sure, *on the theory of descent,*that these characters have been inherited from a common ancestor" (p. 426).

Again:-

"*On my view of characters being of real importance for classification only in so far as they reveal descent,*we can clearly understand," &c. (p. 427).

"On my view" became "on the view" in 1872.

Again:-

"The more aberrant any form is, the greater must be the number of connecting forms which,*on my theory,* have been exterminated and utterly lost" (p. 429).

The words "on my theory" were excised in 1869.

Again:-

"Finally, we have seen that *natural selection. . . explains* that great and universal feature in the affinities of all organic beings, namely, their subordination in group under group. *We use the element of descent*in classing the individuals of both sexes, &c.; . . . *we use descent* in classing acknowledged varieties; . . . and I believe this element of descent is the hidden bond of connection which naturalists have sought under the term of the natural system" (p. 433).

Lamarck was of much the same opinion, as I showed in "Evolution Old and New." He wrote:- "An arrangement should be considered systematic, or arbitrary, when it does not conform to the genealogical order taken by nature in the development of the things arranged, and when, by consequence, it is not founded on well-considered analogies. There is a natural order in every department of nature; it is the order in which its several component items have been successively developed." {195a} The point, however, which should more particularly engage our attention is that Mr. Darwin in the passage last quoted uses "natural selection" and "descent" as though they were convertible terms.

Again:-

"Nothing can be more hopeless than to attempt to explain this similarity of pattern in members of the same class by utility or the doctrine of final causes . . . *On the ordinary view of the independent creation of each being,*we can only say that so it is . . . *The explanation is manifest on the theory of the natural selection of successive slight* modifications," &c. (p. 435).

This now stands - "The explanation is to a large extent simple, on the theory of the selection of successive, sligh modifications." I do not like "a large extent" of simplicity; but, waiving this, the point at issue is not whether the ordinary course of things ensures a quasi-selection of the types that are best adapted to their surroundings, with accumulation of modification in various directions, and hence wide eventual difference between species descended from common progenitors - no evolutionist since 1750 has doubted this - but whether a general principle underlies the modifications from among which the quasi-selection is made, or whether they are destitute of such principle and referable, as far as we are concerned, to chance only. Waiving this again, we note that the theories of independent creation and of natural selection are contrasted, as though they were the only two alternatives; knowing the two alternatives to be independent creation and descent with modification, we naturally took natural selection to mean descent with modification.

Again:-

"*On the theory of natural selection* we can satisfactorily answer these questions" (p. 437).

"Satisfactorily" now stands "to a certain extent."

Again:-

"*On my view* these terms may be used literally" (pp. 438, 439).

"On my view" became "according to the views here maintained such language may be," &c., in 1869.

Again:-

"I believe all these facts can be explained as follows, *on the view of descent with modification*" (p. 443).

This sentence now ends at "follows."

Again:-

"Let us take a genus of birds, *descended, on my theory, from some one parent species,* and of which the several new species *have become modified through natural selection* in accordance with their divers habits" (p. 446).

The words "on my theory" were cut out in 1869, and the passage now stands, "Let us take a group of birds, descended from some ancient form and modified through natural selection for different habits."

Again:-

"*On my view of descent with modification,* the origin of rudimentary organs is simple" (p. 454).

"On my view" became "*on the view*" in 1869.

Again:-

"*On the view of descent with modification,*" &c. (p. 455).

Again:-

"*On this same view of descent with modification* all the great facts of morphology become intelligible" (p. 456).

Again:-

"That many and grave objections may be advanced against *the theory of descent with modification through natural selection,* I do not deny" (p. 459).

This now stands, "That many and serious objections may be advanced against *the theory of descent with modification through variation and natural selection,* I do not deny."

Again:-

"There are, it must be admitted, cases of special difficulty *on the theory of natural selection*" (p. 460).

"On" has become "opposed to;" it is not easy to see why this alteration was made, unless because "opposed to" is longer.

Again:-

"Turning to geographical distribution, the difficulties encountered *on the theory of descent with modification* are grave enough."

"Grave" has become "serious," but there is no other change (p. 461).

Again:-

"As *on the theory of natural selection* an interminable number of intermediate forms must have existed," &c.

"On" has become "according to" - which is certainly longer, but does not appear to possess any other advantage over "on." It is not easy to understand why Mr. Darwin should have strained at such a gnat as "on," though feeling no discomfort in such an expression as "an interminable number."

Again:-

"This is the most forcible of the many objections which may be urged *against my theory* . . . For certainly, *on my theory*," &c. (p. 463).

The "my" in each case became "the" in 1869.

Again:-

"Such is the sum of the several chief objections and difficulties which may be justly urged *against my theory*" (p. 465).

"My" became "the" in 1869.

Again:-

"Grave as these several difficulties are, *in my judgment* they do not overthrow *the theory of descent with modification*" (p. 466).

This now stands, "Serious as these several objections are, in my judgment they are by no means sufficient to overthrow *the theory of descent with subsequent modification*;" which, again, is longer, and shows at what little, little gnats Mr. Darwin could strain, but is no material amendment on the original passage.

Again:-

"*The theory of natural selection,* even if we looked no further than this, *seems to me to be in itself probable*" (p. 469).

This now stands, "The theory of natural selection, even if we look no further than this, *seems to be in the highest degree probable*." It is not only probable, but was very sufficiently proved long before Mr. Darwin was born, only it must be the right natural selection and not Mr. Charles Darwin's.

Again:-

"It is inexplicable, *on the theory of creation*, why a part developed, &c., . . . *but, on my view,* this part has undergone," &c. (p. 474).

"On my view" became "on our view" in 1869.

Again:-

"Glancing at instincts, marvellous as some are, they offer no greater difficulty than does corporeal structure *on the theory of the natural selection of successive, slight, but profitable modifications*" (p. 474).

Again:-

"*On the view of all the species of the same genus having descended from a common parent,* and having inherited much in common, we can understand how it is," &c. (p. 474).

Again:-

"If we admit that the geological record is imperfect in an extreme degree, then such facts as the record gives, support *the theory of descent with modification.*

" . . . The extinction of species . . . almost inevitably follows on *the principle of natural selection*" (p. 475).

The word "almost" has got a great deal to answer for.

Again:-

"We can understand, *on the theory of descent with modification,* most of the great leading facts in Distribution" (p. 476).

Again:-

"The existence of closely allied or representative species in any two areas, implies, *on the theory of descent with modification,* that the same parents formerly inhabited both areas . . . It must be admitted that these facts receive no explanation *on the theory of creation.* . . The fact . . . is intelligible *on the theory of natural selection,*with its contingencies of extinction and divergence of character" (p. 478).

Again:-

"Innumerable other such facts at once explain themselves *on the theory of descent with slow and slight successive modifications*" (p. 479).

"Any one whose disposition leads him to attach more weight to unexplained difficulties than to the explanation of a certain number of facts, *will certainly reject my theory*" (p. 482).

"My theory" became "the theory" in 1869.

From this point to the end of the book the claim is so ubiquitous, either expressly or by implication, that it is difficult to know what not to quote. I must, however, content myself with only a few more extracts. Mr. Darwin says:-

"It may be asked *how far I extend the doctrine of the modification of species*" (p. 482).

Again:-

"Analogy would lead me one step further, namely, to the belief that all animals and plants have descended from some one prototype . . . Therefore I should infer from analogy that probably all the organic beings which have ever lived on this earth have descended from some one primordial form, into which life was first breathed."

From an amœba - Adam, in fact, though not in name. This last sentence is now completely altered, as well it might be.

Again:-

"When *the views entertained in this volume on the origin of species, or when analogous views are generally admitted,*we can dimly foresee that there will be a considerable revolution in natural history" (p. 434).

Possibly. This now stands, "When the views advanced by me in this volume, and by Mr. Wallace, or when analogous views on the origin of species are generally admitted, we can dimly foresee," &c. When the "Origin of Species" came out we knew nothing of any analogous views, and Mr. Darwin's words passed unnoticed. I do not say that he knew they would, but he certainly ought to have known.

Again:-

"*A grand and almost untrodden field of inquiry will be opened*, on the causes and laws of variation, on correlation of growth on the effects of use and disuse, on the direct action of external conditions, and so forth" (p. 486).

Buffon and Lamarck had trodden this field to some purpose, but not a hint to this effect is vouchsafed to us. Again;-

"*When I view all beings not as special creations, but as the lineal descendants of some few beings which lived long before* the first bed of the Silurian system was deposited, they seem to me to become ennobled . . . We can so far take a prophetic glance into futurity as to foretell that it will be the common and widely spread species, belonging to the larger and dominant groups, which will ultimately prevail and procreate new and dominant species."

There is no alteration in this except that "Silurian" has become "Cambrian."

The idyllic paragraph with which Mr. Darwin concludes his book contains no more special claim to the theory of descent *en bloc* than many another which I have allowed to pass unnoticed; it has been, moreover, dealt with in an earlier chapter (Chapter XII.)

CHAPTER XV - The Excised "My's"

I have quoted in all ninety-seven passages, as near as I can make them, in which Mr. Darwin claimed the theory of descent, either expressly by speaking of "my theory" in such connection that the theory of descent ought to be, and as the event has shown, was, understood as being intended, or by implication, as in the opening passages of the "Origin of Species," in which he tells us how he had thought the matter out without acknowledging obligation of any kind to earlier writers. The original edition of the "Origin of Species" contained 490 pp., exclusive of index; a claim, therefore, more or less explicit, to the theory of descent was made on the average about once in every five pages throughout the book from end to end; the claims were most prominent in the most important parts, that is to say, at the beginning and end of the work, and this made them more effective than they are made even by their frequency. A more ubiquitous claim than this it would be hard to find in the case of any writer advancing a new theory; it is difficult, therefore, to understand how Mr. Grant Allen could have allowed himself to say that Mr. Darwin "laid no sort of claim to originality or proprietorship" in the theory of descent with modification.

Nevertheless I have only found one place where Mr. Darwin pinned himself down beyond possibility of retreat however ignominious, by using the words "my theory of descent with modification." {202a} He often, as I have said, speaks of "my theory," and then shortly afterwards of "descent with modification," under such circumstances that no one who had not been brought up in the school of Mr. Gladstone could doubt that the two expressions referred to the same thing. He seems to have felt that he must be a poor wriggler if he could not wriggle out of this give him any loophole, however small, and Mr. Darwin could trust himself to get out through it; but he did not like saying what left no loophole at all, and "my theory of descent with modification" closed all exits so firmly that it is surprising he should ever have allowed himself to use these words. As I have said, Mr. Darwin only used this direct categorical form of claim in one place; and even here, after it had stood through three editions, two of which had been largely altered, he could stand it no longer, and altered the "my" into "the" in 1866, with the fourth edition of the "Origin of Species."

This was the only one of the original forty-five my's that was cut out before the appearance of the fifth edition in 1869, and its excision throws curious light upon the working of Mr. Darwin's mind. The selection of the most categorical my out of the whole forty-five, shows that Mr. Darwin knew all about his my's, and, while seeing reason to remove this, held that the others might very well stand. He even left "On my *view* of descent with modification," {203a} which, though more capable of explanation than "my theory," &c., still runs it close; nevertheless the excision of even a single my that had been allowed to stand through such close revision as those to which the "Origin of Species" had been subjected betrays uneasiness of mind, for it is impossible that even Mr. Darwin should not have known that though the my excised in 1866 was the most technically categorical, the others were in reality just as guilty, though no tower of Siloam in the shape of excision fell upon them. If, then, Mr. Darwin was so uncomfortable about this one as to cut it out, it is probable he was far from comfortable about the others.

This view derives confirmation from the fact that in 1869, with the fifth edition of the "Origin of Species," there was a stampede of my's throughout the whole work, no less than thirty out of the original forty-five being changed into "the," "our," "this," or some other word, which, though having all the effect of my, still did not say "my" outright. These my's were, if I may say so, sneaked out; nothing was said to explain their removal to the reader or call attention to it. Why, it may be asked, having been considered during the revisions of 1861 and 1866, and with only one exception allowed to stand, why should they be smitten with a homing instinct in such large numbers with the fifth edition? It cannot be maintained that Mr. Darwin had had his attention called now for the first time to the fact that he had used my perhaps a little too freely, and had better be more sparing of it for the future. The my excised in 1866 shows that Mr. Darwin had already considered this question, and saw no reason to remove any but the one that left him no loophole. Why, then, should that which was considered and approved in 1859, 1861, and 1866 (not to mention the second edition of 1859 or 1860) be retreated from with every appearance of panic in 1869? Mr. Darwin could not well have cut out more than he did - not at any rate without saying something about it, and it would not be easy to know exactly what say. Of the fourteen my's that were left in 1869, five more were cut out in 1872, and nine only were allowed eventually to remain. We naturally ask, Why leave any if thirty-six ought to be cut out, or why cut out thirty-six if nine ought to be left - especially when the claim remains practically just the same after the excision as before it?

I imagine complaint had early reached Mr. Darwin that the difference between himself and his predecessors was unsubstantial and hard to grasp; traces of some such feeling appear even in the late Sir Charles Lyell's "Principles of Geology," in which he writes that he had reprinted his abstract of Lamarck's doctrine word for word, "in justice to Lamarck, in order to show how nearly the opinions taught by him at the beginning of this century resembled those now in vogue among a large body of naturalists respecting the infinite variability of species, and the progressive development in past time of the organic world." {205a} Sir Charles Lyell could not have written thus if he had thought that Mr. Darwin had already done "justice to Lamarck," nor is it likely that he stood alone in thinking as he did. It is probable that more reached Mr. Darwin than reached the public, and that the historical sketch prefixed to all editions after the first six thousand copies had been sold - meagre and slovenly as it is - was due to earlier manifestation on the part of some of Mr. Darwin's friends of the feeling that was afterwards expressed by Sir Charles Lyell in the passage quoted above. I suppose the removal of the my that was cut out in 1866 to be due partly to the Gladstonian tendencies of Mr. Darwin's mind, which would naturally make that particular my at all times more or less offensive to him, and partly to the increase of objection to it that must have ensued on the addition of the "brief but imperfect" historical sketch in 1861; it is doubtless only by an oversight that this particular my was not cut out in 1861. The stampede of 1869 was probably occasioned by the appearance in Germany of Professor Haeckel's "History of Creation." This was published in 1868, and Mr. Darwin no doubt foresaw that it would be translated into English, as indeed it subsequently was. In this book some account is given - very badly, but still much more fully than by Mr. Darwin - of Lamarck's work; and even Erasmus Darwin is mentioned - inaccurately - but still he is mentioned. Professor Haeckel says:-

"Although the theory of development had been already maintained at the beginning of this century by several great naturalists, especially by Lamarck and Goethe, it only received complete demonstration and causal foundation nine years ago through Darwin's work, and it is on this account that it is now generally (though not altogether rightly) regarded as exclusively Mr. Darwin's theory." {206a}

Later on, after giving nearly a hundred pages to the works of the early evolutionists - pages that would certainly disquiet the sensitive writer who had cut out the "my" which disappeared in 1866 - he continued:-

"We must distinguish clearly (though this is not usually done) between, firstly, the theory of descent as advanced by Lamarck, which deals only with the fact of all animals and plants being descended from a common source, and secondly, Darwin's theory of natural selection, which shows us *why* this progressive modification of organic forms took place" (p. 93).

This passage is as inaccurate as most of those by Professor Haeckel that I have had occasion to examine have proved to be. Letting alone that Buffon, not Lamarck, is the foremost name in connection with descent, I have already shown in "Evolution Old and New" that Lamarck goes exhaustively into the how and why of modification. He alleges the conservation, or preservation, in the ordinary course of nature, of the most favourable among variations that have been induced mainly by function; this, I have sufficiently explained, is natural selection, though the words "natural selection" are not employed; but it is the true natural selection which (if so metaphorical an expression is allowed to pass) actually does take place with the results ascribed to it by Lamarck, and not the false Charles-Darwinian natural selection that does not correspond with facts, and cannot result in specific differences such as we now observe. But, waiving this, the "my's," within which a little rift had begun to show itself in 1866, might well become as mute in 1869 as they could become without attracting attention, when Mr. Darwin saw the passages just quoted, and the hundred pages or so that lie between them.

I suppose Mr. Darwin cut out the five more my's that disappeared in 1872 because he had not yet fully recovered from his scare, and allowed nine to remain in order to cover his retreat, and tacitly say that he had not done anything and knew nothing whatever about it. Practically, indeed, he had not retreated, and must have been well aware that he was only retreating technically; for he must have known that the absence of acknowledgment to any earlier writers in the body of his work, and the presence of the many passages in which every word conveyed the impression that the writer claimed descent with modification, amounted to a claim as much when the actual word "my" had been taken out as while it was allowed to stand. We took Mr. Darwin at his own estimate because we could not for a moment suppose that a man of means, position, and education, - one, moreover, who was nothing if he was not unself-seeking - could play such a trick upon us while pretending to take us into his confidence; hence the almost universal belief on the part of the public, of which Professors Haeckel and Ray Lankester and Mr. Grant Allen alike complain - namely, that Mr. Darwin is the originator of the theory of descent, and that his variations are mainly functional. Men of science must not be surprised if the readiness with which we responded to Mr. Darwin's appeal to our confidence is succeeded by a proportionate resentment when the peculiar shabbiness of his action becomes more generally understood. For myself, I know not which most to wonder at - the meanness of the writer himself, or the greatness of the service that, in spite of that meanness, he unquestionably rendered.

If Mr. Darwin had been dealing fairly by us, when he saw that we had failed to catch the difference between the Erasmus-Darwinian theory of descent through natural selection from among variations that are mainly functional and his own alternative theory of descent through natural selection from among variations that are mainly accidental, and, above all, when he saw we were crediting him with other men's work, he would have hastened to set us right. "It is with great regret," he might have written, "and with no small surprise, that I find how generally I have been misunderstood as claiming to be the originator of the theory of descent with modification; nothing can be further from my intention; the theory of descent has been familiar to all biologists from the year 1749, when Buffon advanced it in its most comprehensive form, to the present day." If Mr. Darwin had said something to the above effect, no one would have questioned his good faith, but it is hardly necessary to say that nothing of the kind is to be found in any one of Mr. Darwin's many books or many editions; nor is the reason why the requisite correction was never made far to seek. For if Mr. Darwin had said as much as I have put into his mouth above, he should have said more, and would ere long have been compelled to have explained to us wherein the difference between himself and his predecessors precisely lay, and this would not have been easy. Indeed, if Mr. Darwin had been quite open with us he would have had to say much as follows:-

"I should point out that, according to the evolutionists of the last century, improvement in the eye, as in any other organ, is mainly due to persistent, rational, employment of the organ in question, in such slightly modified manner as experience and changed surroundings may suggest. You will have observed that, according to my system, this goes for very little, and that the accumulation of fortunate accidents, irrespectively of the use that may be made of them, is by far the most important means of modification. Put more briefly still, the distinction between me and my predecessors lies in this; - my predecessors thought they knew the main normal cause or principle that underlies variation, whereas I think that there is no general principle underlying it at all, or that even if there is, we know hardly anything about it. This is my distinctive feature; there is no deception; I shall not consider the arguments of my predecessors, nor show in what respect they are insufficient; in fact, I shall say nothing whatever about them. Please to understand that I alone am in possession of the master key that can unlock the bars of the future progress of evolutionary science; so great an improvement, in fact, is my discovery that it justifies me in claiming the theory of descent generally, and I accordingly claim it. If you ask me in what my discovery consists, I reply in this; - that the variations which we are all agreed accumulate are caused - by variation. {209a} I admit that this is not telling you much about them, but it is as much as I think proper to say at present; above all things, let me caution you against thinking that there is any principle of general application underlying variation."

This would have been right. This is what Mr. Darwin would have had to have said if he had been frank with us; it is not surprising, therefore, that he should have been less frank than might have been wished. I have no doubt that many a time between 1859 and 1882, the year of his death, Mr. Darwin bitterly regretted his initial error, and would have been only too thankful to repair it, but he could only put the difference between himself and the early evolutionists clearly before his readers at the cost of seeing his own system come tumbling down like a pack of cards; this was more than he could stand, so he buried his face, ostrich-like, in the sand. I know no more pitiable figure in either literature or science.

As I write these lines (July 1886) I see a paragraph in *Nature* which I take it is intended to convey the impression that Mr. Francis Darwin's life and letters of his father will appear shortly. I can form no idea whether Mr. F. Darwin's forthcoming work is likely to appear before this present volume; still less can I conjecture what it may or may not contain; but I can give the reader a criterion by which to test the good faith with which it is written. If Mr. F. Darwin puts the distinctive feature that differentiates Mr. C. Darwin from his predecessors clearly before his readers, enabling them to seize and carry it away with them once for all - if he shows no desire to shirk this question, but, or the contrary, faces it and throws light upon it, then we shall know that his work is sincere, whatever its shortcomings may be in other respects; and when people are doing their best to help us and make us understand all that they understand themselves, a great deal may be forgiven them. If, on the other hand, we find much talk about the wonderful light which Mr. Charles Darwin threw on evolution by his theory of natural selection, without any adequate attempt to make us understand the difference between the natural selection, say, of Mr. Patrick Matthew, and that of his more famous successor, then we may know that we are being trifled with; and that an attempt is being again made to throw dust in our eyes.

CHAPTER XVI - Mr. Grant Allen's "Charles Darwin"

It is here that Mr. Grant Allen's book fails. It is impossible to believe it written in good faith, with no end in view, save to make something easy which might otherwise be found difficult; on the contrary, it leaves the impression of having been written with a desire to hinder us, as far as possible, from understanding things that Mr. Allen himself understood perfectly well.

After saying that "in the public mind Mr. Darwin is perhaps most commonly regarded as the discoverer and founder of the evolution hypothesis," he continues that "the grand idea which he did really originate was not the idea of 'descent with modification,' but the idea of 'natural selection,'" and adds that it was Mr. Darwin's "peculiar glory" to have shown the "nature of the machinery" by which all the variety of animal and vegetabletypes. "The theory of evolution," says Mr. Allen, "already existed in a more or less shadowy and undeveloped shape;" it was Mr. Darwin's "task in life to raise this theory from the rank of a mere plausible and happy guess to the rank of a highly elaborate and almost universally accepted biological system" (pp. 3-5).

We all admit the value of Mr. Darwin's work as having led to the general acceptance of evolution. No one who remembers average middle-class opinion on this subject before 1860 will deny that it was Mr. Darwin who brought us all round to descent with modification; but Mr. Allen cannot rightly say that evolution had only existed before Mr. Darwin's time in "a shadowy, undeveloped state," or as "a mere plausible and happy guess." It existed in the same form as that in which most people accept it now, and had been carried to its extreme development, before Mr. Darwin's father had been born. It is idle to talk of Buffon's work as "a mere plausible and happy guess," or to imply that the first volume of the "Philosophie Zoologique" of Lamarck was a less full and sufficient demonstration of descent with modification than the "Origin of Species" is. It has its defects, shortcomings, and mistakes, but it is an incomparably sounder work than the "Origin of Species;" and though it contains the deplorable omission of any reference to Buffon, Lamarck does not first grossly misrepresent Buffon, and then tell him to go away, as Mr. Darwin did to the author of the "Vestiges" and to Lamarck. If Mr. Darwin was believed and honoured for saying much the same as Lamarck had said, it was because Lamarck had borne the brunt of the laughing. The "Origin of Species" was possible because the "Vestiges" had prepared the way for it. The "Vestiges" were made possible by Lamarck and Erasmus Darwin, and these two were made possible by Buffon. Here a somewhat sharper line can be drawn than is usually found possible when defining the ground covered by philosophers. No one broke the ground for Buffon to anything like the extent that he broke it for those who followed him, and these broke it for one another.

Mr. Allen says (p. 11) that, "in Charles Darwin's own words, Lamarck 'first did the eminent service of arousing attention to the probability of all change in the organic as well as in the inorganic world being the result of law, and not of miraculous interposition.'" Mr. Darwin did indeed use these words, but Mr. Allen omits the pertinent fact that he did not use them till six thousand copies of his work had been issued, and an impression been made as to its scope and claims which the event has shown to be not easily effaced; nor does he say that Mr. Darwin only pays these few words of tribute in a quasi-preface, which, though prefixed to his later editions of the "Origin of Species," is amply neutralised by the spirit which I have shown to be omnipresent in the body of the work itself. Moreover, Mr. Darwin's statement is inaccurate to an unpardonable extent; his words would be fairly accurate if applied to Buffon, but they do not apply to Lamarck.

Mr. Darwin continues that Lamarck "seems to attribute all the beautiful adaptations in nature, such as the long neck of the giraffe for browsing on the branches of trees," to the effects of habit. Mr. Darwin should not say tha Lamarck "seems" to do this. It was his business to tell us what led Lamarck to his conclusions, not what "seemed" to do so. Any one who knows the first volume of the "Philosophie Zoologique" will be aware that there is no "seems" in the matter. Mr. Darwin's words "seem" to say that it really could not be worth any practical naturalist's while to devote attention to Lamarck's argument; the inquiry might be of interest to antiquaries, but Mr. Darwin had more important work in hand than following the vagaries of one who had been so completely exploded as Lamarck had been. "Seem" is to men what "feel" is to women; women who feel, and men who grease every other sentence with a "seem," are alike to be looked on with distrust.

"Still," continues Mr. Allen, "Darwin gave no sign. A flaccid, cartilaginous, unphilosophic evolutionism had full possession of the field for the moment, and claimed, as it were, to be the genuine representative of the young anc vigorous biological creed, while he himself was in truth the real heir to all the honours of the situation. He was i possession of the master-key which alone could unlock the bars that opposed the progress of evolution, and still h waited. He could afford to wait. He was diligently collecting, amassing, investigating; eagerly reading every new systematic work, every book of travels, every scientific journal, every record of sport, or exploration, or discovery, tc extract from the dead mass of undigested fact whatever item of implicit value might swell the definite co-ordinatec series of notes in his own commonplace books for the now distinctly contemplated 'Origin of Species.' His way was to make all sure behind him, to summon up all his facts in irresistible array, and never to set out upon a public progress until he was secure against all possible attacks of the ever-watchful and alert enemy in the rear," &c. (p. 73).

It would not be easy to beat this. Mr. Darwin's worst enemy could wish him no more damaging eulogist.

Of the "Vestiges" Mr. Allen says that Mr. Darwin "felt sadly" the inaccuracy and want of profound technical knowledge everywhere displayed by the anonymous author. Nevertheless, long after, in the "Origin of Species," the great naturalist wrote with generous appreciation of the "Vestiges of Creation" - "In my opinion it has don excellent service in this country in calling attention to the subject, in removing prejudice, and in thus preparing the ground for the reception of analogous views."

I have already referred to the way in which Mr. Darwin treated the author of the "Vestiges," and have stated the facts at greater length in "Evolution Old and New," but it may be as well to give Mr. Darwin's words in full; he wrote as follows on the third page of the original edition of the "Origin of Species":-

"The author of the 'Vestiges of Creation' would, I presume, say that, after a certain unknown number of generations some bird had given birth to a woodpecker, and some plant to the mistletoe, and that these had been produced perfect as we now see them; but this assumption seems to me to be no explanation, for it leaves the case of the coadaptation of organic beings to each other and to their physical conditions of life untouched and unexplained."

The author of the "Vestiges" did, doubtless, suppose that *"some* bird" had given birth to a woodpecker, or more strictly, that a couple of birds had done so - and this is all that Mr. Darwin has committed himself to - but no one better knew that these two birds would, according to the author of the "Vestiges," be just as much woodpeckers, and just as little woodpeckers, as they would be with Mr. Darwin himself. Mr. Chambers did not suppose that a woodpecker became a woodpecker *per saltum* though born of some widely different bird, but Mr. Darwin's words have no application unless they convey this impression. The reader will note that though the impression is conveyed, Mr. Darwin avoids conveying it categorically. I suppose this is what Mr. Allen means by saying that he "made all things sure behind him." Mr. Chambers did indeed believe in occasional sports; so did Mr. Darwin, and we have seen that in the later editions of the "Origin of Species" he found himself constrained to lay greater stres on these than he had originally done. Substantially, Mr. Chambers held much the same opinion as to the suddenness or slowness of modification as Mr. Darwin did, nor can it be doubted that Mr. Darwin knew this perfectly well.

What I have said about the woodpecker applies also to the mistletoe. Besides, it was Mr. Darwin's business not to presume anything about the matter; his business was to tell us what the author of the "Vestiges" had said, or to refer us to the page of the "Vestiges" on which we should find this. I suppose he was too busy "collecting, amassing, investigating," &c., to be at much pains not to misrepresent those who had been in the field before him. There is no other reference to the "Vestiges" in the "Origin of Species" than this suave but singularly fraudulent passage.

In his edition of 1860 the author of the "Vestiges" showed that he was nettled, and said it was to be regretted Mr

Darwin had read the "Vestiges" "almost as much amiss as if, like its declared opponents, he had an interest in misunderstanding it;" and a little lower he adds that Mr. Darwin's book "in no essential respect contradicts the 'Vestiges,'" but that, on the contrary, "while adding to its explanations of nature, it expressed the same general ideas." {216a} This is substantially true; neither Mr. Darwin's nor Mr. Chambers's are good books, but the main object of both is to substantiate the theory of descent with modification, and, bad as the "Vestiges" is, it is ingenuous as compared with the "Origin of Species." Subsequently to Mr. Chambers' protest, and not till, as I have said, six thousand copies of the "Origin of Species" had been issued, the sentence complained of by Mr. Chamber was expunged, but without a word of retractation, and the passage which Mr. Allen thinks so generous was inserted into the "brief but imperfect" sketch which Mr. Darwin prefixed - after Mr. Chambers had been effectually snuffed out - to all subsequent editions of his "Origin of Species." There is no excuse for Mr. Darwin's not having said at least this much about the author of the "Vestiges" in his first edition; and on finding that he had misrepresented him in a passage which he did not venture to retain, he should not have expunged it quietly, but should have called attention to his mistake in the body of his book, and given every prominence in his power to the correction.

Let us now examine Mr. Allen's record in the matter of natural selection. For years he was one of the foremost apostles of Neo-Darwinism, and any who said a good word for Lamarck were told that this was the "kind of mystica nonsense" from which Mr. Allen "had hoped Mr. Darwin had for ever saved us." {216b} Then in October 1883 came an article in "Mind," from which it appeared as though Mr. Allen had abjured Mr. Darwin and all his works.

"There are only two conceivable ways," he then wrote, "in which any increment of brain power can ever have arisen in any individual. The one is the Darwinian way, by spontaneous variation, that is to say, by variation due to minute physical circumstances affecting the individual in the germ. The other is the Spencerian way, by functional increment, that is to say, by the effect of increased use and constant exposure to varying circumstances during conscious life."

Mr. Allen calls this the Spencerian view, and so it is in so far as that Mr. Spencer has adopted it. Most people will call it Lamarckian. This, however, is a detail. Mr. Allen continues:-

"I venture to think that the first way, if we look it clearly in the face, will be seen to be practically unthinkable; and that we have no alternative, therefore, but to accept the second."

I like our looking a "way" which is "practically unthinkable" "clearly in the face." I particularly like "practically unthinkable." I suppose we can think it in theory, but not in practice. I like almost everything Mr. Allen says or does; it is not necessary to go far in search of his good things; dredge up any bit of mud from him at random and w are pretty sure to find an oyster with a pearl in it, if we look it clearly in the face; I mean, there is sure to be something which will be at any rate "almost" practically unthinkable. But however this may be, when Mr. Allen wrote his article in "Mind" two years ago, he was in substantial agreement with myself about the value of natura selection as a means of modification - by natural selection I mean, of course, the commonly known Charles Darwinian natural selection from fortuitous variations; now, however, in 1885, he is all for this same natural selection again, and in the preface to his "Charles Darwin" writes (after a handsome acknowledgment of "Evolution Old and New") that he "differs from" me "fundamentally in" my "estimate of the worth of Charles Darwin's distinctive discovery of natural selection."

This he certainly does, for on page 81 of the work itself he speaks of "the distinctive notion of natural selection" a having, "like all true and fruitful ideas, more than once flashed," &c. I have explained *usque ad nauseam,* and will henceforth explain no longer, that natural selection is no "distinctive notion" of Mr. Darwin's. Mr. Darwin's "distinctive notion" is natural selection from among fortuitous variations.

Writing again (p. 89) of Mr. Spencer's essay in the "Leader," {218a} Mr. Allen says:-

"It contains, in a very philosophical and abstract form, the theory of 'descent with modification' without the distinctive Darwinian adjunct of 'natural selection' or survival of the fittest. Yet it was just that lever dexterously applied, and carefully weighted with the whole weight of his endlessly accumulated inductive instances, that finally enabled our modern Archimedes to move the world."

Again:-

"To account for adaptation, for the almost perfect fitness of every plant and every animal to its position in life, for the existence (in other words) of definitely correlated parts and organs, we must call in the aid of survival of th fittest. Without that potent selective agent, our conception of the becoming of life is a mere chaos; order and organisation are utterly inexplicable save by the brilliant illuminating ray of the Darwinian principle" (p. 93).

And yet two years previously this same principle, after having been thinkable for many years, had become "unthinkable."

Two years previously, writing of the Charles-Darwinian scheme of evolution, Mr. Allen had implied it as his opinion "that all brains are what they are in virtue of antecedent function." "The one creed," he wrote - referring to Mr Darwin's - "makes the man depend mainly upon the accidents of molecular physics in a colliding germ cell and sperm cell; the other makes him depend mainly on the doings and gains of his ancestors as modified and altered by himself."

This second creed is pure Erasmus-Darwinism and Lamarck.

Again:-

"It seems to me easy to understand how survival of the fittest may result in progress*starting from such functionally produced gains* (italics mine), but impossible to understand how it could result in progress, if it had to start in mere accidental structural increments due to spontaneous variation alone." {219a}

Which comes to saying that it is easy to understand the Lamarckian system of evolution, but not the Charles-Darwinian. Mr. Allen concluded his article a few pages later on by saying

"The first hypothesis" (Mr. Darwin's) "is one that throws no light upon any of the facts. The second hypothesis" (which is unalloyed Erasmus Darwin and Lamarck) "is one that explains them all with transparent lucidity." Yet in his "Charles Darwin" Mr. Allen tells us that though Mr. Darwin "did not invent the development theory, he made it believable and comprehensible" (p. 4).

In his "Charles Darwin" Mr. Allen does not tell us how recently he had, in another place, expressed an opinion about the value of Mr. Darwin's "distinctive contribution" to the theory of evolution, so widely different from the one he is now expressing with characteristic appearance of ardour. He does not explain how he is able to execute such rapid changes of front without forfeiting his claim on our attention; explanations on matters of this sort seem out of date with modern scientists. I can only suppose that Mr. Allen regards himself as having taken a brief, as it were, for the production of a popular work, and feels more bound to consider the interests of the gentleman who pays him than to say what he really thinks; for surely Mr. Allen would not have written as he did in such a distinctly philosophical and scientific journal as "Mind" without weighing his words, and nothing has transpired lately, *apropos* of evolution, which will account for his present recantation. I said in my book "Selections," &c., that when Mr. Allen made stepping-stones of his dead selves, he jumped upon them to some tune. I was a little scandalised then at the completeness and suddenness of the movement he executed, and spoke severely; I have sometimes feared I may have spoken too severely, but his recent performance goes far to warrant my remarks.

If, however, there is no dead self about it, and Mr. Allen has only taken a brief, I confess to being not greatly edified. I grant that a good case can be made out for an author's doing as I suppose Mr. Allen to have done; indeed I am not sure that both science and religion would not gain if every one rode his neighbour's theory, as at a donkey-race, and the least plausible were held to win; but surely, as things stand, a writer by the mere fact of publishing a book professes to be giving a *bonâ fide* opinion. The analogy of the bar does not hold, for not only is it perfectly understood that a barrister does not necessarily state his own opinions, but there exists a strict though unwritten code to protect the public against the abuses to which such a system must be liable. In religion and science no such code exists - the supposition being that these two holy callings are above the necessity for anything of the kind. Science and religion are not as business is; still, if the public do not wish to be taken in, they must be at some pains to find out whether they are in the hands of one who, while pretending to be a judge, is in reality a paid advocate, with no one's interests at heart except his client's, or in those of one who, however warmly he may plead, will say nothing but what springs from mature and genuine conviction.

The present unsettled and unsatisfactory state of the moral code in this respect is at the bottom of the supposed antagonism between religion and science. These two are not, or never ought to be, antagonistic. They should never want what is spoken of as reconciliation, for in reality they are one. Religion is the quintessence of science, and science the raw material of religion; when people talk about reconciling religion and science they do not mean what they say; they mean reconciling the statements made by one set of professional men with those made by another set whose interests lie in the opposite direction - and with no recognised president of the court to keep them within due bounds this is not always easy.

Mr. Allen says:-

"At the same time it must be steadily remembered that there are many naturalists at the present day, especially among those of the lower order of intelligence, who, while accepting evolutionism in a general way, and therefore always describing themselves as Darwinians, do not believe, and often cannot even understand, the distinctive Darwinian addition to the evolutionary doctrine - namely, the principle of natural selection. Such hazy and indistinct thinkers as these are still really at the prior stage of Lamarckian evolution" (p. 199).

Considering that Mr. Allen was at that stage himself so recently, he might deal more tenderly with others who still find "the distinctive Darwinian adjunct" "unthinkable." It is perhaps, however, because he remembers his difficulties that Mr. Allen goes on as follows:-

"It is probable that in the future, while a formal acceptance of Darwinism becomes general, the special theory of natural selection will be thoroughly understood and assimilated only by the more abstract and philosophical minds."

By the kind of people, in fact, who read the *Spectator* and are called thoughtful; and in point of fact less than a twelvemonth after this passage was written, natural selection was publicly abjured as "a theory of the origin of species" by Mr. Romanes himself, with the implied approval of the *Times.*

"Thus," continues Mr. Allen, "the name of Darwin will often no doubt be tacked on to what are in reality the principles of Lamarck."

It requires no great power of prophecy to foretell this, considering that it is done daily by nine out of ten who call themselves Darwinians. Ask ten people of ordinary intelligence how Mr. Darwin explains the fact that giraffes have long necks, and nine of them will answer "through continually stretching them to reach higher and higher boughs." They do not understand that this is the Lamarckian view of evolution, not the Darwinian; nor will Mr. Allen's book greatly help the ordinary reader to catch the difference between the two theories, in spite of his frequent reference to Mr. Darwin's "distinctive feature," and to his "master-key." No doubt the British public will get to understand all about it some day, but it can hardly be expected to do so all at once, considering the way in which Mr. Allen and so many more throw dust in its eyes, and will doubtless continue to throw it as long as an honest penny is to be turned by doing so. Mr. Allen, then, is probably right in saying that "the name of Darwin will no doubt be often tacked on to what are in reality the principles of Lamarck," nor can it be denied that Mr. Darwin, by his practice of using "the theory of natural selection" as though it were a synonym for "the theory of descent with modification," contributed to this result.

I do not myself doubt that he intended to do this, but Mr. Allen would say no less confidently he did not. He writes of Mr. Darwin as follows:-

"Of Darwin's pure and exalted moral nature no Englishman of the present generation can trust himself to speak with becoming moderation."

He proceeds to trust himself thus:-

"His love of truth, his singleness of heart, his sincerity, his earnestness, his modesty, his candour, his absolute sinking of self and selfishness - these, indeed are all conspicuous to every reader on the very face of every word he ever printed."

This "conspicuous sinking of self" is of a piece with the "delightful unostentatiousness *which every one must have noticed*" about which Mr. Allen writes on page 65. Does he mean that Mr. Darwin was "ostentatiously unostentatious," or that he was "unostentatiously ostentatious"? I think we may guess from this passage who it was that in the old days of the *Pall Mall Gazelle* called Mr. Darwin "a master of a certain happy simplicity."

Mr. Allen continues:-

"Like his works themselves, they must long outlive him. But his sympathetic kindliness, his ready generosity, the staunchness of his friendship, the width and depth and breadth of his affections, the manner in which 'he bore with those who blamed him unjustly without blaming them again' - these things can never be so well known to any other generation of men as to the three generations that walked the world with him" (pp. 174, 175).

Again:-

"He began early in life to collect and arrange a vast encyclopædia of facts, all finally focussed with supreme skill upon the great principle he so clearly perceived and so lucidly expounded. He brought to bear upon the question an amount of personal observation, of minute experiment, of world-wide book knowledge, of universal scientific abilit such as never, perhaps, was lavished by any other man upon any other department of study. His conspicuous and beautiful love of truth, his unflinching candour, his transparent fearlessness and honesty of purpose, his childlik simplicity, his modesty of demeanour, his charming manner, his affectionate disposition, his kindliness to friends, his courtesy to opponents, his gentleness to harsh and often bitter assailants, kindled in the minds of men of science everywhere throughout the world a contagious enthusiasm only equalled perhaps among the disciples of Socrates and the great teachers of the revival of learning. His name became a rallying-point for the children of light in ever country" (pp. 196, 197).

I need not quote more; the sentence goes on to talk about "firmly grounding" something which philosophers and speculators might have taken a century or two more "to establish in embryo;" but those who wish to see it must turn to Mr. Allen's book.

If I have formed too severe an estimate of Mr. Darwin's work and character - and this is more than likely - the fulsomeness of the adulation lavished on him by his admirers for many years past must be in some measure my excuse. We grow tired even of hearing Aristides called just, but what is so freely said about Mr. Darwin puts us in mind more of what the people said about Herod - that he spoke with the voice of a God, not of a man. So we saw Professor Ray Lankester hail him not many years ago as the "greatest of living men." {224a}

It is ill for any man's fame that he should be praised so extravagantly. Nobody ever was as good as Mr. Darwin looked, and a counterblast to such a hurricane of praise as has been lately blowing will do no harm to his ultimate reputation, even though it too blow somewhat fiercely. Art, character, literature, religion, science (I have named them in alphabetical order), thrive best in a breezy, bracing air; I heartily hope I may never be what is commonly called successful in my own lifetime - and if I go on as I am doing now, I have a fair chance of succeeding in not succeeding.

CHAPTER XVII - Professor Ray Lankester and Lamarck

Being anxious to give the reader a sample of the arguments against the theory of natural selection from among variations that are mainly either directly or indirectly functional in their inception, or more briefly against the Erasmus-Darwinian and Lamarckian systems, I can find nothing more to the point, or more recent, than Professor Ray Lankester's letter to the *Athenæum* of March 29, 1884, to the latter part of which, however, I need alone cal attention. Professor Ray Lankester says:-

"And then we are introduced to the discredited speculations of Lamarck, which have found a worthy advocate in Mr. Butler, as really solid contributions to the discovery of the *veræ causæ* of variation! A much more important attempt to do something for Lamarck's hypothesis, of the transmission to offspring of structural peculiarities acquired by the parents, was recently made by an able and experienced naturalist, Professor Semper of Wurzburg. His book on 'Animal Life,' &c., is published in the 'International Scientific Series.' Professor Semper adduces an immense number and variety of cases of structural change in animals and plants brought about in the individual by adaptation (during its individual life-history) to new conditions. Some of these are very marked changes, such as the loss of its horny coat in the gizzard of a pigeon fed on meat; *but in no single instance could Professor Semper show* - although it was his object and desire to do so if possible - that such change was transmitted from parent to offspring. Lamarckism looks all very well on paper, but, as Professor Semper's book shows, when put to the test of observation and experiment it collapses absolutely."

I should have thought it would have been enough if it had collapsed without the "absolutely," but Professor Ray Lankester does not like doing things by halves. Few will be taken in by the foregoing quotation, except those who do not greatly care whether they are taken in or not; but to save trouble to readers who may have neither Lamarck nor Professor Semper at hand, I will put the case as follows:-

Professor Semper writes a book to show, we will say, that the hour-hand of the clock moves gradually forward, in spite of its appearing stationary. He makes his case sufficiently clear, and then might have been content to leave it; nevertheless, in the innocence of his heart, he adds the admission that though he had often looked at the clock for a long time together, he had never been able actually to see the hour-hand moving. "There now," exclaims Professor Ray Lankester on this, "I told you so; the theory collapses absolutely; his whole object and desire is to show that the hour-hand moves, and yet when it comes to the point, he is obliged to confess that he cannot see it do so." It is not worth while to meet what Professor Ray Lankester has been above quoted as saying about Lamarckism beyond quoting the following passage from a review of "The Neanderthal Skull on Evolution" in the "Monthly Journal of Science" for June, 1885 (p. 362):-

"On the very next page the author reproduces the threadbare objection that the 'supporters of the theory have never yet succeeded in observing a single instance in all the millions of years invented (!) in its support of one species of animal turning into another.' Now, *ex hypothesi,* one species turns into another not rapidly, as in a transformation scene, but in successive generations, each being born a shade different from its progenitors. Hence to observe such a change is excluded by the very terms of the question. Does Mr. Saville forget Mr. Herbert Spencer's apologue of the ephemeron which had never witnessed the change of a child into a man?"

The apologue, I may say in passing, is not Mr. Spencer's; it is by the author of the "Vestiges," and will be found on page 161 of the 1853 edition of that book; but let this pass. How impatient Professor Ray Lankester is of an attempt to call attention to the older view of evolution appears perhaps even more plainly in a review of this same book of Professor Semper's that appeared in "Nature," March 3, 1881. The tenor of the remarks last quoted shows that though what I am about to quote is now more than five years old, it may be taken as still giving us the position which Professor Ray Lankester takes on these matters. He wrote:-

"It is necessary," he exclaims, "to plainly and emphatically state" (Why so much emphasis? Why not "it should be stated"?) "that Professor Semper and a few other writers of similar views" {227a} (I have sent for the number of "Modern Thought" referred to by Professor Ray Lankester but find no article by Mr. Henslow, and do not, therefore, know what he had said) "are not adding to or building on Mr. Darwin's theory, but are actually opposing all that is essential and distinctive in that theory, by the revival of the exploded notion of 'directly transforming agents' advocated by Lamarck and others."

It may be presumed that these writers know they are not "adding to or building on" Mr. Darwin's theory, and do not wish to build on it, as not thinking it a sound foundation. Professor Ray Lankester says they are "actually opposing," as though there were something intolerably audacious in this; but it is not easy to see why he should be more angry with them for "actually opposing" Mr. Darwin than they may be with him, if they think it worth while, for "actually defending" the exploded notion of natural selection - for assuredly the Charles-Darwinian system is now more exploded than Lamarck's is.

What Professor Ray Lankester says about Lamarck and "directly transforming agents" will mislead those who take his statement without examination. Lamarck does not say that modification is effected by means of "directly transforming agents;" nothing can be more alien to the spirit of his teaching. With him the action of the external conditions of existence (and these are the only transforming agents intended by Professor Ray Lankester) is not direct, but indirect. Change in surroundings changes the organism's outlook, and thus changes its desires; desires changing, there is corresponding change in the actions performed; actions changing, a corresponding change is by-and-by induced in the organs that perform them; this, if long continued, will be transmitted; becoming augmented by accumulation in many successive generations, and further modifications perhaps arising through further changes in surroundings, the change will amount ultimately to specific and generic difference. Lamarck knows no drug, nor operation, that will medicine one organism into another, and expects the results of adaptive effort to be so gradual as to be only perceptible when accumulated in the course of many generations. When, therefore, Professor Ray Lankester speaks of Lamarck as having "advocated directly transforming agents," he either does not know what he is talking about, or he is trifling with his readers. Professor Ray Lankester continues:-

"They do not seem to be aware of this, for they make no attempt to examine Mr. Darwin's accumulated facts and arguments." Professor Ray Lankester need not shake Mr. Darwin's "accumulated facts and arguments" at us. We have taken more pains to understand them than Professor Ray Lankester has taken to understand Lamarck, and by this time know them sufficiently. We thankfully accept by far the greater number, and rely on them as our sheet-anchors to save us from drifting on to the quicksands of Neo-Darwinian natural selection; few of them, indeed, are Mr. Darwin's, except in so far as he has endorsed them and given them publicity, but I do not know that this detracts from their value. We have paid great attention to Mr. Darwin's facts, and if we do not understand all his arguments - for it is not always given to mortal man to understand these - yet we think we know what he was driving at. We believe we understand this to the full as well as Mr. Darwin intended us to do, and perhaps better. Where the arguments tend to show that all animals and plants are descended from a common source we find them much the same as Buffon's, or as those of Erasmus Darwin or Lamarck, and have nothing to say against them; where, on the other hand, they aim at proving that the main means of modification has been the fact that if an animal has been "favoured" it will be "preserved" - then we think that the animal's own exertions will, in the long run, have had more to do with its preservation than any real or fancied "favour." Professor Ray Lankester continues:-

"The doctrine of evolution has become an accepted truth" (Professor Ray Lankester writes as though the making of truth and falsehood lay in the hollow of Mr. Darwin's hand. Surely "has become accepted" should be enough; Mr. Darwin did not make the doctrine true) "entirely in consequence of Mr. Darwin's having demonstrated the mechanism." (There is no mechanism in the matter, and if there is, Mr. Darwin did not show it. He made some words which confused us and prevented us from seeing that "the preservation of favoured races" was a cloak for "luck," and that this was all the explanation he was giving) "by which the evolution is possible; it was almost universally rejected, while such undemonstrable agencies as those arbitrarily asserted to exist by Professor Semper and Mr. George Henslow were the only means suggested by its advocates."

Undoubtedly the theory of descent with modification, which received its first sufficiently ample and undisguised exposition in 1809 with the "Philosophie Zoologique" of Lamarck, shared the common fate of all theories that revolutionise opinion on important matters, and was fiercely opposed by the Huxleys, Romaneses, Grant Allens, and Ray Lankesters of its time. It had to face the reaction in favour of the Church which began in the days of the First Empire, as a natural consequence of the horrors of the Revolution; it had to face the social influence and then almost Darwinian reputation of Cuvier, whom Lamarck could not, or would not, square; it was put forward by one who was old, poor, and ere long blind. What theory could do more than just keep itself alive under conditions so unfavourable? Even under the most favourable conditions descent with modification would have been a hard plant to rear, but, as things were, the wonder is that it was not killed outright at once. We all know how large a share social influences have in deciding what kind of reception a book or theory is to meet with; true, these influences are not permanent, but at first they are almost irresistible; in reality it was not the theory of descent that was matched against that of fixity, but Lamarck against Cuvier; who can be surprised that Cuvier for a time should have had the best of it?

And yet it is pleasant to reflect that his triumph was not, as triumphs go, long lived. How is Cuvier best known now? As one who missed a great opportunity; as one who was great in small things, and stubbornly small in great ones. Lamarck died in 1831; in 1861 descent with modification was almost universally accepted by those most competent to form an opinion. This result was by no means so exclusively due to Mr. Darwin's "Origin of Species" as is commonly believed. During the thirty years that followed 1831 Lamarck's opinions made more way than Darwinians are willing to allow. Granted that in 1861 the theory was generally accepted under the name of Darwin, not under that of Lamarck, still it was Lamarck and not Darwin that was being accepted; it was descent, not descent with modification by means of natural selection from among fortuitous variations, that we carried away with us from the "Origin of Species." The thing triumphed whether the name was lost or not. I need not waste the reader's time by showing further how little weight he need attach to the fact that Lamarckism was not immediately received with open arms by an admiring public. The theory of descent has become accepted as rapidly, if I am not mistaken, as the Copernican theory, or as Newton's theory of gravitation.

When Professor Ray Lankester goes on to speak of the "undemonstrable agencies" "arbitrarily asserted" to exist by Professor Semper, he is again presuming on the ignorance of his readers. Professor Semper's agencies are in no way more undemonstrable than Mr. Darwin's are. Mr. Darwin was perfectly cogent as long as he stuck to Lamarck's demonstration; his arguments were sound as long as they were Lamarck's, or developments of, and riders upon, Buffon, Erasmus Darwin, and Lamarck, and almost incredibly silly when they were his own. Fortunately the greater part of the "Origin of Species" is devoted to proving the theory of descent with modification, by arguments against which no exception would have been taken by Mr. Darwin's three great precursors, except in so far as the variations whose accumulation results in specific difference are supposed to be fortuitous - and, to do Mr. Darwin justice, the fortuitousness, though always within hail, is kept as far as possible in the background.

"Mr. Darwin's arguments," says Professor Ray Lankester, "rest on the *proved* existence of minute, many-sided, irrelative Mr. Darwin throughout the body of the "Origin of Species" is not supposed to know what his variations are or are not produced by; if they come, they come, and if they do not come, they do not come. True, we have seen that in the last paragraph of the book all this was changed, and the variations were ascribed to the conditions of existence, and to use and disuse, but a concluding paragraph cannot be allowed to override a whole book throughout which the variations have been kept to hand as accidental. Mr. Romanes is perfectly correct when he says {232a} that "natural selection" (meaning the Charles-Darwinian natural selection) "trusts to the chapter of accidents in the matter of variation" this is all that Mr. Darwin can tell us; whether they come from directly transforming agents or no he neither knows nor says. Those who accept Lamarck will know that the agencies are not, as a rule, directly transforming, but the followers of Mr. Darwin cannot.

"But showing themselves," continues Professor Ray Lankester, "at each new act of reproduction, as part of the phenomena of heredity such minute 'sports' or 'variations' are due to constitutional disturbance" (No doubt. The difference, however, between Mr. Darwin and Lamarck consists in the fact that Lamarck believes he knows what it is that so disturbs the constitution as generally to induce variation, whereas Mr. Darwin says he does not know), "and appear not in individuals subjected to new conditions" (What organism can pass through life without being subjected to more or less new conditions? What life is ever the exact fac-simile of another? And in a matter of such extreme delicacy as the adjustment of psychical and physical relations, who can say how small a disturbance of established equilibrium may not involve how great a rearrangement?), "but in the offspring of all, though more freely in the offspring of those subjected to special causes of constitutional disturbance. Mr. Darwin has further proved that these slight variations can be transmitted and intensified by selective breeding."

Mr. Darwin did, indeed, follow Buffon and Lamarck in at once turning to animals and plants under domestication in order to bring the plasticity of organic forms more easily home to his readers, but the fact that variations can be transmitted and intensified by selective breeding had been so well established and was so widely known long before Mr. Darwin was born, that he can no more be said to have proved it than Newton can be said to have proved the revolution of the earth on its own axis. Every breeder throughout the world had known it for centuries. I believe even Virgil knew it.

"They have," continues Professor Ray Lankester, "in reference to breeding, a remarkably tenacious, persistent character, as might be expected from their origin in connection with the reproductive process."

The variations do not normally "originate in connection with the reproductive process," though it is during this process that they receive organic expression. They originate mainly, so far as anything originates anywhere, in the life of the parent or parents. Without going so far as to say that no variation can arise in connection with the reproductive system - for, doubtless, striking and successful sports do occasionally so arise - it is more probable that the majority originate earlier. Professor Ray Lankester proceeds:-

"On the other hand, mutilations and other effects of directly transforming agents are rarely, if ever, transmitted." Professor Ray Lankester ought to know the facts better than to say that the effects of mutilation are rarely, if ever transmitted. The rule is, that they will not be transmitted unless they have been followed by disease, but that where disease has supervened they not uncommonly descend to offspring. {234a} I know Brown-Séquard considered it to be the morbid state of the nervous system consequent upon the mutilation that is transmitted, rather than the immediate effects of the mutilation, but this distinction is somewhat finely drawn.

When Professor Ray Lankester talks about the "other effects of directly transforming agents" being rarely transmitted, he should first show us the directly transforming agents. Lamarck, as I have said, knows them not. "It is little short of an absurdity," he continues, "for people to come forward at this epoch, when evolution is at length accepted solely because of Mr. Darwin's doctrine, and coolly to propose to replace that doctrine by the old notion so often tried and rejected."

Whether this is an absurdity or no, Professor Lankester will do well to learn to bear it without showing so much warmth, for it is one that is becoming common. Evolution has been accepted not "because of" Mr. Darwin's doctrine, but because Mr. Darwin so fogged us about his doctrine that we did not understand it. We thought we were backing his bill for descent with modification, whereas we were in reality backing it for descent with modification by means of natural selection from among fortuitous variations. This last really is Mr. Darwin's theory, except in so far as it is also Mr. A. R. Wallace's; descent, alone, is just as much and just as little Mr. Darwin's doctrine as it is Professor Ray Lankester's or mine. I grant it is in great measure through Mr. Darwin's books that descent has become so widely accepted; it has become so through his books, but in spite of, rather than by reason of, his doctrine. Indeed his doctrine was no doctrine, but only a back-door for himself to escape by in the event of flood or fire; the flood and fire have come; it remains to be seen how far the door will work satisfactorily.

Professor Ray Lankester, again, should not say that Lamarck's doctrine has been "so often tried and rejected." M. Martins, in his edition of the "Philosophie Zoologique," {235a} said truly that Lamarck's theory had never yet had the honour of being seriously discussed. It never has - not at least in connection with the name of its propounder. To mention Lamarck's name in the presence of the conventional English society naturalist has always been like shaking a red rag at a cow; he is at once infuriated; "as if it were possible," to quote from Isidore Geoffroy St. Hilaire, whose defence of Lamarck is one of the best things in his book,{235b} "that so great labour on the part of so great a naturalist should have led him to 'a fantastic conclusion' only - to 'a flighty error,' and, as has been often said, though not written, to 'one absurdity the more.' Such was the language which Lamarck heard during his protracted old age, saddened alike by the weight of years and blindness; this was what people did not hesitate to utter over his grave, yet barely closed, and what, indeed, they are still saying - commonly too, without any knowledge of what Lamarck maintained, but merely repeating at second hand bad caricatures of his teaching.

"When will the time come when we may see Lamarck's theory discussed, and I may as well at once say refuted, in some important points, with at any rate the respect due to one of the most illustrious masters of our science? Anc when will this theory, the hardihood of which has been greatly exaggerated, become freed from the interpretation: and commentaries by the false light of which so many naturalists have formed their opinion concerning it? If it author is to be condemned, let it, at any rate, not be before he has been heard."

Lamarck was the Lazarus of biology. I wish his more fortunate brethren, instead of intoning the old Churcl argument that he has "been refuted over and over again," would refer us to some of the best chapters in the writers who have refuted him. My own reading has led me to become moderately well acquainted with the literature of evolution, but I have never come across a single attempt fairly to grapple with Lamarck, and it is plain that neither Isidore Geoffroy nor M. Martins knows of such an attempt any more than I do. When Professor Ray Lankester puts his finger on Lamarck's weak places, then, but not till then, may he complain of those who try to replace Mr. Darwin's doctrine by Lamarck's.

Professor Ray Lankester concludes his note thus:-

"That such an attempt should be made is an illustration of a curious weakness of humanity. Not infrequently, after a long contested cause has triumphed, and all have yielded allegiance thereto, you will find, when few generations have passed, that men have clean forgotten what and who it was that made that cause triumphant, and ignorantly will set up for honour the name of a traitor or an impostor, or attribute to a great man as a merit deeds and thoughts which he spent a long life in opposing."

Exactly so; that is what one rather feels, but surely Professor Ray Lankester should say "in trying to filch while pretending to oppose and to amend." He is complaining here that people persistently ascribe Lamarck's doctrine to Mr. Darwin. Of course they do; but, as I have already perhaps too abundantly asked, whose fault is this? If a mar knows his own mind, and wants others to understand it, it is not often that he is misunderstood for any length of time. If he finds he is being misapprehended in a way he does not like, he will write another book and make his meaning plainer. He will go on doing this for as long time as he thinks necessary. I do not suppose, for example, that people will say I originated the theory of descent by means of natural selection from among fortunate accidents or even that I was one of its supporters as a means of modification; but if this impression were to prevail, I cannc think I should have much difficulty in removing it. At any rate no such misapprehension could endure for more than twenty years, during which I continued to address a public who welcomed all I wrote, unless I myself aided and abetted the mistake. Mr. Darwin wrote many books, but the impression that Darwinism and evolution, or descent with modification, are identical is still nearly as prevalent as it was soon after the appearance of the "Origin of Species;" the reason of this is, that Mr. Darwin was at no pains to correct us. Where, in any one of his many later books, is there a passage which sets the matter in its true light, and enters a protest against the misconception of which Professor Ray Lankester complains so bitterly? The only inference from this is, that Mr. Darwin was not displeased at our thinking him to be the originator of the theory of descent with modification, and did not want u to know more about Lamarck than he could help. If we wanted to know about him, we must find out what he had said for ourselves, it was no part of Mr. Darwin's business to tell us; he had no interest in our catching the distinctive difference between himself and that writer; perhaps not; but this approaches closely to wishing us to misunderstand it. When Mr. Darwin wished us to understand this or that, no one knew better how to show it to us.

We were aware, on reading the "Origin of Species," that there was a something about it of which we had not full hold; nevertheless we gave Mr. Darwin our confidence at once, partly because he led off by telling us that we must trust him to a great extent, and explained that the present book was only an instalment of a larger work which, wher it came out, would make everything perfectly clear; partly, again, because the case for descent with modification, which was the leading idea throughout the book, was so obviously strong, but perhaps mainly because every one said Mr. Darwin was so good, and so much less self-heeding than other people; besides, he had so "patiently" and "carefully" accumulated "such a vast store of facts" as no other naturalist, living or dead, had ever yet even tried to get together; he was so kind to us with his, "May we not believe?" and his "Have we any right to infer that the Creator?" &c. "Of course we have not," we exclaimed, almost with tears in our eyes - "not if you ask us in that way." Now that we understand what it was that puzzled us in Mr. Darwin's work we do not think highly either of the chief offender, or of the accessories after the fact, many of whom are trying to brazen the matter out, and on smaller scale to follow his example.

CHAPTER XVIII - Per Contra

"'The evil that men do lives after them" {239a} is happily not so true as that the good lives after them, while the ill is buried with their bones, and to no one does this correction of Shakespeare's unwonted spleen apply more fully than to Mr. Darwin. Indeed it was somewhat thus that we treated his books even while he was alive; the good, descent, remained with us, while the ill, the deification of luck, was forgotten as soon as we put down his work. Let me now, therefore, as far as possible, quit the ungrateful task of dwelling on the defects of Mr. Darwin's work and character, for the more pleasant one of insisting upon their better side, and of explaining how he came to be betrayed into publishing the "Origin of Species" without reference to the works of his predecessors.

In the outset I would urge that it is not by any single book that Mr. Darwin should be judged. I do not believe that any one of the three principal works on which his reputation is founded will maintain with the next generation the place it has acquired with ourselves; nevertheless, if asked to say who was the man of our own times whose work had produced the most important, and, on the whole, beneficial effect, I should perhaps wrongly, but still both instinctively and on reflection, name him to whom I have, unfortunately, found myself in more bitter opposition than to any other in the whole course of my life. I refer, of course, to Mr. Darwin.

His claim upon us lies not so much in what is actually found within the four corners of any one of his books, as in the fact of his having written them at all - in the fact of his having brought out one after another, with descent always for its keynote, until the lesson was learned too thoroughly to make it at all likely that it will be forgotten. Mr. Darwin wanted to move his generation, and had the penetration to see that this is not done by saying a thing once for all and leaving it. It almost seems as though it matters less what a man says than the number of times he repeats it, in a more or less varied form. It was here the author of the "Vestiges of Creation" made his most serious mistake. He relied on new editions, and no one pays much attention to new editions - the mark a book makes is almost always made by its first edition. If, instead of bringing out a series of amended editions during the fifteen years' law which Mr. Darwin gave him, Mr. Chambers had followed up the "Vestiges" with new book upon new book, he would have learned much more, and, by consequence, not have been snuffed out so easily once for all as he was in 1859 when the "Origin of Species" appeared.

The tenacity of purpose which appears to have been one of Mr. Darwin's most remarkable characteristics was visible even in his outward appearance. He always reminded me of Raffaelle's portrait of Pope Julius the Second, which, indeed, would almost do for a portrait of Mr. Darwin himself. I imagine that these two men, widely as the sphere of their action differed, must have been like each other in more respects than looks alone. Each, certainly, had a hand of iron; whether Pope Julius wore a velvet glove or no, I do not know; I rather think not, for, if I remember rightly, he boxed Michael Angelo's ears for giving him a saucy answer. We cannot fancy Mr. Darwin boxing any one's ears; indeed there can be no doubt he wore a very thick velvet glove, but the hand underneath it was none the less of iron. It was to his tenacity of purpose, doubtless, that his success was mainly due; but for this he must inevitably have fallen before the many inducements to desist from the pursuit of his main object, which beset him in the shape of ill health, advancing years, ample private means, large demands upon his time, and a reputation already great enough to satisfy the ambition of any ordinary man.

I do not gather from those who remember Mr. Darwin as a boy, and as a young man, that he gave early signs of being likely to achieve greatness; nor, as it seems to me, is there any sign of unusual intellectual power to be detected in his earliest book. Opening this "almost" at random I read - "Earthquakes alone are sufficient to destroy the prosperity of any country. If, for instance, beneath England the now inert subterraneous forces should exert those powers which most assuredly in former geological ages they have exerted, how completely would the entire condition of the country be changed! What would become of the lofty houses, thickly-packed cities, great manufacturies *(sic)*, the beautiful public and private edifices? If the new period of disturbance were to commence by some great earthquake in the dead of night, how terrific would be the carnage! England would be at once bankrupt all papers, records, and accounts would from that moment be lost. Government being unable to collect the taxes, and failing to maintain its authority, the hand of violence and rapine would go uncontrolled. In every large town famine would be proclaimed, pestilence and death following in its train." {240a} Great allowance should be made for a first work, and I admit that much interesting matter is found in Mr. Darwin's journal; still, it was hardly to be expected that the writer who at the age of thirty-three could publish the foregoing passage should twenty years later achieve the reputation of being the profoundest philosopher of his time.

I have not sufficient technical knowledge to enable me to speak certainly, but I question his having been the great observer and master of experiment which he is generally believed to have been. His accuracy was, I imagine, generally to be relied upon as long as accuracy did not come into conflict with his interests as a leader in the scientific world; when these were at stake he was not to be trusted for a moment. Unfortunately they were directly or indirectly at stake more often than one could wish. His book on the action of worms, however, was shown by Professor Paley and other writers {242a} to contain many serious errors and omissions, though it involved no personal question; but I imagine him to have been more or less *hébété* when he wrote this book. On the whole I should doubt his having been a better observer of nature than nine country gentlemen out of ten who have a taste for natural history.

Presumptuous as I am aware it must appear to say so, I am unable to see more than average intellectual power even in Mr. Darwin's later books. His great contribution to science is supposed to have been the theory of natural selection, but enough has been said to show that this, if understood as he ought to have meant it to be understood, cannot be rated highly as an intellectual achievement. His other most important contribution was his provisional theory of pan-genesis, which is admitted on all hands to have been a failure. Though, however, it is not likely that posterity will consider him as a man of transcendent intellectual power, he must be admitted to have been richly endowed with a much more valuable quality than either originality or literary power - I mean with *savoir faire*. The cards he held - and, on the whole, his hand was a good one - he played with judgment; and though not one of those who would have achieved greatness under any circumstances, he nevertheless did achieve greatness of no mean order. Greatness, indeed, of the highest kind - that of one who is without fear and without reproach - will not ultimately be allowed him, but greatness of a rare kind can only be denied him by those whose judgment is perverted by temper or personal ill-will. He found the world believing in fixity of species, and left it believing - in spite of his own doctrine - in descent with modification.

I have said on an earlier page that Mr. Darwin was heir to a discredited truth, and left behind him an accredited fallacy. This is true as regards men of science and cultured classes who understood his distinctive feature, or thought they did, and so long as Mr. Darwin lived accepted it with very rare exceptions; but it is not true as regards the unreading, unreflecting public, who seized the salient point of descent with modification only, and troubled themselves little about the distinctive feature. It would almost seem as if Mr. Darwin had reversed the usual practice of philosophers and given his esoteric doctrine to the world, while reserving the exoteric for his most intimate and faithful adherents. This, however, is a detail; the main fact is, that Mr. Darwin brought us all round to evolution. True, it was Mr. Darwin backed by the *Times* and the other most influential organs of science and culture, but it was one of Mr. Darwin's great merits to have developed and organised this backing, as part of the work which he knew was essential if so great a revolution was to be effected.

This is an exceedingly difficult and delicate thing to do. If people think they need only write striking and well-considered books, and that then the *Times* will immediately set to work to call attention to them, I should advise them not to be too hasty in basing action upon this hypothesis. I should advise them to be even less hasty in basing it upon the assumption that to secure a powerful literary backing is a matter within the compass of any one who chooses to undertake it. No one who has not a strong social position should ever advance a new theory, unless a life of hard fighting is part of what he lays himself out for. It was one of Mr. Darwin's great merits that he had a strong social position, and had the good sense to know how to profit by it. The magnificent feat which he eventually achieved was unhappily tarnished by much that detracts from the splendour that ought to have attended it, but a magnificent feat it must remain.

Whose work in this imperfect world is not tarred and tarnished by something that detracts from its ideal character? It is enough that a man should be the right man in the right place, and this Mr. Darwin pre-eminently was. If he had been more like the ideal character which Mr. Allen endeavours to represent him, it is not likely that he would have been able to do as much, or nearly as much, as he actually did; he would have been too wide a cross with his generation to produce much effect upon it. Original thought is much more common than is generally believed. Most people, if they only knew it, could write a good book or play, paint a good picture, compose a fine oratorio; but it takes an unusually able person to get the book well reviewed, persuade a manager to bring the play out, sell the picture, or compass the performance of the oratorio; indeed, the more vigorous and original any one of these thing may be, the more difficult will it prove to even bring it before the notice of the public. The error of most origina people is in being just a trifle too original. It was in his business qualities - and these, after all, are the most essential to success, that Mr. Darwin showed himself so superlative. These are not only the most essential to success, but it is only by blaspheming the world in a way which no good citizen of the world will do, that we can deny them to be the ones which should most command our admiration. We are in the world; surely so long as we are in it we should be of it, and not give ourselves airs as though we were too good for our generation, and would lay ourselves out tc please any other by preference. Mr. Darwin played for his own generation, and he got in the very amplest measure the recognition which he endeavoured, as we all do, to obtain.

His success was, no doubt, in great measure due to the fact that he knew our little ways, and humoured them; but if he had not had little ways of his own, he never could have been so much *au fait* with ours. He knew, for example, we should be pleased to hear that he had taken his boots off so as not to disturb his worms when watching them by night, so he told us of this, and we were delighted. He knew we should like his using the word "sag," so he used it, {245a} and we said it was beautiful. True, he used it wrongly, for he was writing about tesselated pavement, and builders assure me that "sag" is a word which applies to timber only, but this is not to the point; the point was, that Mr. Darwin should have used a word that we did not understand; this showed that he had a vast fund of knowledge at his command about all sorts of practical details with which he might have well been unacquainted. We do not deal the same measure to man and to the lower animals in the matter of intelligence; the less we understand these last, the less, we say, not we, but they can understand; whereas the less we can understand a man, the more intelligent we are apt to think him. No one should neglect by-play of this description; if I live to be strong enough to carry i through, I mean to play "cambre," and I shall spell it "camber." I wonder Mr. Darwin never abused this word. Laugh at him, however, as we may for having said "sag," if he had not been the kind of man to know the value o these little hits, neither would he have been the kind of man to persuade us into first tolerating, and then cordially accepting, descent with modification. There is a correlation of mental as well as of physical growth, and we coul not probably have had one set of Mr. Darwin's qualities without the other. If he had been more faultless, he might have written better books, but we should have listened worse. A book's prosperity is like a jest's - in the ear of him that hears it.

Mr. Spencer would not - at least one cannot think he would - have been able to effect the revolution which will henceforth doubtless be connected with Mr. Darwin's name. He had been insisting on evolution for some years before the "Origin of Species" came out, but he might as well have preached to the winds, for all the visible effect that had been produced. On the appearance of Mr. Darwin's book the effect was instantaneous; it was like the change in the condition of a patient when the right medicine has been hit on after all sorts of things have been tried and failed. Granted that it was comparatively easy for Mr. Darwin, as having been born into the household of one of the prophets of evolution, to arrive at conclusions about the fixity of species which, if not so born, he might neve have reached at all; this does not make it any easier for him to have got others to agree with him. Any one, again, may have money left him, or run up against it, or have it run up against him, as it does against some people, but it is only a very sensible person who does not lose it. Moreover, once begin to go behind achievement and there is an end of everything. Did the world give much heed to or believe in evolution before Mr. Darwin's time? Certainly not. Did we begin to attend and be persuaded soon after Mr. Darwin began to write? Certainly yes. Did we ere long go over *en masse*? Assuredly. If, as I said in "Life and Habit," any one asks who taught the world to believe in evolution, the answer to the end of time must be that it was Mr. Darwin. And yet the more his work is looked at, the more marvellous does its success become. It seems as if some organisms can do anything with anything. Beethoven picked his teeth with the snuffers, and seems to have picked them sufficiently to his satisfaction. So Mr. Darwin with one of the worst styles imaginable did all that the clearest, tersest writer could have done. Strange, that such a master of cunning (in the sense of my title) should have been the apostle of luck, and one so terribly unluck as Lamarck, of cunning, but such is the irony of nature. Buffon planted, Erasmus Darwin and Lamarck watered, bu it was Mr. Darwin who said, "That fruit is ripe," and shook it into his lap.

With this Mr. Darwin's best friends ought to be content; his admirers are not well advised in representing him as endowed with all sorts of qualities which he was very far from possessing. Thus it is pretended that he was one of those men who were ever on the watch for new ideas, ever ready to give a helping hand to those who were trying to advance our knowledge, ever willing to own to a mistake and give up even his most cherished ideas if truth required them at his hands. No conception can be more wantonly inexact. I grant that if a writer was sufficiently at once incompetent and obsequious Mr. Darwin was "ever ready," &c. So the Emperors of Austria wash a few poor people's feet on some one of the festivals of the Church, but it would not be safe to generalise from this yearly ceremony, and conclude that the Emperors of Austria are in the habit of washing poor people's feet. I can understand Mr. Darwin's not having taken any public notice, for example, of "Life and Habit," for though I did not attack him in force in that book, it was abundantly clear that an attack could not be long delayed, and a man may be pardoned for not doing anything to advertise the works of his opponents; but there is no excuse for his never having referred to Professor Hering's work either in "Nature," when Professor Ray Lankester first called attention to it (July 13, 1876), or in some one of his subsequent books. If his attitude towards those who worked in the same field as himself had been the generous one which his admirers pretend, he would have certainly come forward, not necessarily as adopting Professor Hering's theory, but still as helping it to obtain a hearing.

His not having done so is of a piece with his silence about Buffon, Erasmus Darwin, and Lamarck in the early editions of the "Origin of Species," and with the meagre reference to them which is alone found in the later ones. It is of a piece also with the silence which Mr. Darwin invariably maintained when he saw his position irretrievably damaged, as, for example, by Mr. Spencer's objection already referred to, and by the late Professor Fleeming Jenkin in the *North British Review* (June 1867). Science, after all, should form a kingdom which is more or less not of this world. The ideal scientist should know neither self nor friend nor foe - he should be able to hob-nob with those whom he most vehemently attacks, and to fly at the scientific throat of those to whom he is personally most attached; he should be neither grateful for a favourable review nor displeased at a hostile one; his literary and scientific life should be something as far apart as possible from his social; it is thus, at least, alone that any one will be able to keep his eye single for facts, and their legitimate inferences. We have seen Professor Mivart lately taken to task by Mr. Romanes for having said {248a} that Mr. Darwin was singularly sensitive to criticism, and made it impossible for Professor Mivart to continue friendly personal relations with him after he had ventured to maintain his own opinion. I see no reason to question Professor Mivart's accuracy, and find what he has said to agree alike with my own personal experience of Mr. Darwin, and with all the light that his works throw upon his character.

The most substantial apology that can be made for his attempt to claim the theory of descent with modification is to be found in the practice of Lamarck, Mr. Patrick Matthew, the author of the "Vestiges of Creation," and Mr. Herbert Spencer, and, again, in the total absence of complaint which this practice met with. If Lamarck might write the "Philosophie Zoologique" without, so far as I remember, one word of reference to Buffon, and without being complained of, why might not Mr. Darwin write the "Origin of Species" without more than a passing allusion to Lamarck? Mr. Patrick Matthew, again, though writing what is obviously a *résumé* of the evolutionary theories of his time, makes no mention of Lamarck, Erasmus Darwin, or Buffon. I have not the original edition of the "Vestiges of Creation" before me, but feel sure I am justified in saying that it claimed to be a more or less Minerva-like work, that sprang full armed from the brain of Mr. Chambers himself. This at least is how it was received by the public; and however violent the opposition it met with, I cannot find that its author was blamed for not having made adequate mention of Lamarck. When Mr. Spencer wrote his first essay on evolution in the *Leader* (March 20, 1852) he did indeed begin his argument, "Those who cavalierly reject the doctrine of Lamarck," &c., so that his essay purports to be written in support of Lamarck; but when he republished his article in 1858, the reference to Lamarck was cut out.

I make no doubt that it was the bad example set him by the writers named in the preceding paragraph which betrayed Mr. Darwin into doing as they did, but being more conscientious than they, he could not bring himself to do it without having satisfied himself that he had got hold of a more or less distinctive feature, and this, of course made matters worse. The distinctive feature was not due to any deep-laid plan for pitchforking mind out of the universe, or as part of a scheme of materialistic philosophy, though it has since been made to play an important part in the attempt to further this; Mr. Darwin was perfectly innocent of any intention of getting rid of mind, and did not, probably, care the toss of sixpence whether the universe was instinct with mind or no - what he did care about was carrying off the palm in the matter of descent with modification, and the distinctive feature was an adjunct with which his nervous, sensitive, Gladstonian nature would not allow him to dispense.

And why, it may be asked, should not the palm be given to Mr. Darwin if he wanted it, and was at so much pains to get it? Why, if science is a kingdom not of this world, make so much fuss about settling who is entitled to what? At best such questions are of a sorry personal nature, that can have little bearing upon facts, and it is these that alone should concern us. The answer is, that if the question is so merely personal and unimportant, Mr. Darwin may as well yield as Buffon, Erasmus Darwin, and Lamarck; Mr. Darwin's admirers find no difficulty in appreciating the importance of a personal element as far as he is concerned; let them not wonder, then, if others, while anxious to give him the laurels to which he is entitled, are somewhat indignant at the attempt to crown him with leaves that have been filched from the brows of the great dead who went before him. *Palmam qui meruit ferat*. The instinct which tells us that no man in the scientific or literary world should claim more than his due is an old and, I imagine, a wholesome one, and if a scientific self-denying ordinance is demanded, we may reply with justice, *Que messieurs les Charles-Darwinies commencent.* Mr. Darwin will have a crown sufficient for any ordinary brow remaining in the achievement of having done more than any other writer, living or dead, to popularise evolution. This much may be ungrudgingly conceded to him, but more than this those who have his scientific position most at heart will be well advised if they cease henceforth to demand.

CHAPTER XIX - Conclusion

And now I bring this book to a conclusion. So many things requiring attention have happened since it was begun that I leave it in a very different shape to the one which it was originally intended to bear. I have omitted much that I had meant to deal with, and have been tempted sometimes to introduce matter the connection of which with my subject is not immediately apparent. Such however, as the book is, it must now go in the form into which it has grown almost more in spite of me than from *malice prepense* on my part. I was afraid that it might thus set me at defiance, and in an early chapter expressed a doubt whether I should find it redound greatly to my advantage with men of science; in this concluding chapter I may say that doubt has deepened into something like certainty. I regret this, but cannot help it.

Among the points with which it was most incumbent upon me to deal was that of vegetable intelligence. A reader may well say that unless I give plants much the same sense of pleasure and pain, memory, power of will, and intelligent perception of the best way in which to employ their opportunities that I give to low animals, my argument falls to the ground. If I declare organic modification to be mainly due to function, and hence in the closest correlation with mental change, I must give plants, as well as animals, a mind, and endow them with power to reflect and reason upon all that most concerns them. Many who will feel little difficulty about admitting that animal modification is upon the whole mainly due to the secular cunning of the animals themselves will yet hesitate before they admit that plants also can have a reason and cunning of their own.

Unwillingness to concede this is based principally upon the error concerning intelligence to which I have already referred - I mean to our regarding intelligence not so much as the power of understanding as that of being understood by ourselves. Once admit that the evidence in favour of a plant's knowing its own business depends more on the efficiency with which that business is conducted than either on our power of understanding how it can be conducted, or on any signs on the plant's part of a capacity for understanding things that do not concern it, and there will be no further difficulty about supposing that in its own sphere a plant is just as intelligent as an animal, and keeps a sharp look-out upon its own interests, however indifferent it may seem to be to ours. So strong has been the set of recent opinion in this direction that with botanists the foregoing now almost goes without saying though few five years ago would have accepted it.

To no one of the several workers in this field are we more indebted for the change which has been brought about in this respect than to my late valued and lamented friend Mr. Alfred Tylor. Mr. Tylor was not the discoverer of the protoplasmic continuity that exists in plants, but he was among the very first to welcome this discovery, and his experiments at Carshalton in the years 1883 and 1884 demonstrated that, whether there was protoplasmic continuity in plants or no, they were at any rate endowed with some measure of reason, forethought, and power of self adaptation to varying surroundings. It is not for me to give the details of these experiments. I had the good fortune to see them more than once while they were in progress, and was present when they were made the subject of a paper read by Mr. Sydney B. J. Skertchly before the Linnean Society, Mr. Tylor being then too ill to read it himself. The paper has since been edited by Mr. Skertchly, and published. {253a} Anything that should be said further about it will come best from Mr. Skertchly; it will be enough here if I give the *résumé* of it prepared by Mr. Tylor himself.

In this Mr. Tylor said:- "The principles which underlie this paper are the individuality of plants, the necessity for some co-ordinating system to enable the parts to act in concert, and the probability that this also necessitates the admission that plants have a dim sort of intelligence.

"It is shown that a tree, for example, is something more than an aggregation of tissues, but is a complex being performing acts as a whole, and not merely responsive to the direct influence of light, &c. The tree knows more than its branches, as the species know more than the individual, the community than the unit.

"Moreover, inasmuch as my experiments show that many plants and trees possess the power of adapting themselves to unfamiliar circumstances, such as, for instance, avoiding obstacles by bending aside before touching, or by altering the leaf arrangement, it seems probable that at least as much voluntary power must be accorded to such plants as to certain lowly organised animals.

"Finally, a connecting system by means of which combined movements take place is found in the threads of protoplasm which unite the various cells, and which I have now shown to exist even in the wood of trees.

"One of the important facts seems to be the universality of the upward curvature of the tips of growing branches of trees, and the power possessed by the tree to straighten its branches afterwards, so that new growth shall by similar means be able to obtain the necessary light and air.

"A house, to use a sanitary analogy, is functionally useless without it obtains a good supply of light and air. The architect strives so to produce the house as to attain this end, and still leave the house comfortable. But the house, though dependent upon, is not produced by, the light and air. So a tree is functionally useless, and cannot even exist without a proper supply of light and air; but, whereas it has been the custom to ascribe the heliotropic and other motions to the direct influence of those agents, I would rather suggest that the movements are to some extent due to the desire of the plant to acquire its necessaries of life."

The more I have reflected upon Mr. Tylor's Carshalton experiments, the more convinced I am of their great value. No one, indeed, ought to have doubted that plants were intelligent, but we all of us do much that we ought not to do, and Mr. Tylor supplied a demonstration which may be henceforth authoritatively appealed to.

I will take the present opportunity of insisting upon a suggestion which I made in "Alps and Sanctuaries" (New edition, pp. 152, 153), with which Mr. Tylor was much pleased, and which, at his request, I made the subject of a few words that I ventured to say at the Linnean Society's rooms after his paper had been read. "Admitting," I said, "the common protoplasmic origin of animals and plants, and setting aside the notion that plants preceded animals, we are still faced by the problem why protoplasm should have developed into the organic life of the world, along two main lines, and only two - the animal and the vegetable. Why, if there was an early schism - and this there clearly was - should there not have been many subsequent ones of equal importance? We see innumerable sub-divisions of animals and plants, but we see no other such great subdivision of organic life as that whereby it ranges itself, for the most part readily, as either animal or vegetable. Why any subdivision? - but if any, why not more than two great classes?"

The two main stems of the tree of life ought, one would think, to have been formed on the same principle as the boughs which represent genera, and the twigs which stand for species and varieties. If specific differences arise mainly from differences of action taken in consequence of differences of opinion, then, so ultimately do generic; so therefore, again, do differences between families; so therefore, by analogy, should that greatest of differences in virtue of which the world of life is mainly animal, or vegetable. In this last case as much as in that of specific difference, we ought to find divergent form the embodiment and organic expression of divergent opinion. Form is mind made manifest in flesh through action: shades of mental difference being expressed in shades of physical difference, while broad fundamental differences of opinion are expressed in broad fundamental differences of bodily shape.

Or to put it thus:-

If form and habit be regarded as functionally interdependent, that is to say, if neither form nor habit can vary without corresponding variation in the other, and if habit and opinion concerning advantage are also functionally interdependent, it follows self-evidently that form and opinion concerning advantage (and hence form and cunning) will be functionally interdependent also, and that there can be no great modification of the one without corresponding modification of the other. Let there, then, be a point in respect of which opinion might be early and easily divided - a point in respect of which two courses involving different lines of action presented equally-balanced advantages - and there would be an early subdivision of primordial life, according as the one view or the other was taken.

It is obvious that the pros and cons for either course must be supposed very nearly equal, otherwise the course which presented the fewest advantages would be attended with the probable gradual extinction of the organised beings that adopted it, but there being supposed two possible modes of action very evenly balanced as regards advantage and disadvantages, then the ultimate appearance of two corresponding forms of life is a *sequitur* from the admission that form varies as function, and function as opinion concerning advantage. If there are three, four, five or six such opinions tenable, we ought to have three, four, five, or six main subdivisions of life. As things are, we have two only. Can we, then, see a matter on which opinion was likely to be easily and early divided into two, and only two, main divisions - no third course being conceivable? If so, this should suggest itself as the probable source from which the two main forms of organic life have been derived.

I submit that we can see such a matter in the question whether it pays better to sit still and make the best of what comes in one's way, or to go about in search of what one can find. Of course we, as animals, naturally hold that it is better to go about in search of what we can find than to sit still and make the best of what comes; but there is still so much to be said on the other side, that many classes of animals have settled down into sessile habits, while a perhaps even larger number are, like spiders, habitual liers in wait rather than travellers in search of food. I would ask my reader, therefore, to see the opinion that it is better to go in search of prey as formulated, and finding its organic expression, in animals; and the other - that it is better to be ever on the look-out to make the best of what chance brings up to them - in plants. Some few intermediate forms still record to us the long struggle during which the schism was not yet complete, and the halting between two opinions which it might be expected that some organisms should exhibit.

"Neither class," I said in "Alps and Sanctuaries," "has been quite consistent. Who ever is or can be? Every extreme - every opinion carried to its logical end - will prove to be an absurdity. Plants throw out roots and boughs and leaves; this is a kind of locomotion; and, as Dr. Erasmus Darwin long since pointed out, they do sometimes approach nearly to what may be called travelling; a man of consistent character will never look at a bough, a root, or a tendril without regarding it as a melancholy and unprincipled compromise" (New edition, p. 153).

Having called attention to this view, and commended it to the consideration of my readers, I proceed to another which should not have been left to be touched upon only in a final chapter, and which, indeed, seems to require a book to itself - I refer to the origin and nature of the feelings, which those who accept volition as having had a large share in organic modification must admit to have had a no less large share in the formation of volition. Volition grows out of ideas, ideas from feelings. What, then, is feeling, and the subsequent mental images or ideas?

The image of a stone formed in our minds is no representation of the object which has given rise to it. Not only, as has been often remarked, is there no resemblance between the particular thought and the particular thing, but thoughts and things generally are too unlike to be compared. An idea of a stone may be like an idea of another stone, or two stones may be like one another; but an idea of a stone is not like a stone; it cannot be thrown at anything, it occupies no room in space, has no specific gravity, and when we come to know more about stones, we find our ideas concerning them to be but rude, epitomised, and highly conventional renderings of the actual facts mere hieroglyphics, in fact, or, as it were, counters or bank-notes, which serve to express and to convey commodities with which they have no pretence of analogy.

Indeed we daily find that, as the range of our perceptions becomes enlarged either by invention of new appliances or after use of old ones, we change our ideas though we have no reason to think that the thing about which we are thinking has changed. In the case of a stone, for instance, the rude, unassisted, uneducated senses see it as above all things motionless, whereas assisted and trained ideas concerning it represent motion as its most essential characteristic; but the stone has not changed. So, again, the uneducated idea represents it as above all things mindless, and is as little able to see mind in connection with it as it lately was to see motion; it will be no greater change of opinion than we have most of us undergone already if we come presently to see it as no less full of elementary mind than of elementary motion, but the stone will not have changed.

The fact that we modify our opinions suggests that our ideas are formed not so much in involuntary self-adjusting mimetic correspondence with the objects that we believe to give rise to them, as by what was in the outset voluntary, conventional arrangement in whatever way we found convenient, of sensation and perception-symbols, which had nothing whatever to do with the objects, and were simply caught hold of as the only things we could grasp. It would seem as if, in the first instance, we must have arbitrarily attached some one of the few and vague sensations which we could alone at first command, to certain motions of outside things as echoed by our brain, and used them to think and feel the things with, so as to docket them, and recognise them with greater force, certainty, and clearness - much as we use words to help us to docket and grasp our feelings and thoughts, or written characters to help us to docket and grasp our words.

If this view be taken we stand in much the same attitude towards our feelings as a dog may be supposed to do towards our own reading and writing. The dog may be supposed to marvel at the wonderful instinctive faculty by which we can tell the price of the different railway stocks merely by looking at a sheet of paper; he supposes thi power to be a part of our nature, to have come of itself by luck and not by cunning, but a little reflection will show that feeling is not more likely to have "come by nature" than reading and writing are. Feeling is in all probability the result of the same kind of slow laborious development as that which has attended our more recent arts and our bodily organs; its development must be supposed to have followed the same lines as that of our other arts, and indeed of the body itself, which is the *ars artium* - for growth of mind is throughout coincident with growth of organic resources, and organic resources grow with growing mind.

Feeling is the art the possession of which differentiates the civilised organic world from that of brute inorganic matter, but still it is an art; it is the outcome of a mind that is common both to organic and inorganic, and which the organic has alone cultivated. It is not a part of mind itself; it is no more this than language and writing are parts of thought. The organic world can alone feel, just as man can alone speak; but as speech is only the development of powers the germs of which are possessed by the lower animals, so feeling is only a sign of the employment and development of powers the germs of which exist in inorganic substances. It has all the characteristics of an art, and though it must probably rank as the oldest of those arts that are peculiar to the organic world, it is one which is still in process of development. None of us, indeed, can feel well on more than a very few subjects, and many can hardly feel at all.

But, however this may be, our sensations and perceptions of material phenomena are attendant on the excitation of certain motions in the anterior parts of the brain. Whenever certain motions are excited in this substance, certain sensations and ideas of resistance, extension, &c., are either concomitant, or ensue within a period too brief for our cognisance. It is these sensations and ideas that we directly cognise, and it is to them that we have attached the idea of the particular kind of matter we happen to be thinking of. As this idea is not like the thing itself, so neither is i like the motions in our brain on which it is attendant. It is no more like these than, say, a stone is like the individual characters, written or spoken, that form the word "stone," or than these last are, in sound, like the word "stone" itself, whereby the idea of a stone is so immediately and vividly presented to us. True, this does not involve that our idea shall not resemble the object that gave rise to it, any more than the fact that a looking-glass bears no resemblance to the things reflected in it involves that the reflection shall not resemble the things reflected; the shifting nature, however, of our ideas and conceptions is enough to show that they must be symbolical, and conditioned by changes going on within ourselves as much as by those outside us; and if, going behind the ideas which suffice for daily use, we extend our inquiries in the direction of the reality underlying our conception, we find reason to think that the brain-motions which attend our conception correspond with exciting motions in the object that occasions it, and that these, rather than anything resembling our conception itself, should be regarded as the reality.

This leads to a third matter, on which I can only touch with extreme brevity.

Different modes of motion have long been known as the causes of our different colour perceptions, or at any rate as associated therewith, and of late years, more especially since the promulgation of Newlands'{260a} law, it has been perceived that what we call the kinds or properties of matter are not less conditioned by motion than colour is. The substance or essence of unconditioned matter, as apart from the relations between its various states (which we believe to be its various conditions of motion) must remain for ever unknown to us, for it is only the relations between the conditions of the underlying substance that we cognise at all, and where there are no conditions, there is nothing for us to seize, compare, and, hence, cognise; unconditioned matter must, therefore, be as inconceivable by us as unmattered condition; {261a} but though we can know nothing about matter as apart from its conditions or states, opinion has been for some time tending towards the belief that what we call the different states, or kinds, of matter are only our ways of mentally characterising and docketing our estimates of the different kinds of motion going on in this otherwise uncognisable substratum.

Our conception, then, concerning the nature of any matter depends solely upon its kind and degree of unrest, that i to say, on the characteristics of the vibrations that are going on within it. The exterior object vibrating in a certain way imparts some of its vibrations to our brain - but if the state of the thing itself depends upon its vibrations, must be considered as to all intents and purposes the vibrations themselves - plus, of course, the underlying substance that is vibrating. If, for example, a pat of butter is a portion of the unknowable underlying substance in such-and-such a state of molecular disturbance, and it is only by alteration of the disturbance that the substance can be altered - the disturbance of the substance is practically equivalent to the substance: a pat of butter is such-and such a disturbance of the unknowable underlying substance, and such-and-such a disturbance of the underlying substance is a pat of butter. In communicating its vibrations, therefore, to our brain a substance does actually communicate what is, as far as we are concerned, a portion of itself. Our perception of a thing and its attendan feeling are symbols attaching to an introduction within our brain of a feeble state of the thing itself. Our recollection of it is occasioned by a feeble continuance of this feeble state in our brains, becoming less feeble through the accession of fresh but similar vibrations from without. The molecular vibrations which make the thing an idea of which is conveyed to our minds, put within our brain a little feeble emanation from the thing itself - if w come within their reach. This being once put there, will remain as it were dust, till dusted out, or till it decay, or till it receive accession of new vibrations.

The vibrations from a pat of butter do, then, actually put butter into a man's head. This is one of the commonest of expressions, and would hardly be so common if it were not felt to have some foundation in fact. At first the man does not know what feeling or complex of feelings to employ so as to docket the vibrations, any more than he knows what word to employ so as to docket the feelings, or with what written characters to docket his word; but he gets over this, and henceforward the vibrations of the exterior object (that is to say, the thing) never set up their characteristic disturbances, or, in other words, never come into his head, without the associated feeling presenting itself as readily as word and characters present themselves, on the presence of the feeling. The more butter a man sees and handles, the more he gets butter on the brain - till, though he can never get anything like enough to be strictly called butter, it only requires the slightest molecular disturbance with characteristics like those of butter to bring up a vivid and highly sympathetic idea of butter in the man's mind.

If this view is adopted, our memory of a thing is our retention within the brain of a small leaven of the actual thir itself, or of what *quâ* us is the thing that is remembered, and the ease with which habitual actions come to be performed is due to the power of the vibrations having been increased and modified by continual accession from without till they modify the molecular disturbances of the nervous system, and therefore its material substance which we have already settled to be only our way of docketing molecular disturbances. The same vibrations, therefore, form the substance remembered, introduce an infinitesimal dose of it within the brain, modify the substance remembering, and, in the course of time, create and further modify the mechanism of both the sensory and motor nerves. Thought and thing are one.

I commend these two last speculations to the reader's charitable consideration, as feeling that I am here travelling beyond the ground on which I can safely venture; nevertheless, as it may be some time before I have another opportunity of coming before the public, I have thought it, on the whole, better not to omit them, but to give them thus provisionally. I believe they are both substantially true, but am by no means sure that I have expressed them either clearly or accurately; I cannot, however, further delay the issue of my book.

Returning to the point raised in my title, is luck, I would ask, or cunning, the more fitting matter to be insisted upon in connection with organic modification? Do animals and plants grow into conformity with their surroundings because they and their fathers and mothers take pains, or because their uncles and aunts go away? For the survival of the fittest is only the non-survival or going away of the unfittest - in whose direct line the race is not continued and who are therefore only uncles and aunts of the survivors. I can quite understand its being a good thing for any race that its uncles and aunts should go away, but I do not believe the accumulation of lucky accidents could result in an eye, no matter how many uncles and aunts may have gone away during how many generations.

I would ask the reader to bear in mind the views concerning life and death expressed in an early chapter. They seem to me not, indeed, to take away any very considerable part of the sting from death; this should not be attempted or desired, for with the sting of death the sweets of life are inseparably bound up so that neither can be weakened without damaging the other. Weaken the fear of death, and the love of life would be weakened. Strengthen it, and we should cling to life even more tenaciously than we do. But though death must always remain as a shock and change of habits from which we must naturally shrink - still it is not the utter end of our being, which, until lately, it must have seemed to those who have been unable to accept the grosser view of the resurrection with which we were familiarised in childhood. We too now know that though worms destroy this body, yet in our flesh shall we so far see God as to be still in Him and of Him - biding our time for a resurrection in a new and more glorious body; and moreover, that we shall be to the full as conscious of this as we are at present of much that concerns us as closely as anything can concern us.

The thread of life cannot be shorn between successive generations, except upon grounds which will in equity involve its being shorn between consecutive seconds, and fractions of seconds. On the other hand, it cannot be left unshorn between consecutive seconds without necessitating that it should be left unshorn also beyond the grave, as well as in successive generations. Death is as salient a feature in what we call our life as birth was, but it is no more than this. As a salient feature, it is a convenient epoch for the drawing of a defining line, by the help of which we may bette grasp the conception of life, and think it more effectually, but it is a *façon de parler* only; it is, as I said in "Life and

Habit," {264a} "the most inexorable of all conventions," but our idea of it has no correspondence with eterna underlying realities.

Finally, we must have evolution; consent is too spontaneous, instinctive, and universal among those most able to form an opinion, to admit of further doubt about this. We must also have mind and design. The attempt to eliminate intelligence from among the main agencies of the universe has broken down too signally to be agair ventured upon - not until the recent rout has been forgotten. Nevertheless the old, far-foreseeing *Deus ex machinâ* design as from a point outside the universe, which indeed it directs, but of which it is no part, is negatived by the facts of organism. What, then, remains, but the view that I have again in this book endeavoured to uphold - I mean, the supposition that the mind or cunning of which we see such abundant evidence all round us, is, like the kingdom of heaven, within us, and within all things at all times everywhere? There is design, or cunning, but it is a cunning not despotically fashioning us from without as a potter fashions his clay, but inhering democratically within the body which is its highest outcome, as life inheres within an animal or plant.

All animals and plants are corporations, or forms of democracy, and may be studied by the light of these, as democracies, not infrequently, by that of animals and plants. The solution of the difficult problem of reflex action for example, is thus facilitated, by supposing it to be departmental in character; that is to say, by supposing it to be action of which the department that attends to it is alone cognisant, and which is not referred to the centra government so long as things go normally. As long, therefore, as this is the case, the central government is unconscious of what is going on, but its being thus unconscious is no argument that the department is unconscious also.

I know that contradiction in terms lurks within much that I have said, but the texture of the world is a warp and woof of contradiction in terms; of continuity in discontinuity, and discontinuity in continuity; of unity in diversity and of diversity in unity. As in the development of a fugue, where, when the subject and counter subject have been enounced, there must henceforth be nothing new, and yet all must be new, so throughout organic life - which is as a fugue developed to great length from a very simple subject - everything is linked on to and grows out of that which comes next to it in order - errors and omissions excepted. It crosses and thwarts what comes next to it with difference that involves resemblance, and resemblance that involves difference, and there is no juxtaposition of things that differ too widely by omission of necessary links, or too sudden departure from recognised methods of procedure.

To conclude; bodily form may be almost regarded as idea and memory in a solidified state - as an accumulation of things each one of them so tenuous as to be practically without material substance. It is as a million pounds formed by accumulated millionths of farthings; more compendiously it arises normally from, and through, action. Action arises normally from, and through, opinion. Opinion, from, and through, hypothesis. "Hypothesis," as the derivation of the word itself shows, is singularly near akin to "underlying, and only in part knowable, substratum;" and what is this but "God" translated from the language of Moses into that of Mr. Herbert Spencer? The conception of God is like nature - it returns to us in another shape, no matter how often we may expel it. Vulgarised as it has been by Michael Angelo, Raffaelle, and others who shall be nameless, it has been like every other *corruptio optimi - pessimum:* used as a hieroglyph by the help of which we may better acknowledge the height and depth of our own ignorance, and at the same time express our sense that there is an unseen world with which we in some mysterious way come into contact, though the writs of our thoughts do not run within it - used in this way, the idea and the word have been found enduringly convenient. The theory that luck is the main means of organic modification is the most absolute denial of God which it is possible for the human mind to conceive - while the view that God is in all His creatures, He in them and they in Him, is only expressed in other words by declaring that the main means of organic modification is, not luck, but cunning.

Footnotes:

{17a} "*Nature*," Nov. 12, 1885.

{20a} "Hist. Nat. Gén.," tom. ii. p. 411, 1859.

{23a} "Selections, &c." Trübner & Co., 1884. [Out of print.]

{29a} "Selections, &c., and Remarks on Romanes' 'Mental Intelligence in Animals,'" Trübner & Co., 1884. pp. 228,

229. [Out of print.]

{35a} Quoted by M. Vianna De Lima in his "Exposé Sommaire," &c., p. 6. Paris, Delagrave, 1886.

{40a} I have given the passage in full on p. 254a of my "Selections," &c. [Now out of print.] I observe that Canon Kingsley felt exactly the same difficulty that I had felt myself, and saw also how alone it could be met. He makes the wood-wren say, "Something told him his mother had done it before him, and he was flesh of her flesh, life of her life, and had inherited her instinct (as we call hereditary memory, to avoid the trouble of finding out what it is and how it comes)." - *Fraser,* June, 1867. Canon Kingsley felt he must insist on the continued personality of the two generations before he could talk about inherited memory. On the other hand, though he does indeed speak of this as almost a synonym for instinct, he seems not to have realised how right he was, and implies that we should find some fuller and more satisfactory explanation behind this, only that we are too lazy to look for it.

{44a} 26 Sept., 1877. "Unconscious Memory." ch. ii.

{52a} This chapter is taken almost entirely from my book, "Selections, &c.. and Remarks on Romanes' 'Mental Evolution in Animals.'" Trübner, 1884. [Now out of print.]

{52b} "Mental Evolution in Animals," p. 113. Kegan Paul, Nov., 1883.

{52c} Ibid. p. 115.

{52d} Ibid. p. 116.

{53a} "Mental Evolution in Animals." p. 131. Kegan Paul, Nov., 1883.

{54a} Vol. I, 3rd ed., 1874, p. 141, and Problem I. 21.

{54b} "Mental Evolution in Animals," pp. 177, 178. Nov., 1883.

{55a} "Mental Evolution in Animals," p. 192.

{55b} *Ibid.* p. 195.

{55c} *Ibid.* p. 296. Nov., 1883.

{56a} "Mental Evolution in Animals," p. 33. Nov., 1883.

{56b} *Ibid.*, p. 116.

{56c} *Ibid.,* p. 178.

{59a} "Evolution Old and New," pp. 357, 358.

{60a} "Mental Evolution in Animals," p. 159. Kegan Paul & Co., 1883.

{61a} "Zoonomia," vol. i. p. 484.

{61b} "Mental Evolution in Animals," p. 297. Kegan Paul & Co., 1883.

{61c} *Ibid.*, p. 201. Kegan Paul & Co., 1883.

{62a} "Mental Evolution in Animals," p. 301. November, 1883.

{62b} Origin of Species," ed. i. p. 209.

{62c} *Ibid.*, ed. vi., 1876. p. 206.

{62d} "Formation of Vegetable Mould," etc., p. 98.

{62e} Quoted by Mr. Romanes as written in the last year of Mr. Darwin's life.

{63a} Macmillan, 1883.

{66a} "Nature," August 5, 1886.

{67a} London, H. K. Lewis, 1886.

{70a} "Charles Darwin." Longmans, 1885.

{70b} Lectures at the London Institution, Feb., 1886.

{70c} "Charles Darwin." Leipzig. 1885.

{72a} See Professor Hering's "Zur Lehre von der Beziehung zwischen Leib und Seele. Mittheilung über Fechner's psychophysisches Gesetz."

{73a} Quoted by M. Vianna De Lima in his "Exposé Sommaire des Théories Transformistes de Lamarck, Darwin, et Hæckel." Paris, 1886, p. 23.

{81a} "Origin of Species," ed. i., p. 6; see also p. 43.

{83a} "I think it can be shown that there is such a power at work in 'Natural Selection' (the title of my book)." - "Proceedings of the Linnean Society for 1858," vol. iii., p. 51.

{86a} "On Naval Timber and Arboriculture," 1831, pp. 384, 385. See also "Evolution Old and New," pp. 320, 321.

{87a} "Origin of Species," p. 49, ed. vi.

{92a} "Origin of Species," ed. i., pp. 188, 189.

{93a} Page 9.

{94a} Page 226.

{96a} "Journal of the Proceedings of the Linnean Society." Williams and Norgate, 1858, p. 61.

{102a} "Zoonomia," vol. i., p. 505.

{104a} See "Evolution Old and New." p. 122.

{105a} "Phil. Zool.," i., p. 80.

{105b} *Ibid.,* i. 82.

{105c} *Ibid.* vol. i., p. 237.

{107a} See concluding chapter.

{122a} Report, 9, 26.

{135a} Ps. cii. 25-27, Bible version.

{136a} Ps. cxxxix., Prayer-book version.

{140a} *Contemporary Review,* August, 1885, p. 84.

{142a} London, David Bogue, 1881, p. 60.

{144a} August 12, 1886.

{150a} Paris, Delagrave, 1886.

{150b} Page 60.

{150c} "Œuvre complètes," tom. ix. p. 422. Paris, Garnier frères, 1875.

{150d} "Hist. Nat.," tom. i., p. 13, 1749, quoted "Evol. Old and New," p. 108.

{156a} "Origin of Species," ed. vi., p. 107.

{156b} *Ibid.,* ed. vi., p. 166.

{157a} "Origin of Species," ed. vi., p. 233.

{157b} *Ibid.*

{157c} *Ibid.,* ed. vi., p. 109.

{157d} *Ibid.,* ed. vi., p. 401.

{158a} "Origin of Species," ed. i., p. 490.

{161a} "Origin of Species," ed. vi., 1876, p. 171.

{163a} "Charles Darwin," p. 113.

{164a} "Animals and Plants under Domestication," vol. ii., p. 367, ed. 1875.

{168a} Page 3.

{168b} Page 4.

{169a} It should be remembered this was the year in which the "Vestiges of Creation" appeared.

{173a} "Charles Darwin," p. 67.

{173b} H. S. King & Co., 1876.

{174a} Page 17.

{195a} "Phil. Zool.," tom. i., pp. 34, 35.

{202a} "Origin of Species," p. 381, ed. i.

{203a} Page 454, ed. i.

{205a} "Principles of Geology," vol. ii., chap. xxxiv., ed. 1872.

{206a} "Natürliche Schöpfungsgeschichte," p. 3. Berlin, 1868.

{209a} See "Evolution Old and New," pp. 8, 9.

{216a} "Vestiges," &c., ed. 1860; Proofs, Illustrations, &c., p. xiv.

{216b} *Examiner,* May 17, 1879, review of "Evolution Old and New."

{218a} Given in part in "Evolution Old and New."

{219a} "Mind," p. 498, Oct., 1883.

{224a} "Degeneration," 1880, p. 10.

{227a} E.g. the Rev. George Henslow, in "Modern Thought," vol. ii., No. 5, 1881.

{232a} "Nature," Aug. 6, 1886.

{234a} See Mr. Darwin's "Animals and Plants under Domestication," vol. i., p. 466, &c., ed. 1875.

{235a} Paris, 1873, Introd., p. vi.

{235b} "Hist. Nat. Gen.," ii. 404, 1859.

{239a} As these pages are on the point of going to press, I see that the writer of an article on Liszt in the "Athenæum" makes the same emendation on Shakespeare's words that I have done.

{240a} "Voyages of the *Adventure* and *Beagle*," vol. iii., p. 373. London, 1839.

{242a} See Professor Paley, "Fraser," Jan., 1882, "Science Gossip," Nos. 162, 163, June and July, 1878, and "Nature," Jan. 3, Jan. 10, Feb. 28, and March 27, 1884.

{245a} "Formation of Vegetable Mould," etc., p. 217. Murray, 1882.

{248a} "Fortnightly Review," Jan., 1886.

{253a} "On the Growth of Trees and Protoplasmic Continuity." London, Stanford, 1886.

{260a} Sometimes called Mendelejeff's (see "Monthly Journal of Science," April, 1884).

{261a} I am aware that attempts have been made to say that we can conceive a condition of matter, although there is no matter in connection with it - as, for example, that we can have motion without anything moving (see "Nature," March 5, March 12, and April 9, 1885) - but I think it little likely that this opinion will meet general approbation.

{264a} Page 53.